NIGHT OF A THOUSAND DARLAS

ALSO BY BROOKE ABRAMS

Penelope in Retrograde

NIGHT OF A THOUSAND DARLAS

A NOVEL

BROOKE ABRAMS

Published by Lake Union Publishing, Seattle

www.apub.com

ISBN-13: 9781662521119 (hardcover)
ISBN-13: 9781662521102 (paperback)
ISBN-13: 9781662521126 (digital)

Cover design by Alicia Tatone
Cover image: ©jgroup, ©CSA Images, ©panic_attack, ©artJazz / Getty

Printed in the United States of America

First edition

For the generations of women who have made my life infinitely better: Esther, Ana María, Maria de Jesús, Shirley, Karen, Chelsey, and Hattie

Some memories are realities and are better than anything that can ever happen to one again.

—Willa Cather, My Ántonia

Chapter 1

I shouldn't be in a book club.

Don't get me wrong, I like the idea of a book club. Getting together with a group of friends with a glass of wine and a nice cheese board to discuss a good book sounds like a little slice of heaven on earth. But like most ideas I've tried in an effort to find my *thing*—that hobby or activity that parents look for when their kids no longer need them to act as a personal chauffeur—joining a book club is proving to be more work than it's worth.

Case in point, it's Tuesday morning, and I'm furiously trying to make it through *The Vagina Monologues*, and I'm failing miserably. It's not that I don't think the work is profound and important. It's just that I prefer the books I read to have fewer vocal vaginas and more shirtless men. I'm flexible about how much the men do or don't talk, but in my experience, less is always better.

I glance out the window from my perch at the kitchen counter. The mail truck stops at each of the matching little black boxes outside the matching houses on Cornelia Street. I sip my coffee and watch as the postal worker opens my neighbor's box and shoves a handful of white envelopes inside it. She struggles to open my mailbox, eventually having to get out of the truck so she can achieve proper leverage. I instinctively slink back behind my book, keeping it high enough to cover my face but low enough to watch the struggle continue. Eventually, the box opens, spitting out a dozen or so envelopes and advertisements. I'm not sure when the last time that I checked it was, but judging by the mess on my lawn, it's probably been a while.

The mail woman peers into the box and shakes her head in what I assume to be disgust, which seems unfair considering I didn't ask anyone to send me mail. If she were to check my email right now, she'd find zero unread messages. I don't even have any spam in my email, and if you ask me, isn't most of the paper mail people receive today just spam in physical form?

She looks up at my little Craftsman bungalow, and the two of us lock eyes.

"Crap," I mutter under my breath.

She motions to the box and then the ground, her facial expression twisted into a classic stink eye. I wave and mouth *Sorry* as I head out the front door.

"Whoops," I say, hurrying down the sidewalk. I notice the woman's name tag, Arlene. "I guess it's been a few days. Hi." I wave awkwardly. "I'm Liza, by the way."

"I'm aware," Arlene says, sternly. "You've got a week's worth of letters with your name all over it. You know I can have your mail service shut off if nobody retrieves it, don't you?"

"Oh, that would be so nice of you." It takes me longer than it should to realize that this woman is not offering me a complimentary postal service. "I'll try to do a better job."

I scoop up my mail from the ground while Arlene reaches into the box and piles the remaining bills and advertisements in my arms.

"Is it possible for you to only bring me important mail?" I ask, holding up a shiny postcard offering a discount on Brazilian waxes to new customers. "Stuff like this I'm just never going to use, and it seems like such a waste of paper—and your time. You know, with email, I can just unsubscribe. It's so easy. You should see my email. Clean as a whistle."

Somewhere between the Brazilian wax discount postcard and mentioning my email, Arlene appears to have unsubscribed from our conversation.

"Here's your mail for today, ma'am." She plops a stack of envelopes in my arms, which are now overflowing. "Tomorrow, you're probably going to get some more. That's how mail works. It's just going to keep on showing up until you die. Got it?"

"That doesn't exactly sound efficient, but I understand." I nod.

Arlene mutters something under her breath. She rolls her eyes before getting back into her truck and driving down the street. I have a feeling she and I won't be exchanging holiday cards.

I carry my heap of mail inside, dropping it on the counter next to my copy of *The Vagina Monologues*. I consider putting all of it, the book included, into my shredding pile when something catches my attention: an oversize turquoise envelope with gold-flake trim and hand lettering. It stands out like a peacock in a coop full of chickens. I can't remember the last time I got an invitation in the mail, which makes this beautiful monstrosity of an envelope feel like something special. A treat, even.

At least that's what I think until I open it.

I stop reading and run up the stairs to retrieve my phone and then back down into the kitchen to call my brother. I gasp for breath. It's not a far distance. I'm just out of shape. "Miles. Have you checked your mail today?"

"What?" My brother's voice comes across muffled through my cell. "Are you OK, Liza? You sound out of breath." He lowers his voice. "Did you just have a little morning delight with that hot math teacher who keeps liking all your posts on Insta? And on a Tuesday morning, no less. You cheeky devil."

Miles doesn't have kids, a normal job, or a grasp of what it's like to share a household with a teenager. If he did, he'd understand that a casual morning hookup would require the same amount of planning that NASA undertakes when launching a rocket into space.

"No." I shake my head. "That guy owns, like, seven cats and keeps all their pictures on his desk. I need to delete Instagram. Wait. You're getting me sidetracked. Mail. Have you checked it?"

His voice cuts out with an incoming call from our sister.

"Wait, Kat's calling. I'm going to dial her in and do a three-way call."

"Is that still a thing? I don't think I even know how to do that on a cell phone."

"Focus, Miles! Just don't hang up." I tap the "merge call" button on my screen. "Hey, Kat. I've got—"

"Did you get it?" Kat cuts me off, the anxiousness in her tone palpable. "What the hell does this mean? I've been trying to call her, and the stupid answering machine just keeps picking up. She's got to be the last human alive who doesn't have a cell phone."

"Who are we talking about?" Miles asks.

"Mom!" Kat and I shout in unison.

"Don't yell at me," Miles snaps. "Two minutes ago, I was in a hot-yoga class, standing behind a gorgeous man with the flexibility of salt-water taffy. Excuse me for needing a minute!"

"Mom sent us an invitation," I say, forcing myself to steady my breath.

"To what?"

"Her funeral," Kat exclaims. "The woman sent us an invitation to her freaking funeral, and now she won't even answer her phone."

"Oh my god." Miles's voice rises an octave. "Is she dead? Did Mom die while I was in hot yoga? She'll never forgive me. I'm the worst publicist ever. The woman raised me and—"

"Calm down, Miles," Kat hisses. "She just called me last night to ask if I could order her a new toaster on Amazon because hers, and I quote, 'must've grown legs and walked away.' I mean, I guess technically she could be dead. I haven't heard from her this morning, but if she *is* dead, then it's completely unrelated to this funeral stunt."

"She's not even old enough to be dead," Miles argues. "She's in her seventies, which is basically like being in your fifties. That's how aging works now. We're all twenty years younger."

"As someone who is almost in her forties, I can assure you I do not feel like I'm in my twenties," Kat says.

"So is she or is she not dead?" I ask.

"I highly doubt she's dead," Kat tries to assure me. "Like I'm 99.9 percent sure."

"I'm getting in my car," Miles says.

"Are you going to drive all the way out to the ranch to check on her?" I ask.

Mom's ranch, better known as Day Ranch, is located in the middle of nowhere in Riverside County, California. Both Miles and Kat live in LA, which means they're looking at a two-hour drive with traffic to get there.

"No." The rumble of Miles's car engine echoes through the Bluetooth speaker. "I'm going home to make sure I got an invitation. Then I'll drive out there."

"What if she didn't send you one?" I tease.

"Then the woman might as well be dead to me," he replies.

"I'm supposed to be in Temecula in an hour to look at a property with a client," Kat says. "I don't think I'll have time to drive out today. Liza, will you keep calling in the meantime?"

"I have to go in and teach."

"Can't you just call in a sub?" Kat asks. "It's a high school drama class in Colorado, not brain surgery."

"Ooh, maybe you can ask the teacher with the cats to cover for you," Miles adds.

"Miles, you're Mom's publicist, and you don't know if she's currently dead, alive, or somewhere in between, because you're too busy doing hot Pilates," I argue.

"It was hot yoga, and Kat's already established that she's probably not dead," Miles fires back. "Right, Kat?"

Kat doesn't reply. I check the screen, and sure enough, she's gone.

"She hung up," I say.

"Typical Kat. She barks orders and ducks out. I swear, it's like she thinks she's the unofficial manager of this family." He pauses for a moment. "You do think Mom is OK, right? I haven't checked in on her in a couple of weeks."

It's been longer for me. A month. Possibly two? Mom and I aren't very close, but we're not estranged. I would definitely know if she were anywhere near death—at least I thought I would, up until a few moments ago. Miles is probably the closest to her out of the three of us, which I guess goes to show that none of us are as connected with her as we should be.

"I'm sure she's fine."

"What does the invitation say?"

"It says—"

I'm interrupted by my daughter's heavy footsteps trailing down the stairs. She grabs the keys to my car from the hook near the door and gives me one of those incredulous stares that come so naturally to teenagers.

"We're going to be late." Avery nods toward the door. "C'mon."

"Miles, I'll take a picture of it and text you," I say. "Call me if you hear anything?"

"Will do," he replies.

I hang up and collect my purse, teaching bag, and lunch sack. Being a teacher means looking a little like a bag lady. I do a quick makeup and hair check in the downstairs bathroom, which mainly consists of making sure my dark brown hair doesn't look like it hasn't been washed in over a week, even though that's exactly how long it's been. Thank god for the creator of dry shampoo. I swipe a little bit of gloss on my lips and consider whether or not I have time to apply eyeliner. Avery honks the horn on my Prius twice, signaling that I don't. It's ironic that the child who made me late to work for the last eleven years because she always needed just five more minutes to rest is now the one blaring a horn at me because, god forbid, I need five minutes to look like a semi-together adult.

"Why are you in such a hurry?" I ask, despite already knowing the answer to the question. "Did you adjust the mirrors? What about the seat? I'm taller than you."

"Mom, I know what I'm doing," she says, putting the car in reverse. "And you know why I'm in a hurry."

Avery has a boyfriend, or at least I think she does. She will neither confirm nor deny any rumors about her and Matthew Martinez, the high school quarterback. It's so cliché, but also a little cute, I suppose. I just wish she'd talk to me about him so I wasn't relegated to getting details about my sixteen-year-old daughter's love life from cafeteria gossip. I get that having your mom work at your high school isn't exactly ideal. Toss in the fact that I was a teenager when I had Avery and we look practically like twins, and it makes the two of us being at the same school a little awkward.

"Officially I know nothing," I say, making sure my seat belt is as tight as possible. "Now if you want to confirm—"

She adjusts the volume on the car stereo. "Can we skip the usual interrogation and just have a chill ride instead?"

Chill isn't my strong suit, but I've got bigger mysteries to crack this morning. "Sure," I say, pulling Mom's death invitation out of my purse.

I run my finger along the thick card stock and read the invitation in its entirety again, hoping for a crumb of logic to make sense out of all this.

YOU ARE CORDIALLY INVITED

TO THE

FINAL CURTAIN CALL

OF

DARLA DAY

OCTOBER 20TH

Day Ranch
1771 Day Road, Hemet, CA

The time has come to pay our final respects to America's Darling. Services will be held October 20th at dusk. Light refreshments and hors d'oeuvres will be served.

Dress code for the evening is Night of a Thousand Darlas. Guests' dress should be inspired by one of the many iconic looks that Darla has worn throughout her fashionable life. For references, please visit Darla's website.

Accommodations for guests traveling to be provided by the Heavenly Motor Lodge at a special discounted rate.

Please include any dietary restrictions with RSVP to George Wilson, Day Ranch Manager.

There are no crumbs. There is no hidden message in this madness. It's just pure insanity. I snap a photo of the invitation and text it to Miles along with a string of angry-face emojis.

"What's that?" Avery points with her chin at the invitation on my lap, veering the Prius into the right-turn lane. A truck honks at us. "Jeez, what's his problem?"

"He probably just doesn't want to die today, Avery."

"I wasn't even close to him," she grumbles.

"Usually, people don't honk at you if you're not close to them."

I rub my temples with my index fingers in slow counterclockwise circles. I have six hours of running lines and working on sets for our fall performance of *Grease* with a bunch of hormonal teenagers. It's too damn early to have a headache already.

My phone rings, setting off the car's Bluetooth speakers. I try to switch the setting over to private before I answer, but Avery accepts the call from the steering wheel before I have the chance.

"Hey, Dad," Avery says, cheerfully. She jerks the car to a last-minute stop at a red light. "What's up?"

The only thing more unexpected than getting an invitation to my mother's funeral is getting a call from Scotty Samson, Avery's father, this early in the morning.

"Ave? Hey, honey, I'm trying to get ahold of your mom. Is she around?"

"You're not supposed to talk on the phone while you're driving," I scold her.

"You're the one with your phone hooked up to the car," she says. "And it's my dad. I didn't realize you were going to start controlling when I was allowed to talk to him on the phone now too."

"I am not trying to control when you talk to your father," I say. "It's not safe for you to be on the phone and drive. I'm not even sure it's safe for you to listen to music and drive."

"Is everything OK?" Scotty asks.

"Everything is fine," I say. Avery guns the green light, causing the tires to screech across the asphalt. "I'll call you back later today. If I manage to survive that long."

I hang up just as Avery makes an unnecessarily sharp turn into the teachers' parking lot at Crimson Clover Academy. She squeezes into a parking spot between an oversize SUV and the varsity wrestling coach's lifted truck with a rubber scrotum hanging from the tow hitch. I'm not sure what possesses a person to attach fake genitalia to their vehicle, but today is not the day to ponder such philosophical questions. No, I can already tell that today is going to require every shred of my mental wherewithal to simply survive.

"What's this?" Avery finally snags the invitation from my lap. Her hazel eyes, hidden behind thick, dark lashes, skim over it. "Grandma's dead?"

"No. She's just being dramatic."

"Cool." She places the invitation on the dash. "I've got practice tonight, and then some of the girls are going to grab food after. Can I borrow some cash?"

I reach into my purse and hand her two tens. "Are there going to be any boys joining—"

"Gotta go. Bye, Mom."

She slams the driver's side door so hard it sets my teeth on edge. I let out a primal, frustrated sort of growl. Does being an ATM count as a hobby? Because if so, I'm killing it.

Chapter 2

There are three universal truths when it comes to teaching: Windy days are the worst for student behavior. September is the absolute longest month of the school year. And a classroom full of quiet students without a teacher present is always something to be suspicious of. The last truth is the one I encounter when I walk into my classroom a few minutes late this morning. It also happens to be the truth I find the most terrifying.

My entire first-period class is huddled in the back corner of the room. They're partially hidden behind a freshly painted prop made to look like lockers. It's like they've unintentionally created a scene from *Grease*, and I half expect to find them sharing a pack of Camels. I set my purse down on my desk with a thud and clear my throat, expecting all of them to jump to attention and fall in line, but they're so focused that not a single student seems to notice or care. In my experience, the only thing that can hold the attention of a group of fourteen-year-olds that intently is a new video game that they'll all inevitably become obsessed with for the foreseeable future, or a YouTube video of a cat who looks suspiciously like Adam Driver.

"Alright, class." I lean against my metal desk. "Let's get started."

A few heads turn my way, followed by a few more, but there's no sense of urgency. If anything, it feels like they're all in on some inside joke.

"Just a reminder that all cell phones are prohibited—"

My phone belts out the *Golden Girls* theme song—my ringtone specifically for Miles—from inside my teaching bag, setting off a cacophony of exaggerated *ooh*s and threats of lunch detention. There's a pretty strict schoolwide cell-phone ban that applies to both staff and students, which I would've finished reminding them about had I not broken the policy. I rummage through my bag like a raccoon in a back-alley dumpster until I finally find my phone.

"Calm down, everyone," I say, silencing the ringer. I put my phone on "do not disturb" because Miles is nothing if not persistent. "Now, let's break into groups. We've got poodle skirts that need to be hemmed and plywood that needs to be turned into a convertible. Actors, we've got a few script adjustments to make, but I'm pretty sure we'll breeze right through them."

An unexpected spark of laughter breaks out among the students. Years of teaching have taught me that freshmen speak their own language, and trying to understand what they think is funny is a useless task. I ignore the little outburst and move on.

"Alright, any questions before we get started?"

Gwendolyn Rash's hand shoots up. I often find myself dreading Gwen's questions. Her parents are both morning news anchors, and she's basically Christiane Amanpour in training.

"Yes, Gwen?"

"Can I ask you a question unrelated to the play?"

A wave of muffled laughter crosses the room, but Gwen just stares at me with a completely straight face. Normally, I wouldn't indulge in a distraction like this, but something tells me no work will be accomplished today unless somebody addresses whatever elephant is hiding in this room.

"I suppose," I say, unable to hide the annoyance in my tone. "Go on."

"Does someone need to have special qualifications to be a drama teacher?"

"Huh?" A few scattered snickers escape across the class. "If you're asking if I went to school to be a teacher, then my diploma is literally hanging over my desk."

"That's not what I mean." She taps her chin with her pencil, and suddenly I really do feel like I'm in an interview hot seat. "Teaching drama is different from teaching math or history. I would assume you have to have some sort of special qualifications."

"No," I say, flatly, my patience worn thin. Kat's earlier comment echoes in my head. "It's not brain surgery."

Chaos erupts, and I can feel myself start to lose my cool. Normally, my classroom management is pretty flawless. Maybe it's a windy day. Maybe it's a full moon too. Or maybe I'm just coming down from the earlier adrenaline spike thanks to Mom's death-gram.

She can't actually be dead, can she? I mean, I know I'm not the most knowledgeable when it comes to the inner workings of the US Postal Service, but I don't think mail moves that fast. Somebody would've called us. Right? Am I a terrible daughter for coming to work? Should I be trying to get ahold of her right now? A bead of sweat runs down my chest. I'll call as soon as this period finishes.

The sharp rattle of the old wall phone catches me off guard, and I let out a little yelp. More laughing. Actually, at this point it feels more like heckling.

"Get to work," I say, sternly, as I walk across the room. "The next person who laughs gets detention." I pick up the receiver. "This is Ms.—"

"Where the hell have you been?" Miles's voice booms through the speaker.

"Why are you calling me at school?" I hiss, trying to shield myself with a filing cabinet. I lower my voice. "Is Mom OK?"

"How should I know? And I'm calling you at school because you put me on 'do not disturb.' What kind of a person doesn't answer their cell phone when their mother's earthly whereabouts are in limbo?"

"A person with twenty pairs of eyeballs watching her every move." I glance over my shoulder at the class and aggressively mouth, *Get to work.* "Why are you calling me and not her?"

"Because people won't stop calling me. She leaked the funeral, Liza. There's a blind item in *Page Six* about an A-List celebrity-turned-troubled-soap-opera-actress hosting a secret celebration of life this weekend. It's already been picked up by GMA and all the usual gossip blogs."

My stomach drops.

Well, that explains it. If Mom is in the news, then I must be too. I rest my head against the wall, resisting the urge to bang it repeatedly until I lose consciousness. That might scare the children. My mother was once a highly sought-after actress. She was the It Girl of the eighties, and she won an Oscar in the early nineties, but that's not how she's best remembered today.

In the early 2000s, she and I did a soap opera called *Sunset Breeze*. Breeze! Brain surgeon! That's why those little shits were laughing. It all makes sense. I played a sexy Doogie Howser rip-off—a teenage neurosurgeon who spent more time on the beach in a bikini than in an actual operating room—and Mom played an undercover FBI agent/surgeon. Daytime TV in the early 2000s was unhinged.

"Oh god, the comments are awful," Miles gasps.

"Don't read the comments," I whisper. "Don't read them. Don't read them. Don't—"

"You know I can't not read them," Miles says. "It's my job. NotSoAnonymous45 says, 'It's probably some whackadoodle euthanasia party. Hollywood is filled with crazies.' OK, well, I can't argue the crazy, but—"

"Does it say anything about me?" I slide down the side of the filing cabinet, trying my best to melt into the linoleum floor. "Because I'm pretty sure my first-period class knows about *Sunset Breeze*."

"Let me do a quick search," Miles says. "Oh, here we go. 'The Day Family Dynasty: Where Are They Now?'"

His voice trails off as he reads, and I press my head so hard against the receiver, it hurts my cheek.

"What does it say?"

"'Miles Vance hasn't had a major client added to his list since his mother signed him,'" he mumbles. "Well, that's just rude and completely not true. Who the hell—"

"Me, Miles!" I snap. "I'm the one freaking out here!"

A shudder of laughter echoes in the otherwise dead-silent classroom. I crawl behind my desk and turn on the noise machine I use to help me focus when I'm grading. Normally, I listen to "babbling brook," but this moment calls for "raging river."

"'Liza Day, the mother of action superstar Scott "Scotty" Samson's only child, is still unmarried,'" Miles reads.

"The most interesting thing that someone could possibly say about me is that I'm 'still unmarried.'"

"It also says that you're a teacher and . . . oh my."

"'Oh my' what?" I whisper-yell.

"Is that how you really dress for work?"

My stomach has gone from churning and dropping to full-on spin cycle. He can see me, which means that there's a picture of me on the internet, and not in an Instagram- or Facebook-curated kind of way that I can control. There's a picture of me on the internet that I did not put there, next to the phrase "still unmarried."

"I just sent you the link to the article," Miles says.

"I don't have my phone."

"What do you mean, you don't have your phone?"

"I mean getting my phone would require my students to see me, and I don't know that I'm in the mental headspace for that to happen right now. Just describe it to me."

"Alright." He clears his throat. "You're wearing this kind of dowdy black sweater that looks like you found it under a bridge, and your hair, well, it would definitely benefit from a blowout. Now your face—"

"I'll just wait and look at it myself, Stacy London."

"Honey, if I was Stacy London, you'd be in tears," he quips. "I'm going to try to do some damage control on this mess. Oh, and find out if Mom is dead."

"Well, if she's not, then I'm going to kill her."

He ends the call, and I let the phone fall out of my hand and onto the floor. I consider staying down here until the end of first period or until I die. Whichever comes first. Because that's what you do when your life as you know it becomes one of those whale carcasses that washes up on the shore from time to time. The kind that draws crowds of people to gawk at until it finally blows up, splattering smelly debris like a sadistic piñata.

"Ms. Day," Gwen calls. "Are you OK?"

"Yup," I grunt. If there's one common language between high school teacher and student, it's sarcasm. "Never better."

There's a flurry of hushed whispers, followed by a few giggles, but I'm too defeated to even attempt to control them. I glance at my cell phone on my desk, equal parts curious and terrified about what might be on it. What I still can't wrap my brain around is how my students found any of this. I mean, they don't know who Darla Day is, and they sure as hell don't care to. Come to think of it, the article Miles mentioned didn't lead with anything about *Sunset Breeze*. It led with Scotty, and none of the kids have ever made a big deal about Avery's dad being an actor. Maybe there's something else awful that happened today, and I've just been so wrapped up in Mom's funeral drama that I haven't noticed. I think back to Scotty's call from earlier this morning. Oh god. What if there's a story about him that somehow links back to me and—

"You can't look at the sun because it's too bright, but that's alright. We've still got the breeze, blowing through the palm trees. It's Sunset Breeze.*"*

I bolt upright. I'd know that god-awful theme song anywhere. The way the *e* sound on the last "breeze" drags out for an eternity. It makes my skin crawl.

They're watching the show. My students are watching my old soap opera, which up until a few minutes ago I thought was impossible. You can't even find clips of it on YouTube. Scotty's team more or less had them erased from the internet after he bought out the rights to it when he started filming the Brock Lucas series and became a *real* actor.

I get to my feet, wrath pulsing through my veins. I'm ready to hand out detentions like Oprah passing out cars. These kids will rue the day they brought a soap opera into my classroom.

"Hey, Ms. Day. You were kind of a babe back in the day," Colton James says in his best Danny Zuko / John Travolta voice.

Ew.

He turns his laptop toward me, and there I am in my swimsuit on my student's computer in my classroom. I am officially in hell.

"How did you get that?" I swallow back a dry heave. "Did you hack into something? Did you use LimeWire?"

"What's a lime wire?" he asks.

I grab his computer and try to drag the cursor to the top of the screen, but my fingers are too shaky to hold it still.

"Where did you find this?" I snap my head in Gwendolyn's direction and point at her. "You. Did your parents find this? Did they do some little investigative journaling because I didn't give you the role you wanted? Is that what happened?"

"What? No!" Gwen shakes her head nervously. "My parents are ethical journalists."

"Baloney!" I snap. "There's no such thing."

"You were on the welcome screen of Netflix this morning." Gwen hands me her cell phone and points to a picture of me in a bathing suit with a stethoscope dangling from my neck. "See?"

Yes. Yes, I see. And now I also want to rip my eyeballs out. All three seasons are there for the whole world to see, and there's nothing I can do to stop it.

"I have to go," I say, as I head toward my desk and collect my various bags. "Gwen, you're in charge of the class."

"For how long?" she asks. "And can I have my phone back?"

"You're in charge until a sub shows up," I call over my shoulder.

"But what about my phone?"

I glance down at the phone still in my hand. "Phones are prohibited in class."

There. Now there's at least one less student with instant access to my teenage, bikini-clad self. Maybe that's what I need to do. Just confiscate all the students' phones. And laptops. And TVs. Honestly, I just need to take out the Wi-Fi. If I can control the Wi-Fi, then I can basically control the whole school. Then I just have to worry about every other place in the world where there's internet and a screen.

Chapter 3

I call Scotty the moment I reach the parking lot. He doesn't pick up, but I am not deterred. I will keep calling until he answers or blocks me because that's what you do when twenty freshmen have access to a show that features you performing emergency brain surgery in a string bikini.

By the fourth call, he answers. "Sorry, I was on the phone with my agent and—"

"What the hell, Scotty?" I blurt out, catching the school parking-lot monitor off guard. He spills his coffee across his work pants and gives me a scowl. "Sorry. So sorry."

"It's fine," Scotty replies.

"No, I'm not sorry to you. I'm sorry to the man whose pants I just wet."

"What?"

"Scotty, did you know that *Sunset Breeze* was going to be on Netflix today?"

"I didn't know it would happen today," he says, calmly. He's always so calm. It drives me nuts because it reminds me of how uncalm I can be. "At least not until this morning."

"And you didn't think to mention that when you called, or at the very least follow up with a text?" I huff.

"My attorney sent you a letter. Several actually."

Why does the US Postal Service keep ruining my life?

"I don't believe in mail," I say. "I'm not a subscriber."

"What?" Now he's the one who sounds lost and confused. "Look, I sold the rights, and I wanted to make sure everyone who was part of the original series received their compensation. My attorney drafted everything up. You should've received a check."

Checks should come in special envelopes. Maybe bright gold or neon green. Something that screams *I have money inside*. Of course, that might lead to quite a bit of mail theft. Whatever. The system is broken.

I reach into my purse for my keys. "Dammit."

"I can have my attorney send it again."

"No, not dammit to that." I put the call on speaker as I squat down on the ground to check all my bags for my keys. "I think Avery has the car keys." A car door slams, followed by another. An engine starts. I gather my bags to move, because being run over in the school parking lot isn't on my morning bingo card. "Scotty, I'll have to call you . . . Hey! That's my car!"

"Are you OK?"

I don't answer him. I shove my phone in my pocket and drop my bags and break out into a sprint. Well, it feels like a sprint. In reality, I probably look like a five-year-old trying to round the bases in a Little League game, trying my best to avoid falling on my ass. I cut through a row of cars to beat my car to the exit.

Scotty's muffled yells from my pocket catch my attention. "Are you OK?"

I take the phone from my pocket. "Someone is trying to steal my car. Don't worry. I've got it under control. I think."

The Prius takes the corner fast, tires screeching against the asphalt, exactly the way it did earlier today . . . when Avery was driving.

"Shit."

"Liza, I think you need to call the police," Scotty shouts.

The car comes close enough into view for me to see through the front windshield. Close enough for me to see the passenger, Matthew Martinez, and the driver, my daughter. She mouths what looks like a series of expletives. Most likely the same series of expletives that are running through my head. She kills the engine, and something tells me it won't be the only thing that dies in this parking lot.

"It's fine," I lie. Things couldn't be any more *unfine*. "Just a prank. I'll call you back."

I end the call and walk up to the passenger side of the car. I tap on the glass and wait for Matthew to roll down the window. An artificial vanilla odor wafts from the inside of my car, and that's when I notice the vape pen in the cup holder.

"Hi, Ms. Day," he says, sheepishly. "We were just . . . uh . . . well."

"Get out of my car, Matthew," I snarl.

"Yep." He nods overzealously, like a bobblehead. "You can call me Matt, by the way."

"I won't be calling you anything." I open the car door.

"That works too."

He scrambles out of the car, his backpack falling onto the asphalt and spilling its contents everywhere, most of which rolls under my car. What doesn't end up under my car is a three-pack of condoms. The icing on the cake of this absolute shitstorm of a morning. I pick up the condoms with the tips of my fingernails.

"Those are—"

"Yours, Matthew?" I dangle them in front of him. "Are they yours? Well, now they're mine, and if you want them back, you can ask your parents to pick them up from the school office."

"Mom!" Avery snaps. "Can you calm down? Please?"

"This is me being calm, Avery Leigh." I shove past Matthew—not Matt—and plop into the passenger seat. I grab the vape pen and hold it out the window. "Don't forget this."

"That's actually not mine, Ms. Day," he says.

I glance at Avery and sigh. "Of course it's not."

I roll up the window and instruct Avery to park the car, which she does. The tires don't even screech this time.

"Is there anything else you want to tell me? Any other secrets you've been hanging on to, or does grand theft auto, sex, and smoking about cover it?"

She doesn't say anything. She just folds her arms across her chest and stares out the window, her face frozen in an expression of absolute contempt. Not regret. Not remorse. Not even a hint of guilt. Matthew at least had the decency to look ashamed, but not Avery.

She won't even look at me. Her long, chocolate-brown hair hangs along the side of her face like a curtain, making it impossible to see her expression. If it weren't for her white-knuckled grip on the steering wheel, I wouldn't be able to tell that she's bothered at all.

"Can I go back to class?" she asks, coolly.

"That's it? That's all you want to say to me?"

"What's the point? You're not going to listen to anything I have to say right now."

"You don't get to decide that. I'm the mom. You're the kid. That means you have to do something even if you don't see the point in it."

"Fine." She turns to face me. "I'm sorry for taking the car without telling you. That was wrong, and I shouldn't have done it. Now can I go to class?"

"Is this because of what happened this summer?" My voice is just above a whisper. "Is this a way for you to punish me or to get back at me?"

"Not everything is about you, Mom."

"That's not what I'm suggesting, and you know it." I pinch the bridge of my nose and let out a heavy sigh. "It was an impossible situation, Avery."

It happened in July. July has always been Avery's month with her dad. They go on these big trips together and have the best time exploring new places and new cuisines. They become like two peas in a pod, and honestly, nothing makes me happier than seeing the two of them together like that. It's a relationship I could never imagine having with my father.

For fifteen years, I made sure Avery had at least one uninterrupted month of time with her dad, but that all changed this past summer. Scotty and I have always maintained a strict policy of keeping Avery's life as separate from his career as possible, and until this year it was never an issue. Scotty couldn't rearrange his film schedule for the latest installment of the Brock Lucas franchise. He was filming all summer in New York, and of course, Avery wanted to be there. For years, she begged to spend time on set. The girl's been obsessed with acting ever since she could walk. Scotty wanted her there just as much as she wanted to be there.

But I wasn't OK with it. I couldn't get on board with her spending a month surrounded by actors and agents and a director known for always being on the hunt for a new, undiscovered muse. A film set is no place for a teenage girl. It's a place where even the strongest of kids are subject to constant criticism about everything from the shape of their body to the sound of their voice. I didn't doubt that Scotty would protect Avery, but I also didn't doubt that if Avery was offered even a small, uncredited part, he wouldn't be able to tell her no.

All it would take is one part, and she'd be hooked. She'd fight me tooth and nail to drop out of school early. She'd probably even try to get herself emancipated, because that's what Day women are like when it comes to acting. It's like a drug, and we'll do anything we can for another hit.

So, I put my foot down, and for the first time, Avery and I found ourselves on opposite sides of a line drawn in the sand. Unknowingly, I started a war between the two of us. It started with weeks of her giving me the cold shoulder, which then slowly morphed into Avery spending as much time out of the house as humanly possible. I thought the start of the school year might bring back some balance to our dysfunction, but that proved to be only the tip of a much deeper iceberg.

Avery dropped out of drama. I wasn't even aware of it until I got my school roster and saw that she wasn't on it. It was a last-minute switch that her counselor approved after she forged my signature. When I asked her why she did it, Avery just looked at me and said, "It's what you wanted, Mom. Now you don't have to worry about me acting. Not now. Not ever. You win."

"How did we get like this, Ave?" My anger starts to subside ever so slightly and is quickly replaced with an overwhelming sense of heartbreak and failure. "When did we decide that this was what our relationship was going to be like?"

She doesn't say anything. She won't. The girl who used to tell me her every thought, the comings and goings of her school day right down to what her friends packed for lunch, now barely says a word to me. The bell chimes, signaling the end of first period, and in an instant, her hands are off the steering wheel and on the door handle.

"Can we talk about this after practice?" she asks, her face decidedly pointed toward the door.

"I thought you were going out with the team for dinner after practice. I thought that's why you needed money. Was that just another lie?"

"No." Her voice softens. "I just didn't think I would be allowed to go."

"Oh. Well, you're right. You aren't allowed."

"So can I leave?"

"Fine." I motion toward the door. "But Avery, this can never happen again. Do you understand me?"

"I guess."

She slams the door closed. I watch her like a hawk until I see the school door close behind her. Part of me wants to barricade it closed and keep her locked up until I know what to do with her. Am I ever going to know what to do with her? For a moment, I consider calling Scotty. Not because I think he's going to know how to make this situation better, but because I'm so tired of feeling like an island.

My siblings don't have kids. The one time I ever asked them for help parenting Avery was when she was two and going through this phase where she'd run away from me whenever we left the house. It's kind of a full-circle moment now that I think about it. Anyway, she'd run, and once she went out into the street and just missed being sideswiped by a bicyclist. Up until that moment, I'd been trying to gentle parent her and felt like I was failing miserably. I was young, just twenty-one, and trying my best to raise myself and a baby on my own while going to school. Kat and Miles came to visit for the weekend, and both showed up with baby leashes.

It's cute, Miles argued. *It has a monkey on it and everything.*

They don't make baby shock collars, Kat said. *But the lady at Buy Buy Baby says this could hold back a pit bull if it needed to.*

To be fair, I did use the leash—Miles's, with the monkey, not the one possibly made for dogs—when we took Avery to a carnival. It did what it was supposed to, but the judgy looks from everyone around us were enough for me to throw both leashes away after my siblings left. I bought one of those baby carriers that you can wear instead, and I kept Avery strapped onto me like a baby sloth until she was four.

God, I wish I could do that now.

My phone buzzes with a text from Kat.

Kat: Mom's not dead.
Miles: Spoiler alert much?
Liza: So what's with the funeral?
Kat: Not sure yet.
Liza: Keep me posted.

I move into the driver's seat, and throw it in reverse. My car thuds against something. *Shit.* I glance in my backup camera, which I have a tendency to ignore more often than I care to admit. There's nothing on the screen. For a second, I wonder if I imagined the hit, but there's a tap on my window. It's Matthew Martinez, rubbing his hip, and motioning for me to roll down the window.

"What?" I snap. "You're supposed to be in class. I should write you a detention right now."

"I think I left my phone in your car," he says. "Could you check?"

I want to scream. I want to scream and shout and say every single one of Carlin's seven words you can't say on TV. Instead, I unlock my doors and let Matthew scrounge around under the seat of my car for his phone.

"Found it." He holds it up as if I'm supposed to care. I expect him to close the door and be on his way, but he just stands there like a labrador waiting for me to throw a ball. God, I'd love to throw something at him right now.

"Is there something else I can help you with?" I growl.

"Yeah." He looks down at his feet. "It's about the condoms."

"If you think I'm giving them back to you, then—"

"No. No. That's not what I mean. I just thought you should know we haven't used them."

"So, you're having unprotected sex with my daughter?" My eyeballs might actually start bleeding. "That's what you want me to know?"

"I meant that we haven't had sex." He lowers his voice. "I just thought you might want to know that."

That might actually be the one piece of good news I've had all morning, and that's saying something, considering the fact that I just found out my mother isn't dead.

"Goodbye, Matthew," I say.

"Goodbye, Ms. Day." He starts to close the car door but stops. "Also, if you could wait to reverse until after I move out of the way, that would be great. My hip still kinda hurts from when you hit me with your car."

"Fine."

"Thanks, I appreciate it."

"Oh, and Matthew?"

"Yes?"

"I would appreciate it if you didn't mention to anyone, especially Avery, that I hit you with my car."

"You got it, Ms. Day." He starts to close the door but once again stops. "One more thing. Do you think you could maybe write me a late pass for second period?"

I explain to Matthew that I'm only capable of honoring one of his requests this morning. He chooses not to be run over, which I think is a wise decision for the both of us.

Chapter 4

I pick up a box of wine, a bag of Cool Ranch Doritos, and a lavender-scented face mask from Target. It's moments like this when I appreciate self-checkout. I slip into a pair of my most hideous pajamas, because they are the coziest, and prepare to sink into my couch with my snacks and my mask like the world's saddest superhero, when my phone pings with an email.

I consider ignoring it, but my hyperfixation on having an empty inbox takes over. I pick up my phone and glance at the notification. It's from Principal Long. The subject line reads: *Teacher Code of Conduct Query.*

Shit.

Did Matthew Martinez rat me out? I barely tapped the kid. What kind of high school football player can't handle a little tap from a Prius?

I open the email and quickly wish that it was, in fact, an email about hitting a student with my car.

> Dear Ms. Day,
>
> It's come to my attention and the attention of the school board that your former work as an actress on a soap opera titled *Sunset Breeze* has garnered a fair amount of negative attention from many of our students, bringing a distraction to the academic

learning environment Crimson Clover Academy works to maintain.

As you are aware, upon hiring, all teachers are required to adhere to a code of conduct, which prohibits teachers from: *promoting reckless behavior, engaging in dangerous or lewd acts, and demonstrating poor judgment.* Your affiliation with this soap opera has brought into question your ability to maintain the type of conduct expected of Crimson Clover teachers, and it is requested that you meet in my office tomorrow morning at 7 a.m. to discuss this matter with me and a representative of the school board.

Regards,
Della Long, M.Ed.
Crimson Clover Academy Principal

They're firing me.

I dial Kat's number, and she picks up on the first ring.

"I haven't heard anything else about the funeral," she says. "But you are coming, right? Because I can't go to our mother's funeral without you. Especially not if she's alive."

"I need you to tell me if I'm being fired first." I fill her in on the details of the email, and the two of us dissect each sentence like a couple of forensic scientists. "Maybe the reckless behavior is performing brain surgery underage?"

"Maybe the reckless behavior is simply being a woman," Kat huffs. "This is the patriarchy at its finest. You know that? It makes me sick. Do you think they'd be giving Scotty this difficult of a time if he was a teacher at your school?"

"Uh, I don't know."

"The answer is *no*, Liza. *No.* Because men can do whatever they want, even if it's brain surgery in a bikini; meanwhile a woman can't even talk about freezing her eggs without losing her shot at partner at a real-estate firm that she helped build. It's bullshit."

I start to get the feeling that Kat may be dealing with her own drama. "So, bad day for you too, huh?"

"I'm sitting in my bathtub with a carton of ice cream and a bottle of prosecco." Her voice is muffled, likely from the ice cream. "I canceled all my appointments. I plan on getting completely drunk and bloated before getting into bed and rotting until I need to pick you and Avery up from the airport. You are coming, right?"

The thought of getting on a plane with Avery to attend my not-dead mother's funeral sounds almost as unpleasant as my meeting with the principal tomorrow morning. I decide not to mention the fiasco with Avery and Matthew, and Matthew and the back of my car, to Kat. That feels like drama for another day when she isn't so amped up. In this state of mind, she's liable to look up the Martinez family home address and ship them a bag of flaming dog poo.

"Let me see how tomorrow goes," I say. "Call me if you hear from Mom. OK?"

"Will do."

I decide to take my box of wine, Doritos, and face mask and draw a hot bath too, complete with rose-scented candles. It's a ritual I started the first summer that Avery left to go stay with her dad. The bath and candles, that is. This is my first time including dinner and drinks, but it feels right for the occasion.

The hot water glides over my skin, and every hair on my body stands at attention. I close my eyes and turn on my Stevie Nicks playlist, completely prepared to let the queen lull me into an almost comatose state. I'm not even twenty seconds into *Rhiannon* when my phone pings with a text. *Sigh.* This is why the bath ritual is reserved for when Avery's away. When she's with Scotty, I don't have to leave my phone on. I can unplug.

Before I look at it, I make myself promise that unless it's Avery, I won't respond. The world can survive just fine without me for the next hour. I check the screen. It's Scotty, and suddenly I remember that I actually kind of hate Scotty right now. He's the reason I'm in this bathtub. He's the reason I may lose my job. If it weren't for Scotty, I never would've been in that parking lot today in the first place, which means I wouldn't know about Avery playing Grand Theft Auto with my car.

I take a sip of my wine, which happens to be in a coffee mug instead of a wineglass because I didn't want Avery to come home and see a dirty wineglass. I came home to that scene plenty of times when I was her age, and the last thing I want is to resemble my mother in the slightest way.

I open the text, my fingers poised to eviscerate this man with angry-face emojis.

Scotty: Just got a Google alert. Sunset Breeze is trending on X.

What the hell is X?

Liza: X?
Scotty: It's what Twitter is called now.

My phone rings, and I almost drop it in the tub. Scotty's face flashes across the screen. He's trying to FaceTime. Why in the hell is he trying to FaceTime right now? Phones are for texting and playing sudoku or Wordle. Occasionally they are used for calls, but never, ever do I use my phone to FaceTime.

I send the call to voicemail and text him.

Liza: Can't talk right now.
Liza: Busy.
Scotty: My bad.

Liza: It's fine. Everything OK?

Why am I asking if he's OK? Of course he's OK. He's *trending on X*, whatever that means. He isn't worried about losing his job tomorrow. He didn't nearly murder his daughter's boyfriend with a Toyota, and his daughter doesn't hate him, because she's too busy hating me.

It occurs to me that I probably need to fill Scotty in on the details of today's events. At least the events that include Avery. I've just never had to do anything like this before. Minus the brief leash stage, Avery's basically been the perfect kid. I never even told him about the silent treatment or the fact that she dropped out of drama. I take another sip of wine. Guess there's no time like the present.

I dial his number.

"I thought you were busy." Scotty's voice is thick and gravelly. "You can call me after you're done doing whatever it is you're doing. Teaching?"

I glance at the time. It's just past three p.m. Technically, I should be teaching.

"Just finished up," I say.

"I'm in New York, which I guess means it's six here? Time zones are a mystery to me." He doesn't sound anything like the guy I spoke to in the parking lot this morning. His speech is too slow, his tone too melancholy.

"Are you OK?" I down the last of the wine in my mug. "You sound a little . . . off."

"I've been drinking, if I'm being honest."

We're twinning.

I catch a glimpse of myself in the full-length mirror. I'm bookended by a box of wine at one end of the tub and a now-empty coffee mug that says *Best Mom Ever* on the other end—oh, and I'm naked. *Twinning* might be the wrong word.

"Rough day?" I ask, unsure of how to proceed. Scotty and I are coparents. We're not friends, at least not anymore. I don't know how to comfort him, and quite frankly, I didn't call to comfort him. I called to give him a piece of my mind. A very sharp, stabby piece of my mind.

"They're canceling the franchise and scrapping the last movie we shot over the summer," he says. "That's why I'm in New York. That's why I was on the phone with my agent when you kept calling. He thought maybe there was a way to at least salvage the movie, but it didn't work."

"No more Brock Lucas?"

"Nope." He sighs. "Agent Lucas is officially retired. But not to worry, they're already in development for a spinoff featuring the kid who they brought on to be my partner two movies ago. He's twenty, with abs chiseled out of marble. Looks like a young Keanu Reeves. Getting old sucks."

"You're not old." I refill my mug. "I mean, you might be Hollywood old, but thirty-six isn't real-life old."

"I should've seen it coming. All the signs were there. They fed the young stud more and more lines while slowly cutting mine back. I was too arrogant, though. I thought I could be a Tom Cruise or something and play an action star until I was sixty."

"Is Tom Cruise sixty?" I rest my head against the tub.

"He's over sixty now."

"Well, I've always thought your action movies were much better than his."

"You've never seen any of my movies, Liza." He chuckles. "And I'm willing to bet that other than *Top Gun*, you haven't seen many of Tom's either."

He's not wrong. Action movies aren't my thing. I'm more of a romantic comedy / family dramedy kind of gal. Regardless of my preference, though, I do feel bad for Scotty. His mom worked so hard to help him become an actor. Unlike me, he didn't have any connections. His mom took him on auditions around the clock because it's what he wanted, and to his credit, it's what he was good at. He landed some commercials in the late nineties and later was picked up on a series that died halfway through the first season.

It's because that series failed that he auditioned for *Sunset Breeze*. Mom and I had already been cast, and I got to help with auditions for the part of Ryan West. I must've read with twenty different guys before Scotty walked in and stole the show. I wanted to hate him so much, but it was practically impossible. Scotty was just a natural in front of the camera. He made the script, no matter how ridiculous, come to life in a way nobody else who auditioned for the role did.

It took us a little while to get our footing, both on and off camera. I was nervous and absolutely certain the show was going to get canceled just like every other soap that had filmed in studio 2B the previous five years. The script was messy at best, and our director, Todd Darby, was so out of his element. It was like someone giving a Boy Scout permission to sail the *Titanic*. Sometimes I can't even believe we ever managed to film a single episode. But we did. Eventually, the audience fell in love with Naomi Parker, my character, and Ryan West. The nickname Ryomi was born. God, it made us cringe, but that's how we knew we made it. If you had a couple's nickname in the early and mid-2000s, you were something.

"Child support and all that won't be affected," Scotty says. "And I'll still be able to cover Avery's college. It's part of the reason I decided to make the deal to stream *Sunset Breeze*."

"I'm not worried about that."

"How is she, by the way?"

"Who?" I take another sip.

"Our daughter."

Something about the way he says *our daughter* makes me go all melty inside, which seems dangerous. Very dangerous.

"She's fine," I lie. "Sixteen. You know how that is."

"That's how old you were when we met." He pauses, and I can hear the clinking of ice cubes in a glass. I can visualize him swirling his glass of whiskey, and I can almost smell the scent of his amber-musk cologne.

"That was almost twenty years ago. How is that possible? How have twenty years gone by so fast? I mean, Avery's driving now."

"If that's what you want to call it."

"What if I come out sometime and work with her on it now that my schedule is open?"

"Sure. That would be good." Scotty's never come out to visit us in Colorado. It's always been Avery going to him or the two of them going somewhere on vacation. I don't know what I would do if the two of us were in the same zip code for any stretch of time.

"What about this weekend?"

If there was a panic button on this tub, I'd be jamming it with my fist.

"Busy," I blurt out. "Let me check my schedule and get back to you. OK?"

"Oh." His voice sounds small. "Yeah. That works." Well, now I feel like a jerk. "I better let you go."

"OK."

"Hey, Liza."

"Yeah?"

"Thanks."

"For what?" I ask.

"For doing such a great job with Avery. She's a good kid. She takes after you." The ice clinks again. "Just wanted you to know that."

If only he knew how acutely aware I am of the similarities between me and Avery. I could give an entire monologue right now of all the ways we're alike despite my best efforts to make her different. Because to be like me means to be like my mom, and the world truly only needs one Darla Day in it.

I put myself to bed as soon as I hear Avery come through the front door. I'm too tired to do any real parenting right now. She's home. She's safe. She's not having unprotected sex. At her age, I hadn't even kissed a boy. And that first boy that I kissed turned out to be her father.

Chapter 5

Sunset Breeze, Pilot Episode
Fall 2004

I stare at my reflection in the smudged vanity mirror, trying to spot it, whatever facial tell I must have that made it so easy for Scotty Samson to know that I have never been kissed. Not on-screen, and definitely not off-screen. I squint in the mirror, examining my cheeks and neck. I'm not usually someone who blushes, but I do sometimes get splotchy when I'm nervous. And Scotty Samson definitely makes me nervous. Maybe that's what gave me away.

"I don't know why you stress yourself out like this." Kat sighs. She's sprawled out on the plaid sofa in my dressing room, a leftover from the previous occupant. "You said you were done acting after that last sitcom with the talking anteater got canceled."

"First of all, there was no talking anteater." I roll my eyes. "It was an *Alf* reboot, and I was twelve. You can't trust a twelve-year-old to make logical career decisions."

"Was a twelve-year-old in charge of coming up with the idea of an *Alf* reboot?" Kat snarks.

I throw my makeup wedge at her. I'd throw her out of my dressing room too if it weren't for the fact that she's the only thing keeping me from climbing the walls right now. Today is the first live taping for *Sunset Breeze*, and even though I've performed in front of an audience before, it's been a few years. At sixteen, I'm a little rusty. I felt it all week during dress rehearsals. Mom was on point as per usual, and even acting newbie Scotty had to remind me of my lines more than a handful of times. That was when he suggested that my nerves might have something to do with the fact that I've never been kissed.

To be honest, the kiss wasn't even in the top five of my ever-growing list of worries and concerns for the show's taping this week, although it quickly shot up there after he mentioned it. My primary concern is Mom. Not her ability to perform. The woman has an Academy Award. She could play her new role of Lana Parker, neurosurgeon and secret FBI agent, in her sleep. What concerns me are her heart and her ego, both of which have taken a significant beating over the past few years and will take an even bigger hit if *Sunset Breeze* tanks.

"How do you know which way to tilt your head?" I turn around and face Kat. "Is it like driving?"

"Driving?" Kat's brow lifts.

"Yes, you know, like lanes that you drive in so everybody doesn't crash into one another."

The door to my dressing room opens, and Miles pops his head in. "Have you tried the pasta salad? God, I forgot how much I missed craft services."

"Get in here." Kat motions to him. "You're never going to believe how this one thinks kissing works."

"Kat," I groan.

In my defense, it's not like I've had a ton of opportunities to kiss anyone. I've barely had much of an opportunity to make friends. Between Mom and Dad's marriages and divorces, the only consistent place in my life has been the ranch. Day Ranch had a lot to offer me, but kissing boys wasn't part of the deal.

"Can I just tell you how jealous I am that you get to kiss that Brad Pitt doppelgänger?" Miles clutches his chest with the hand that isn't clutching his pasta salad. "Normally, I prefer *Legends of the Fall* Brad

Pitt—long hair and rugged. But this *Ocean's Eleven* thing he's got going is completely changing my opinion on frosted tips."

"I'm sorry, but how is this supposed to help me?" I reach for my script and begin to look over my lines.

"Alright, alright." Kat stands and takes my script from me. "C'mon now. Up you go."

I stare at my sister in abject horror. "You're not going to ask me to kiss you, are you?"

"Ew." Miles makes a gagging sound. "Please don't ruin this pasta salad for me."

"Oh my god, grow up. Both of you." Kat takes me by the shoulders and stands me up. "I can't believe you haven't already rehearsed this. I'm no actor, but it doesn't seem very efficient to not practice all parts of a script."

"Todd wants it to look authentic," I say, which is not exactly true. The truth is that the cast rehearsals have been so epically bad that we haven't actually gotten through the entire script.

Todd Darby is a relatively new director, and managing big personalities isn't exactly his strong suit. As for the rest of the mostly green cast, it doesn't appear that acting is our collective strong suit. We're awful, and I'm not talking *soap opera* bad. I'm talking *can barely get through a scene without flubbing lines, missing marks, or going off on tangents that make zero sense* bad. Do you have any idea how hard it is to make a show about a coastal hospital that has possibly been infiltrated by Russian spies look bad?

"What's the line before the kiss?" Kat asks.

"'You should stop CPR when the victim demonstrates they are able to breathe without complication on their own,'" I say.

"That's possibly the most unsexy line I've ever heard," Miles says.

"Never mind that," Kat says. "You deliver your line, and then you tilt your head in the direction you want to lean in to for the kiss. Just make it look natural. Let's run through it."

The last thing I want to do is practice my kissing scene with my sister, but once Kat has an idea in her head, that's it. "Fine." I sigh.

She lies on the threadbare floral rug, another leftover from the last actress of the last failed soap-opera series who graced this room. I kneel next to her. In the actual scene, Scotty and I are on the beach. He plays a lifeguard who nearly drowns while trying to rescue a miniature poodle that got swept up in a wave, and I'm the teenage neurosurgeon who likes to spend her lunch running on the beach instead of eating, because god forbid we ever pass up a chance for a woman to run in a bikini.

"So, I've just finished pumping your chest," I say.

"Don't tell me," Kat says, in an overly dramatic tone. "Act it."

"Good grief." I roll my eyes. "You don't even know your line."

"Is it 'kiss me'?" Kat closes her eyes and puckers up.

"I quit." I get up from my spot on the floor and open the door to my dressing room. "Out. The both of you. Now."

"What did I do?" Miles holds up his fork in protest. "I'm just peacefully eating my pasta salad."

"I wouldn't care if you were peacefully conducting a drum circle." I motion toward the door. "I need you both gone. Now. Don't make me call security."

"Fine." Kat sighs. She dusts her Abercrombie jeans off and stands. "I know when my services aren't wanted. C'mon, Miles." She gives me a quick hug and whispers, "Break a leg."

I close the door behind them and lean against it. The sudden silence accompanying my siblings' exit feels more jarring than soothing. It reminds me of the fact that unlike the other shows and even commercials I've done as a young child, this time around I'm on my own. I don't have Mom sitting in my dressing room with me to hype me up. She's got to get herself hyped up. She's got her own lines and nerves to deal with. She's not in Mom mode. She's in full-on actress mode, which is the mode I'm supposed to be in, but I just can't seem to get there.

The door pushes against my back, giving me a little shove.

"Listen, I don't care how bad I suck at kissing, I'm not learning how to do it on my sister." I open the door, and to my horror, Scotty Samson is standing on the other side of it. "Oh shit. It's you."

"Sorry to disappoint." He smirks. "We can't all be your sister."

I hate my life. Why does he always have something clever to say? Why does he always have to look so good and so put together? He's dressed in his lifeguard uniform, complete with a puka-shell necklace and leather REEF sandals. I'm not even dressed in my scrubs yet. I'm supposed to be the experienced professional between the two of us, yet he's always one step ahead of me.

"You going to let me in?" he asks.

"Fine." I move out of the doorframe and let him in. He settles on the sofa. "What do you want?"

"Just wanted to see how you're doing." He picks up one of the floral throw pillows and sniffs it. "Man, I thought I was the only one who ended up with a dressing room that smells like mothballs."

"My room doesn't smell like mothballs," I say, defensively. "It's just not aired out yet."

Truthfully, it does smell a little like mothballs, although Mom noted the scent as being *failure mixed with sadness*. It kind of seems appropriate, considering the fact that for the last five years in a row, this dressing room has belonged to a different actress each year. They call the studio we're filming in cursed. Not a single series that's shot here has made it through a full season.

"You nervous?" Scotty asks.

He looks at me, and for the first time all week, I don't get the sense that he's being a smart-ass. I get the impression that he might be just as nervous as I am.

"A little." I try to play it cool. "There's a lot of medical jargon I have to remember, but it'll be fine."

"I can relate. I've got a bunch of surfer lingo I've got to remember. Really tough stuff like *dude* and *bro*."

I chuckle, but only a little, because Scotty Samson seems like the kind of guy who gets a big head from girls laughing at his jokes.

"I could help you go over your lines, if you want. We've got twenty minutes before we start shooting."

"I'm good," I lie. "My siblings helped me rehearse before they left."

"Right. You kissed your sister. I almost forgot."

"I did *not* kiss my sister," I snarl, wishing I had something I could throw at him. "You're the one from Iowa. Isn't that the sort of stuff you people do there all the time—kiss your cousins and grow corn?"

"I don't know if it's something we do all the time, but it's definitely how I learned to kiss," he teases. "To be clear, I'm saying I learned how to kiss on an ear of corn. Not my cousin. I wasn't her type."

"Well, I'm glad someone in your family has some taste."

"All kidding aside"—he runs his finger along the bumpy pink-and-white shells on his necklace—"I just wanted to let you know that I've never kissed anyone before either."

"Well, this is your first acting job."

"I don't just mean in front of a camera," he says, softly. "I haven't kissed anyone ever."

It's hard to tell whether he's being serious. Nothing about Scotty ever seems serious. Not the way he constantly hid my stethoscope during rehearsals this week, or the way he kept calling me Lisa instead of Liza for days. He's a ham, and everybody seems to love him for it, except me. But right now, he's not acting like he's playing things up for attention. Right now, he just seems like a regular sixteen-year-old kid who might be slightly in over his head when it comes to this whole acting thing.

"Well, neither have I." I turn away from him and face my mirror.

"Really?" He sounds surprised.

"Yes, really." I twist a section of my ponytail around my finger. "I kind of assumed you knew, since you've been teasing me about it all week."

"I was just teasing you because I was nervous. I do that sometimes. It's kind of obnoxious, I guess."

"'Kind of'?"

"OK, fine. Very obnoxious."

"Actually, you've been practically intolerable all week long."

"Duly noted."

I realize that he's trying to apologize, but I'm too fired up to let things go. For the first time in weeks, I feel like I have the upper hand. Like I'm finally getting through his thick head of spiky hair. It's kind of exhilarating.

"I have been nothing but nice to you, and you've made me the butt of all your dumb jokes. And yes, your jokes are dumb, in case you weren't aware."

"Liza—"

"I'm not finished." I start to pace between the sofa and vanity, electricity firing through my veins. "You made me feel like an absolute idiot for having never been kissed before; meanwhile, you're just as much of a kissing virgin as I am."

"Did you just say '*kissing virgin*'?"

"Well, what would you call it?" I rest my hands on my hips. "Do you have a better name for it, or are you just going to mock me some more?"

"No, I don't have a better name." He stands up, blocking my path. "But I also know I don't want to be called that."

"Well, I certainly don't want to be called that either," I huff. "Just like I didn't want to be called Lisa all week, but here we are."

He reaches out and rests his hand on my shoulder unexpectedly. I look at it and then him, trying to discern if he's made some sort of error by placing it there. He doesn't pull it away, and surprisingly, I don't mind it being there. I do want to know why it's there, though.

"What are you doing?" I ask.

"I'm trying to close the physical distance between us," he says, almost robotically.

"Why?"

"Because that's what it says to do in the magazine."

"What magazine?"

He reaches into the back pocket of his board shorts and pulls out a copy of *Teen* magazine that looks like it's from the early nineties. "This." He holds it out to me. "It was in my dressing room. It tells you whether you're a winter or a spring, and what kind of product you should use if you have an oily face."

A smile tugs at my lips as I take the magazine from him. "Are you about to tell me whether I'm an autumn or a summer?"

"It also has kissing advice." He points to a yellow sticky note hanging out from the top of the magazine. "I just kind of thought it could be useful for you and me, since we're going to be having our first kiss on camera for the whole world to see."

"I highly doubt the whole world is going to be tuning in to our pilot episode, Scotty." I open the magazine and skim through the article. "It says here that step one is to ask permission, not close the distance."

"I know." He holds my gaze. "But I figured if you swatted my hand away, I would know that kissing practice would definitely be off the table, and I could spare myself some embarrassment."

"Well, I haven't hit you yet." I look up at him, and for the first time, I don't see the guy who knows everything. I see a regular sixteen-year-old kid who looks just as unsure about everything as I am. I also see someone I want to kiss. "What's the next step?" I ask.

"I'll need to consult the magazine to be sure, but I think we—"

I don't let him finish. Instead, I tilt up on my tippy toes and close the rest of the distance between us. I press my lips against his pillowy-soft mouth without giving a single thought to what angle I should have my face turned. He tastes like peppermint and smells like the ocean, which might be the best combination ever created. When I pull away, he pulls me back to him, and together we melt into a pile of teenage hormones and angst, not stopping until one of the assistants knocks on my door with a five-minute warning.

When we finally reach our kissing scene on the fake beach in front of the green screen, we know exactly what to do, and neither of us seems to mind when the director asks us to do a second and third take.

Chapter 6

I try to sneak out of the house without waking Avery. I don't want our first conversation post blowup to be about my job, and whether I'll still have one at the end of the day. I leave a note for her on the kitchen counter, letting her know I plan to be back in time to take her to school.

My heart races for most of the drive, taking turns with the pounding in my head from last night's wine. I made sure to throw the box away this morning and rinse out the mug. The whole process made me feel icky. It made me wonder how many times Mom did the same thing before she finally stopped caring.

My phone rings, and it's as if I've somehow managed to summon the devil herself just by thinking about her. I click accept on the car's touch screen.

"Mom?" I say it like a question because I can count on one hand the number of times my mom has called me at this hour. It's before seven here, which means it's before six her time. Mom is a solid ten a.m. riser at best. "Are you OK?"

"Salmon or ratatouille?"

I don't even know how to respond to that. Is she taking a poll? I can't hear the word *ratatouille* without thinking about that little rat movie, so I'm inclined to say salmon. But the thought of fish before I've even drank all my coffee sounds vile.

"Why?"

"Huh?"

This is a brilliant conversation. "Mom, why are you asking me about food?"

"Well, you didn't RSVP to George, and I know you received my invitation. I figured I better take things into my own hands. So, what will you be having?"

It's early, so there's a chance I could be wrong, but I don't remember there being a food option on the invitation. "Are you sure you're serving dinner?"

"Liza, what kind of a funeral would it be without a dinner?"

"I don't know. What kind of a funeral is it without a dead person, Mom?" I stop at the intersection right before the school. "Can I call you back? I'm actually on my way to a meeting."

I hear her talking, but it's not to me. Her voice keeps cutting in and out like she's waving the phone around. "George says there isn't a dinner after all. Just appetizers. Which I remember Chauncey—that's the man who's helping me with my funeral—saying was much more in vogue."

The light turns green, and I reluctantly turn into the school parking lot. "OK, Mom. I'm going to have to—"

"So you'll be here, Liza. Right? I mean, you wouldn't miss my funeral. Would you?"

I fight the urge to tell her that I'll attend the second one. "I'm not sure. It's short notice, and I've got a lot going on."

"Well, all funerals are short notice, Liza," she argues. I hate that she says my name so much. Something about the inflection in her tone makes it sound like it's a curse word. "If anything, I'm giving you more notice than daughters usually get."

I pull into a parking spot, this one thankfully not next to a car with genitalia. "Thanks. I think?"

"Is it money?"

"Is what money?"

"The reason you're avoiding coming to my funeral. Is it because you can't afford it on a schoolteacher's salary? I can see if Frank's plane is available. He used to fly your grandparents around all the time. I'm sure his estate would take my call in a pinch."

The Frank she's referring to is Sinatra. My grandparents were moderately famous, but the way Mom talks about them, you'd think they were the Beatles.

"You know he's dead, right? He has been for a very long time, Mom."

"Of course I know that, Liza," she snaps. "But they didn't bury the plane with him. Excuse me for wanting my daughter and only granddaughter to be at my funeral."

Do you ever have the feeling you're trapped in a conversation? Like the person who's talking is also holding you hostage, and the only way to get out of the situation is to do something drastic? Once I went on a date with an elementary school teacher. Nice guy, or so I thought. He taught first grade. Who doesn't like a guy willing to teach children who still have yet to master the ability to tie their shoes and wipe their noses?

Me. That's who. This man talked for an entire hour about the Jurassic Park movies. Thirty minutes in, and I was willing to volunteer to play the role of the goat that gets sacrificed to the T. rex in the first Jurassic Park movie. Forty minutes in, and I considered the fact that I might actually hate men. Once an hour hit, I felt like my soul was exiting my body, and not in a fun, marijuana-induced way. I was going to die at that table if I didn't do something drastic, so that's what I did. I thought of the most unattractive and unhinged way possible to end a conversation.

I think I'm going to shit my pants, I said. *Please don't wait for me. I'm going to the bathroom, and it might take hours.*

This man looked at me with so much disgust you would've thought I'd suggested I was going to shit in *his* pants. I left the table, and we never spoke again.

"Mom." I interrupt her rambling about god knows what. "I'm going to shit my pants. I'll call you later."

I hang up and say a little prayer before heading to the principal's office, where I very likely could end up pooping my pants.

It's early. Most of the teachers and office staff don't show up until closer to eight. I make my way into the office, and the school secretary lets Principal Long know that I'm here. I take a seat in the lobby, feeling very much like a student in trouble for doing something stupid, like, I don't know, stealing her mother's car.

"Liza." Principal Long greets me stoically. There's a woman standing next to her, a board representative most likely, that I don't recognize. "This is Melinda Martinez. She's our board representative."

Martinez.

Maybe it's just a coincidence?

"Nice to finally meet you." She holds out her hand for me to shake. "I keep telling the kids that we need to have a little get-together."

"'The kids'?" I have to remind myself to stop squeezing her hand. This woman holds my fate in it, after all. "Are you Matthew's mom?"

"So formal." She laughs. "Call him Matt."

"Uh-oh," Principal Long says. "I'm worried we might have a conflict of interest here. I wasn't aware that you two had a connection."

You and me both, sister.

"No need to worry, Principal Long," Melinda says. "We all three want what's best for our students. I think we can handle this, don't you, Liza?"

"Sure," I say.

What are the odds that the woman whose kid I hit with my car would be the board member deciding whether I was fit to be a teacher at Crimson Clover?

Maybe it's a good thing. She seems to like Avery. At the very least, she seems to have had an actual conversation with my daughter, which is more than I can say I've had with her son. I don't think you can count *You can pick up your condoms in the school office* as an actual conversation.

We take a seat in the office, Principal Long behind her desk, and Melinda and I next to each other on the opposite side. We look like a lovely lesbian couple prepared to discuss the academic progress of our children.

"Liza, first and foremost, I want you to know that this meeting is purely to gather information. No major decisions will be made today." Principal Long offers me a thin smile, which I suspect she thinks is comforting. How nice to know nobody will fire me today. "With that being said, we are going to ask that you take a leave of absence while the board processes this information."

"Paid, of course," Melinda says, touching my arm. "I know how important money is to teachers."

I don't know what Melinda does for a living, but I'm willing to bet it's *kept woman* or *trophy wife*. I smile and nod because I think that's what these people want from me.

"Is there anything you'd like to say?" Principal Long asks. "In defense of your character. Moral character, that is. Not the character you played on television."

I feel like everybody has a script they're reading from except me.

"I wasn't aware my character was in need of defense." I pause, waiting for them to offer an explanation. They don't. Must not be in the script. "My teaching reviews have always been good. I don't have excessive absences. The students like my class, and our productions have always been well attended and supported."

"To be clear, we're not concerned about your character as an educator," Principal Long says. "It's the show that you were a part of. *Malibu Sun*."

"Sunset Breeze," I correct her.

"Yes, *Sunset Breeze*. Well, as I said in the email, your performance has caused quite a bit of controversy, and—"

"I'm going to cut right to the chase, Liza," Melinda says, patting my arm. Actually, she's really petting it more than patting it. I hate it. "The character you played on that show, well, she's a little slutty."

"What?" I scoff. *Is she serious?* "Look, I know that Naomi—that's the character I played—I know that she shows a lot of skin. In her defense, she spends a lot of time on the beach. But she's not slutty. She has one love interest for all three seasons. Well, minus that time she was accidentally seduced by Ryan's long-lost twin. Uh, Ryan is Naomi's love interest. He's also my daughter's father. Well, the actor who played him. Scotty."

"Let's not split hairs." Melinda pets me with a little more vigor. If she keeps this up, I'm going to end up chafing. "You're seen getting very, very physical on the show. You even have sex on it in the second season."

I don't know if I'm more bothered that this woman has watched me in a sex scene or that she knows the exact season the scene took place in. I pull my arm away in case there's some sort of *Fatal Attraction* situation going on here.

"I didn't actually have sex," I argue. "It's all pretend. It's acting."

"But what message does it send to the children?" Principal Long asks. "I mean, your students have access to all this material. Don't you think it will influence them to . . . you know?"

"Have premarital sex," Melinda says. "If they see a teacher having sex—"

"Can you please stop saying that?" I plead. "I was an actress. I was playing a role. Last spring, Porter Hartford played Scar in our adaption of the *Lion King*, and nobody is running around worried that he might actually try to throw someone off a cliff."

"Murder isn't the same as sex," Melinda says. God, I hope Matthew gets his brains from his father's side of the family. "Sex leads to pregnancy and sexually transmitted diseases."

I wonder how this woman would feel if she realized I have her son's condoms in my purse.

"And murder is just population control," I scoff. Neither woman looks amused by my humor. "Look, I don't really know what to say. I had no idea the show was going to be released. I apologize for the distraction this has caused, but at the end of the day, there's nothing I can do about it. It is what it is."

"Is that your final statement?" Principal Long asks. She has a pencil poised in her hand. "'It is what it is'? Is that correct?"

I'm fired. Maybe not right now. Maybe not today. But the writing's on the wall. I am being fired for a sex scene I filmed twenty years ago. A sex scene that kept everything under the sheets, which I filmed with a pair of sweatpants on.

"Can you add one more thing?" I ask. "Can you write down that I quit?"

"Excuse me?" Principal Long's face drops. "You're quitting?"

"To be clear, we're not asking you to do that," Melinda adds, quickly.

"And if you do quit, you won't be able to collect unemployment or any severance that the board might wish to offer you," Principal Long says.

"I quit." I stand up. "You can write that down." I start for the door but stop. "Oh, and I won't be able to clear my room out until next week. I have a funeral to attend this weekend."

"Oh, I'm sorry to hear that." Melinda stands and opens her arms to me like she expects me to hug her and cry on her shoulder. "Was it somebody you were close to?"

"Just my mother," I deadpan.

"Maybe you should hold off on making any major decisions right now, Liza," Principal Long offers. "It's clear you're in a highly emotional state."

"No, it's fine," I say. "This is what she would've wanted." I reach into my purse, grab the foil-wrapped condoms, and hand them to Melinda. "Your son left these in my car yesterday after I caught him and Avery trying to leave campus."

"Oh god." Her face goes pale.

"Don't worry." I pet her arm, the way she did mine. "He says they don't use them. Enjoy the rest of your day."

That's what my mother would've wanted, if she actually were dead. If you can't control your entrance into a room, make sure you make a memorable exit.

Chapter 7

Avery and I touch down in LA the next day.

She hasn't spoken to me since I quit. Turns out Melinda Martinez isn't nearly as good as her son is when it comes to keeping things to herself. Matthew broke up with Avery in a text. A text I suspect his mother authored rather than him, unless Matthew regularly begins his texts with *Unfortunately it has come to my attention*. Either way, she hates me again, which actually bothers me more than the fact that I'm now unemployed.

"Maybe we could go to the beach one day while we're here," I say as we descend down the airport escalator. "It would be a bit of a drive, but it would be worth it." She doesn't even grunt an acknowledgment. "How long has it been since you've been to the beach? Five years? Maybe—"

"Dad took me last summer," she says, avoiding all possible eye contact with me. "Correction. He took me two summers ago. Last summer I didn't get to see him."

I'm going to call this a win, considering the fact that this is the most she's said to me in days.

"Oh, look! There's Aunt Kat and Uncle Miles." Never in my life have I been more relieved to see my siblings. I hurry off the escalator and practically jump into my sister's arms. She smells like coffee and jasmine, and her embrace feels like home.

"Avery hates me," I whisper. "Please make her stop. I'll do anything."

"Are you planning on using any more of your eggs?" Kat pulls away. "Because I know yours are old, but they're still younger than mine, and I could use eggs."

"'I'll do anything' might've been too broad of a statement," I say. "You know, most people ask how your flight was before they call dibs on your reproductive parts."

"I will never be able to eat eggs again after hearing this one go on and on about hers all morning." Miles gives Avery a hug and then kisses me on the cheek. "Now, sperm-donor shopping, that's something I can take an interest in."

"Is this about the embryos and the brokerage?" I ask.

"And the patriarchy," Miles adds. "And the disappointing nature of heterosexual men in power, which typically results in sexism." He lowers his voice. "It was a very, very long car ride."

"Avery, what do you want for dinner? Your uncle has decided that you're in charge."

"You better check with my mom first," Avery says, flatly.

"Ooh." Miles side-eyes me. "Guess it's pretty chilly in Colorado right now."

"Like the Arctic," I say.

Avery picks Waffle House, marking the first time that any of us have eaten at the breakfast establishment in twenty years, if not longer. She orders eggs in every way imaginable, which nearly makes Miles vomit. Both he and Kat do their best to engage her in conversation, but she's like a stone fortress, barely offering more than a one-word answer.

She gets up to use the restroom, and I follow her, grabbing her wrist before she can shut the stall door on me.

"What are you doing?" she snarls. "You know, if someone walked in right now, they might think you're trying to abduct me."

The thing that nobody tells you when you have kids is the number of times you want to say really mean things to them but you can't because you have to be the adult.

"Look," I say, letting go of her wrist. "You can be a jerk to me, but they're off-limits. Your aunt and uncle have never been anything but kind and loving to you. Being mean to them doesn't hurt me, it hurts them. Got it?"

"Whatever." She tries to close the door again, but I catch it. "What now?"

"I still haven't told your dad about what happened with the car or the boy or the condoms," I say. "And unless you want me to call him right now and discuss all of that at once, I suggest that when you come back out of that stall and return to the table, you show up with a pleasant attitude."

Avery's expression shifts from an angry wolf ready to rip me to shreds to a terrified chihuahua worried I might pounce on her. I've never played the *I'll tell your dad* card, because, frankly, I never needed to. But what choice do I have now? It's not my finest moment, but it's all I've got. If I can threaten her into being a decent human for the next four days, then I'll take it.

"So you're blackmailing me into being nice?" Avery says, cautiously.

"I guess I am."

"Fine." She shakes her head and makes a sound of disapproval. "I'll play your little game, but just know that it's all pretend. Anytime I'm being nice to you or anyone, I'm secretly thinking in my head how much I'd rather be stabbed in the leg with a spork."

"Thanks, honey," I say, as she slams the door on me. "Love you too."

~

After dinner, we say goodbye to Kat for the evening. She'll meet us tomorrow to head to the ranch. Tonight, we're staying at Miles's place. His husband, James, is away on business, so it'll be just us three. Miles gets Avery set up in the guest room, while I sip my wine and snoop around his apartment, careful to keep my distance from Xavier, his pet parrot, who Miles claims is basically like a child, only better. At this point, I think he might be on to something.

His home is effortlessly chic in a way that mine could never be. It's all white walls with gallery-style artwork hung throughout and doors painted black with gold hardware. He has an extensive library of old movies—both VHS and DVD—which he has arranged by genre and subcategorized by leading actors. The Diane Keaton and Meryl Streep sections are my personal favorites.

I linger on a shelf of family pictures. Photos of me and Miles and Kat when we were kids are lined up in chronological order, starting from our first photo as a family at my fourth birthday party. Miles has a different biological mother than Kat and I. Our father had an affair when he was married to Mom the first time. It wasn't until the divorce that Mom realized Miles existed. Dad showed up to my party with Miles and a backpack.

I don't remember what was said or what deals were made that day. All I know is that Miles stayed for my party and never left. I'm just three months older than him, and by the time we celebrated his fourth birthday, he was my best friend. He was probably Mom's favorite child too. She always wanted a boy, and the fact that this one didn't even give her stretch marks made him the apple of her eye.

Surprisingly, Miles was what brought Mom and Dad back together. She ended up adopting him. It would take a few years for Mom to agree to marry Dad again, and it would only take her a few months to realize it was a mistake. But Miles wasn't.

As I skim through the photos, I notice someone's missing. James. There's not a single picture of him or of his family on the shelf. No wedding pictures. Not even the picture of the two of them the day they adopted Xavier.

"So when were you planning on telling us that our sweet little Avery Leigh was actually Emily Rose?" He sinks into his emerald velvet couch as exhausted as if he's just run a marathon. "Should I sleep with my door locked?"

"Where's James?" I point to the shelf. "His pictures are all gone. Why?"

"So that's where we're starting. I was kind of hoping we could stick to the topic of your baggage instead of mine." He takes a sip of his wine. "But if you must know, James and I are taking a break."

"Like a Ross and Rachel sort of thing?"

"More like a Gwyneth Paltrow and Chris Martin conscious uncoupling thing."

"But you love each other. I mean you really, obnoxiously love each other." I sit next to him, folding my legs underneath me. "You have a parrot together."

"We share custody of Xavier," he says. "And we still love each other. We just want different things."

"Like what?"

"He wants a baby. I don't." He takes a long sip of his wine. "Honestly, it's for the best. I wouldn't want to hold him back from his dreams, and he doesn't want to hold me back from mine. Of course, my dreams always involved him, but I'm figuring things out. I'm dating."

"Does Kat know?" I ask. "What about Mom?"

"That I'm dating?" He chuckles. "God no."

"I mean the divorce."

"We haven't actually filed papers yet. We will, eventually, or we won't."

I'm used to Miles being wishy-washy when it comes to most things. He's the only kid I've ever known who couldn't commit to just one favorite color, or one favorite anything for that matter. Except for James. James was Miles's favorite everything, and something makes me think that there's more to this conscious uncoupling than what he's letting on.

My phone pings with a notification, and I walk across the living room into the kitchen to retrieve it from my purse. Miles follows me with his empty glass and my glass, which he's currently working on draining.

I perch on top of the counter and pull out my phone. It's a text from Scotty. The first text I've received since our bathtub gabfest.

Scotty: Hey, do you have a sec to talk?

Miles is leaning over my shoulder, reading, before I can even think about hiding my screen. "Ooh, you two talk casually now? That's new."

"We don't talk casually," I grumble.

Liza: Sorry. Busy.

"You're not busy," Miles says. "I don't mind you taking a call."

"I don't want to talk on the phone right now. We're catching up, and I have so many questions."

"No. No." Miles wags his finger at me. "I'm through trauma dumping. You're up now."

My phone pings again, and Miles snatches it from my hand before I have a chance to look at the text.

"Seriously?" I lunge for the phone, which he keeps just out of reach. "What are we, five?"

"Well, this is interesting." Miles opens the refrigerator door, using it as a shield between us. "Scotty says, 'Call when you can. Looking at renting a house near you and Ave. Want your opinion.' Please explain, Liza."

"There's nothing to explain."

My phone pings again, and this time I swing the refrigerator door at Miles, catching his knee. He lets out a yelp, and I snatch my phone back and shove it in my bra.

"Fine." He holds his hands up in mock surrender. "You win. Just tell me what's going on with you and Scotty."

Maybe it's the wine, or maybe it's the catastrophic level of stress my nerves have been under. Whatever the reason, something dislodges in my subconscious, and I say the thing I'm not supposed to say. The thing I didn't even know I was still thinking.

"I think I might want him again," I say.

"Want? As in . . ." Miles makes a thrusting gesture with his hips that makes me want to laugh and vomit at the same time. "Is that what you mean?"

"He made me feel melty the other night," I say. "He called Avery 'our daughter,' and something inside me just came undone."

"So you love him?" Miles is practically giddy. "You're in love with your baby's daddy. I love that for you."

"I'm not in love with him." I roll my eyes. "Is there something in between love and like?"

"Lust," Miles says.

"Then maybe that's what it is. Maybe I just need to sleep with Scotty, and that will fix everything," I say, fishing my phone out of my bra. "Oh, crap. I hit that little 'voice memo' button. Honestly, why is everyone so obsessed with talking on the phone? What's wrong with good old-fashioned text—"

In a moment of sheer terror, I realize that instead of deleting the voice memo that my boobs recorded, I've actually sent it. I've sent a voice memo proclaiming that I need to sleep with Scotty *to Scotty*.

"Miles. Help. Now." I practically shove my phone into his face. "Fix it. Fix it now!"

"Fix what?"

"Look," I stammer. "The voice. The thing with the voice that's mine that says—"

"Oh god." Miles's jaw basically unhinges itself. "How much did you record?"

"I don't know, Miles! I just need you to make it go away. Delete it. Fix it." I start to feel a little lightheaded. "I might puke or pass out. God, I hope I pass out. At least then I'm unconscious."

"It's fine. I'll just hit unsend, and then . . . oh shit."

"Oh shit? What is 'oh shit'?" I grab onto Miles's shoulder and force myself to look at the phone screen. "Why haven't you deleted it?" He points to the most terrifying word in the English language that I can think of. *Read.* "He's read it? So that's it. My life is over. I thought the worst thing that could possibly happen this week was getting fired."

"You were fired?" Miles gasps. "And you didn't tell me?"

"Technically, I quit. And you didn't tell me about James. Also, this doesn't feel like the right time to—"

"It's ringing." Miles tosses me the phone like it's a hot potato. "Do something. I want no part in this mess."

"You are the reason for the mess." I toss the phone back. "If you would've just left the phone alone, none of this would be happening. You need to fix it."

Miles glances at the phone and then me and then the phone again. "You're right," he says. "I should be the one to fix this."

"So do it!"

He takes my phone and drops it in his glass of wine.

"What are you doing? That's my phone! Plus, I think it's waterproof, so that won't even work. You'd have to leave it in there for hours."

"Do you want to be the one to get it out?" he asks. I shake my head no. "Then we just leave it be. OK?"

"OK."

We both stare at my phone in its little cabernet bath for a while until it stops showing any sign of life. I'm not sure how long it takes, but when I finally climb into bed next to Avery, I'm pretty sure it's well after midnight. I reach for her phone to check the time and notice a string of texts from Matthew, which I won't read or look at because I do respect her privacy within reason. There is one text, though, that catches my attention enough for me to open it. It's from Scotty.

Dad: Can't wait to see you.

Oh, I can. I could wait a million years before ever having to see Scotty Samson again.

Chapter 8

The next day starts with a picture. An aerial shot of Day Ranch with a caravan of paparazzi lining the dirt road that leads to the front half of the property. With the funeral less than twenty-four hours away and the viral and unexplainable popularity of *Sunset Breeze*, Mom's fame has experienced somewhat of a resurrection.

"Who do they think is going to be there?" I ask. "This is Mom's fake funeral. Not Beyoncé's."

Miles zooms in on the photo on his laptop, while Avery and I look over his shoulder. "What is that a statue of?" He points at a pink blobby thing that looks vaguely like a capybara but could just as easily be a penguin. "Is Chauncey Hill planning a funeral or a three-ring circus?"

Miles informs me that Chauncey Hill, the party planner—scratch that, the experience curator—that Mom hired, is somewhat of an artistic savant. He's known for his extravagant events, which typically garner hundreds of guests, if not more, ranging from the rich and famous to the richer and infamous. Since Miles is Mom's publicist, I would've assumed that he'd be excited by all this attention, but Miles seems to be having the exact opposite reaction.

"I need to get there immediately." Miles runs his hand through his curly hair, which twists in every direction. "I should be the point of contact for everything. I want to know who is on the guest list. I want to know the flowers, the lighting, the . . ." He leans in closer to the image on the screen. "Is that a porta potty? For the love of god, what is this man doing? Creating the next Fyre Festival?"

Kat emerges from the balcony just as Miles's voice reaches a pitch I'm sure only dogs can hear. She's been on a call all morning, trying to figure out the logistics for getting us to the ranch while drawing as little attention as humanly possible.

"Alright, we have two options." Kat claps her hands like a football coach calling together a huddle. "The first option is we risk taking the back way into Day Ranch. The paparazzi either haven't discovered that route yet, or they don't think their creepy white vans can brave the rough terrain."

"Can either of your cars brave the rough terrain?" I ask.

"No," Miles says. "Plus, you know I get carsick."

"So, what's the other option?" Avery asks.

"Well." A conspiratorial smile forms across Kat's face. "I have a client who owns a vineyard. He was the one I was showing a property to in Temecula earlier this week. Anyway, he has a helicopter, and—"

"No." I cross my arms in an X motion. "Absolutely not."

"Mom!" Avery pleads. "Come on. That would be so cool."

"Yeah, come on," Miles echoes. "Oh, let's take a vote. All in favor of driving in Kat's car and watching me blow chunks, raise your hand. I see no votes. All in favor of flying into the ranch like a bunch of Kardashians, say aye."

Three very eager *aye*s pierce through my foggy brain. *Like Kardashians?* We are not Kardashians. We are not even Kardashian adjacent.

"No." I double down. "Avery, your dad would kill me if I let you fly in a helicopter."

"No, he wouldn't. Call him."

My knees go a little wobbly. "Huh?"

"Call him." She takes a step toward me and smiles, like she somehow knows that I would rather skinny-dip in a pool of broken glass than call her father. "He actually texted me this morning. He says he's been trying to get ahold of you."

Miles makes a noise that sounds like a cross between a burp and a shocked gasp.

"Fine. I'll call him," I bluff.

She just stares at me. Like she's challenged me to a duel and is just waiting to see if I'm going to pick up my pistol and fire first.

"Go get dressed," I say. "I'll call while you're in the shower."

"I don't believe you."

"I'm going to go back on the balcony and see if I can figure out a third option," Kat says. "Miles, you come with me."

They keep a wide berth, maneuvering around us until they reach the safety of the balcony. Honestly, I wouldn't mind being out there with them right now. It seems less scary.

"I found your phone in a glass of wine last night," she says. "I know there's no way you're going to call him."

My skin crawls, and I desperately want to find a way to climb out of it. God, I don't even want to know what she's thinking, because it's probably all the things that I've thought before about my mother. I never found her phone in a wineglass, but I did on more than one occasion find her passed out next to a wineglass, a wine bottle, and a wine box. Basically, any sort of container that could hold alcohol.

"Your uncle and I were being dumb," I say, unable to look her in the face. "We got a little carried away."

"I don't care about that." She makes a face. "I just don't want you to lie to me like I'm some little kid. So if you have to call my dad in order for me to ride on a helicopter, then I want you to actually do it. If you're just not going to let me, then at least tell me to my face."

I really hate it when she sounds more like an adult than I do. It's rare, especially lately, but it still stings. I glance at the picture still zoomed in on Miles's laptop. Just the thought of the four of us parading in front of all those cameras makes me sick to my stomach. I wouldn't let Avery on a film set because it made me uneasy, and at least there the cameras wouldn't be pointed at her. This would be a million times worse and more chaotic.

"Fine," I say. "We'll take the helicopter."

~

Rows of pecan trees surround two-thirds of the perimeter of Day Ranch. From up here, they look like old guards standing at attention. I look past the cars peppering the dirt road leading to the front of the ranch. I don't want to give them any more of my mental real estate than what they've already taken. Instead, I focus on the land and how it seems to look both bigger and smaller than what I remember. The vastness of the pecan groves—now mostly dried up and abandoned over time—look as though they extend for miles. Meanwhile, Lake Vivian, named after our grandmother, appears half its size. There's something peaceful, almost hypnotic, about coming back to the ranch after a long time away. It commands you to slow down.

There's a big sign at the entrance with copper letters flecked with patina. It hangs across the gate's arch, proudly announcing DAY RANCH: LOVELY DAYS FOUND HERE. When we moved out here after Mom and Dad divorced the first time, Mom hated that sign. She used to flip it the bird every time we drove under it. As far as she was concerned, there was nothing lovely about the ranch. Looking back, I'm not so sure it was the ranch she despised so much as what her living at it meant. It represented what she believed to be a failure. It was the place she went back to after each of her divorces from my father, and before that it was the place her parents tried to keep her sequestered from the real world.

Day Ranch was a last resort for Mom, but for me it was a refuge, from the very first time I stepped foot on the property and met George. He still had hair then—at most he was two or three years younger than my parents—but something about him felt old and comforting. He greeted the three of us kids with banana milkshakes topped with whipped cream and chocolate sprinkles and asked us what we wanted to do that summer. None of us knew how to answer such a question. Our entire existence up until that point had always been decided by someone else. When we couldn't come up with an answer, George told us he just wanted us to be kids, and my god, we were. George showed us how to hunt for crawdads in the streams that barely held water because of the drought. He taught us to ride horses and make s'mores over an open flame. But most importantly, George allowed us to feel safe and *to just be kids*. It was the best gift anyone had ever given me.

That's why when I see George after we land, standing in front of the Big House now, hunched over with age and no more red hair to speak of, my breath catches in my chest and something inside me whispers, *Home.*

"If you would've told me they could get a helicopter on this ranch, I never would've believed you," George shouts over the roar of the engine as the aircraft flies away. "Of course, I never would've thought there would be a life-size pink elephant next to the pool."

"It's been a big week," I say.

"Come here, you." He wraps his arms around me in a big, warm hug. He feels smaller. His bones more angular. Not frail, but also not as strong as I remember. "How are you, kid?"

"A little nauseated. I don't think helicopter travel is meant for me, but I'm OK." I give him one last squeeze before forcing myself to let go. "How about you?"

"Same as always." His gray eyes look over my shoulder to Avery. "Don't tell me this is the same little girl who used to send me drawings of unicorns and fairies."

"Papa George." Avery smiles. "You remember those pictures?"

"Remember them? I kept every single one, chickadee."

She hugs him, and they exchange the normal sort of pleasantries that I always imagined granddaughters and grandfathers doing. My heart swells with a mix of pride and sadness. I'm so glad I established a pen-pal-style relationship for Avery and George, but I'm also a little heartbroken that she never had the luxury of waking up on a summer morning knowing she had the entire day to spend with him. He'd have taught her how to ride a bike in a weekend, and her driving would definitely be better than it is. I wish it hadn't taken a fake funeral for the two of them to see each other again, but I'm glad they at least have this weekend.

George greets Miles, while Kat takes a call with her client to thank him for the special transportation. She tells us to go on without her. She'll catch up. George is about to escort us inside the Big House when my mother comes barreling through the front door. "Has anyone seen Benny?"

She's a dust devil of colorful silk scarves and a long, flowing skirt in a garish leopard print. Long, wavy hair in shades of silver and bronze hangs loose, blowing in the wind. She's a little bit Cher and a little Stevie Nicks, all tied into one fiery little package. It's easy to see why people fell in love with her on-screen. Understanding why they relished her downfall is much more difficult to grasp.

"Liza! My baby girl!" She throws her arms around my neck and kisses my cheeks like I'm a kindergartener returning from my first day of school. "Honey, have you seen Benny?"

"Benny?"

"Yes. Benny." She lets go of me just as quickly as she hugged me. "Small. Long hair. Fat and white."

"Wow," I say. "I don't think that's how we're supposed to describe—"

"Avery!" Mom squeals. "You are gorgeous. Absolutely stunning. A face for the silver screen if there ever was one. I'm going to have you talk to my agent."

"Oh, that's not necessary, Mom," I interject.

"George? Have you seen Benny?"

"Not since I gave him his breakfast," George replies. "Have you checked the bathroom? Sometimes he lingers in there."

I grip Miles's arm. "Please, dear god, tell me that Benny is a dog or a cat and not a hostage."

"I doubt she has the attention span to manage a hostage," Miles says. "Mom. Is Chauncey Hill here?"

"Miles, focus, please. Benny is missing. We must form a search party. Come on now." She motions to us. "Now Benny scares quite easily, so try to present calm energy. Oh, and please don't chase him. He's still recovering from surgery."

"Who's Benny?" Avery nudges me. "A relative?"

"I think he may be a hostage," I say. "But your uncle seems to think he's a dog or a cat."

"Shouldn't we know what we're looking for?" Avery asks.

I'm about to ask Mom who this Benny is when a small army of white, fluffy rabbits the size of soccer balls scurry behind her. I count at least ten, all of which follow Mom like she's the pied piper of the pet shop, and we're all just guests. A straggler hops across my feet, stopping to nibble on my shoelaces.

"Did you put magic mushrooms in my smoothie this morning?" I ask Miles. "Or is this really happening?"

"If it's not really happening, then I'm on the same shit," Miles replies. "George, what's going on? Who's Benny, and what the hell are all these?"

"Benny is your mother's buck," he says.

"Her buck?" Miles cocks his head to the side. "I thought a buck was a deer."

"Male rabbits too," Avery says, holding the shoelace eater. "It's cute. Can we keep it?"

"Absolutely not."

"George, you and Avery go look over by the cottage. Liza and Miles, you two can follow me to the Casita," Mom announces from the end of the driveway. "C'mon now. If we don't get him into the house before noon, he'll absolutely cook in this heat."

It is unseasonably warm for October in California, but not so much that I would imagine it roasting a rabbit. Then again, I'm not familiar with the animal husbandry required for keeping rabbits alive. I decide not to question the science.

"Please don't leave me," I whisper, clinging to Avery's arm. "This is how horror movies start."

"You're scaring Alice," she groans.

"Who the hell is Alice?"

Avery holds up the rabbit and smiles proudly. "Meet Alice."

"Oh no." I shake my head. "Do not think that just because you name something, you get to keep it."

She ignores me, as per usual, leaving me to Elmer Fudd it without her.

"C'mon now, kids. You've got to scan the underbrush." Mom places a hand to her forehead and crouches down low like she's the *Golden Girls* version of Dora the Explorer. "He'll seek out the shade and cool earth. You'll never find him if you just stand there like that."

Part of me would like to point out the fact that when Kat ran away from home, Mom didn't notice for an entire weekend, but that doesn't seem helpful.

"What should I do if I spot him? Make myself look big to exert my dominance?" Miles pantomimes a bear and holds his arms up over his head. "Grr."

"Miles, Benny is an Angora. The breed is naturally docile." Mom sighs as if rabbit breeds and their corresponding behavior traits are common knowledge. "If you did that, you'd probably send him into shock."

"He wouldn't be the only one," I mutter under my breath.

"What was that, Liza?" Mom calls over her shoulder.

"Nothing, Mom," I reply. "Just saying how I hope we find the little guy."

I catch Kat coming around the other side of the porch. "Thank god, we've got reinforcements now."

"Is it Benny again?" She rolls her eyes.

"You know about Benny?" Miles lets his hands fall to his side dramatically. "Mom, why does Kat know about Benny, but I don't? You know, you've been keeping me out of the loop as your publicist from quite a few things lately."

"I didn't realize you were taking new clients, Miles," Mom says. "While I'm not seeking representation for him now, I'll keep you in mind should Benny show an interest in film."

"Sucker," Kat teases Miles. "Mom, have you checked by Dad's old truck? That's where you found him last time, remember?"

"Looking for Benny is a normal occurrence for you?" I ask.

"No." Kat shakes her head. "I came out to see Mom a few weeks ago, when she had some questions about property lines and stuff like that. Benny was on the run then. She'd just had him fixed and apparently his lady rabbits weren't too happy about it."

"I emasculated him." Mom fans herself with one of her scarves. "At least that's what Annie said."

I can't help myself. "Who is Annie?"

"My psychic," Mom says. "Well, Benny's, technically. I use her sister Marla for human-related concerns. That's where I came up with the idea for the funeral."

"From the pet psychic?" Kat can barely keep a straight face. "Or the human psychic?"

"Both."

Mom rants on about her latest reading, as we follow her in the direction of Dad's old truck. It's near the stretch of dirt road that leads to the front of Day Ranch. The same stretch of road that the paparazzi are currently treating like a tailgate party. There's a hedge of bougainvillea and oleander and a couple of hundred yards that act as a buffer, but I still don't like it. Just knowing they are there, lurking, like a pack of hyenas waiting for an easy meal.

I nudge Kat as we get closer to the truck. "They're allowed to just be here?"

"Technically, they aren't breaking any laws. The road is owned by the county," she says. "As long as they don't come on the property, we can't do much."

"It feels wrong."

"I know, but on the bright side, I don't think they can even see us, let alone take a picture."

I doubt it. In my experience, they always find a way to get a shot.

"Oh, Miles!" Mom waves her arms in the air. "Honey, I think I see him under Eddie's old truck. Katherine, you were right. You know, you might be a little bit intuitive yourself. Miles, get him."

"Get him?" Miles makes a face. "Do you have a net or something for me to catch him with?"

"Don't be ridiculous," Mom replies. "You just need to crawl on your belly and fetch him. He'll go right to you. He's very loving. I would do it, but I'll get dirty, and these scarves are vintage."

"Not it," Miles whispers to Kat and me. "Listen, I will do a lot of things, but this is a Gucci polo, and I am not ruining it for an emasculated rabbit."

Kat and I exchange a look.

"This is an all-white, dry-clean-only suit. There's no way I'm getting under a truck in this." Kat folds her arms across her chest. "Liza, your clothes look washable and mass-produced. You do it."

"Oh, c'mon now," Mom begs. "He's starting to pant. Rabbits overheat easily. Please, Liza. I just know he'll warm right up to you."

Lucky me.

"You jerks owe me," I growl, rolling up the sleeves of my washable shirt.

I sprawl on all fours beneath what's left of our father's long-abandoned Dodge. He bought it with the intent to fix it up one day, but like most of our father's plans, he didn't follow through with it. The dry, ruddy earth clings to my jeans and burrows beneath my fingernails. I manage to wriggle half of my body beneath the truck and hold out my hand to Benny. I don't know what I expect him to do. Reach his paw to me? Leap into my arms? He doesn't budge and looks at me, completely unbothered by the situation.

"You have to grab him by the scruff, Liza," Mom commands. "Just grab his scruff and pull."

"What the hell is a scruff?" I whine.

"The neck," Mom says. "Grab his neck."

"What if he bites me because he thinks I'm trying to strangle him?" I shout. "What if—"

A flurry of dirt sprays into my face and my open mouth. I instantly gag and spit before crawling backward from beneath the truck with my eyes snapped shut.

"He maced me," I cough. "The little bastard maced me."

"Oh, don't call him names," Mom says. "You scared him right out from under there with all your shouting."

When I'm finally able to open my eyes again, Benny is snuggled safely in Mom's arms, and my siblings are doubled over laughing at my expense.

"Let's get you into a nice lavender bath," she coos to Benny. "I'll meet everyone in the kitchen just as soon I get Benny squared away. I might give Annie a quick ring. Benny has a tendency to hold on to trauma." She turns on her heels and heads back toward the Big House, leaving the three of us behind.

"Who is that woman, and what has she done with our mother?" I brush the dirt off my jeans. "She wouldn't pay for us to go to therapy, but she's got an on-call shrink for Bugs Bunny?"

"Hopefully we outlive Benny." Miles sighs. "Otherwise, there goes our inheritance."

"I want to go home where things are normal," I say.

"You are home." Kat pats me on the shoulder. "And things have never been normal here."

Chapter 9

Walking into the Big House is like stepping into a time capsule. Grandma Vivian might've been an actress by trade, but her true gift was in design. Grandpa William purchased the pecan orchard and neighboring land back in the fifties, when ranches and Hollywood cowboys were all the rage, but it was Viv who turned Day Ranch into something special. The ranch has been featured in multiple magazines and publications over the decades. While the outside of the Big House has a classic lodge feel about it, the inside is all midcentury modern with a little bit of a cowboy twist. Think clean lines, bold colors, and the occasional cowhide rug or steer-horns ornament.

Miles and Kat gather around the kitchen table, combing through an assortment of Darla memorabilia for Mom's funeral. Old magazines, movie posters, and even a few empty jars of Darling Baby Food with Mom's nine-month-old face plastered across the label.

"The house is finally starting to show its age." I press a corner of peeled wallpaper with my index finger, trying to make it stick.

"Aren't we all?" Miles groans. "Ooh, look at this one."

He holds up a copy of *People* magazine. Mom's on the cover in a floral dress. Her hair is long and dark and pin-straight. "God, she looks just like—"

"Avery." I take the copy from him and give it a closer look. It's from July of 1981. The year *Summertime Madness*, Mom's first breakout film, debuted. "They could be twins, couldn't they?"

"I guess," Miles says. "But I was going to say she looks more like you did at that age. Don't you see it?"

"Not really," I say.

"You looked just like her." Kat takes the magazine and opens it up. She points to a photo of Mom riding a horse. Her head is tilted back, and she's laughing like she doesn't have a care in the world. "You both have that smile. So does Avery."

Most of my formative years as a young girl and actress were spent having people compare my looks to Mom's, and more often than not, the comparisons weren't kind. Comments about my figure being lanky instead of womanly like hers. My breasts were too small. My lips too thin. Mom was a natural at being sexy and seductive, whereas I contained all the natural sex appeal of a raw potato. It wasn't just my body that made me feel inadequate compared to Mom. It was her energy. As cheesy as it sounds, Mom had star power. She could walk into a quiet room and make it come to life without saying a word. She had charisma in spades and the talent to back it. She was the real deal, and at my very best, I was just a knock-off.

"You should show this to Avery," he says. "While we're here, we could watch a couple of Mom's old movies. Maybe even squeeze in a few episodes of *Sunset Breeze*. The Wi-Fi here is crap, but I'm sure Mom's got the entire DVD set hidden around here somewhere."

"What's all this?" Avery asks. She's changed into a flannel shirt and a pair of cut-off jeans, and much to my chagrin, she's still holding Alice. "Is that you, Mom?"

"Told you," Miles says.

"It's your grandma." Kat hands Avery the magazine.

"Grandma was a total babe." Avery pulls out a chair between Miles and Kat, keeping the rabbit on her lap. "This is so cool that she kept all this."

"You wouldn't believe the stuff she keeps," Miles says.

"Here's your mom," Kat says.

She's holding a photo Mom had professionally taken of the two of us when I was ten. We're both wearing matching pink tuxedos with long tails and top hats. Mom went through a phase where she was determined to bring back the variety show. Something like *The Carol Burnett Show*. The concept failed to gain traction, but it did land me my first little gig on a medical drama. The part was billed as *Young girl who swallows watch battery.*

"I still have those tuxedos," Mom huffs, appearing more than a little out of breath after this morning's excursion. She's carrying what looks like an old hatbox bursting at the seams with papers. "You should take them home with you."

"I don't know that I have a need for pink tuxedos," I say.

"Better to have one and not need it than to need a pink tuxedo and be without it." She opens the hatbox just enough to stick her hand in and pull out four pads of brightly colored sticky notes. Mom passes them out to us like she's a blackjack dealer, calling out our names with each color. "Pink for Avery. Yellow for Miles. Purple for Kat, and orange for Liza. Oh, I should really write this down."

"What are we supposed to do with these, Mom?" I ask.

"And what's with the hatbox?" Miles asks.

"The sticky notes are for you to put on items you want in the house," Mom says. "I'll have George box them all up and mail them to you after the funeral."

For a moment, I wonder if I've misheard her. While I wouldn't call Mom a hoarder, she's definitely someone who likes to hang on to things. Hence the pink tuxedos that are nearly thirty years old. But every object that she owns has a story. Everything has a memory. From the peeling wallpaper that Mom will likely insist on fixing with a bit of Scotch tape instead of replacing, to the Formica kitchen table that's older than every person sitting at this table, minus Mom, this house is made up of memories. And good or bad, Mom doesn't just give memories away. She keeps them all, which makes the idea of us calling dibs on them with sticky notes feel all the more wrong.

Avery takes one of her pink sticky notes and places it on Alice.

"Hold on just a minute," I say. "First things first, no." I reach across the table and pluck the pink paper from Alice's back. "And second, what the hell is going on, Mom? You do know you're not actually dying, right?"

"Yeah, this is making me very uncomfortable," Kat says. "I feel like there's something you're not telling us."

Miles places a yellow sticky note on a brass peacock sculpture hanging on the wall. I shoot him a death glare.

"What?" He shrugs. "I can be concerned and call dibs."

"Oh, let's get some food before we dive into all this," Mom says. "There's a charcuterie tray in the fridge, Katherine. Why don't you get that out, and Miles can make some tea? Liza, will you get George? He's looking after the pool. With all the preparations for the party, he's been having to clean it constantly. Chauncey accidentally dropped a tub of tiny glitter balls in it earlier today. It was a disaster, but in a beautiful sort of way. You'll meet him tomorrow. Miles, he's particularly eager to meet you."

"Eager to meet me?" Miles points at his chest. "We've met. Chauncey Hill knows me."

"He didn't say that," Mom says.

"Well, he does," Miles snaps.

"If you say so, honey." Mom smirks. "Let's get the food. I think we're all on the verge of being a little hangry."

I find George skimming the pool, just as Mom said. It's a sparkling turquoise blue, exactly as I remember it. There are some new additions, which I assume are from Chauncey. A giant pink elephant that appears to double as a minibar; a flashy brass dance floor that looks like it could also double as a roller rink; and hundreds of glitter balls suspended over the pool, to name a few.

"Mom wants everyone to come in," I say, standing next to the pool's edge. "The pool looks beautiful." I kneel next to the diving board and slide my shoes off before dipping my toes in. "It feels nice too."

"Your mother likes to come out here at night and watch the stars," he says softly. "I can't keep up with this place like I used to, so I prioritize what's important. Her pool is important."

There's a melancholy to him that I hadn't noticed before. He hangs the pool skimmer back in place and pats his hands dry on the back of his Wranglers.

"George, why's Mom doing all this?" I motion toward the elephant and dance floor. "Do you know she wants us to put sticky notes on all her stuff? The woman who wouldn't throw away the cast from when I broke my arm when I was five is now getting rid of everything. That's not like her."

"People change, Liza."

"Mom is not like most people," I say. "Is something wrong? Is she sick? Is she dying?"

"We're all dying, kid."

"I know, but if there was a reason for me to worry, you'd tell me. Right?"

"You've never needed anyone to give you a reason to worry." He holds out his hand to help me up. "Can I give you a little advice?"

"Sure." I nod.

"Let this weekend happen. Follow her lead. You don't always have to be in control, kid." He lowers his voice. "Just wait until you get to be my age and realize that even when you think you're in control, you're really not."

"Is that supposed to make me feel better?"

"That's up to you."

Together, we walk up to the Big House, holding hands just as we did countless times before. I'm not a touchy-feely person—I never have been—but holding George's hand feels as natural to me as breath in my lungs.

Once we're all gathered around the table, each of us with iced tea and a tiny plate full of cheese, meats, crackers, and dried fruits, Mom raises her glass. "A toast," she says, waiting for us to raise our glasses of iced tea. "To the lovely Days. May we find them wherever life leads us."

My siblings and I exchange unsure glances as we clink our glasses.

"I want to thank all of you for coming to my last curtain call," Mom says. "I know you're wondering why you're here, and the truth is, I'm not one to beat around the bush. I do like surprises, though. But I'm also not one to spoil a good time, and a good time we have planned for us. Of course, there is always business to attend to before pleasure, isn't there?" She nods as if agreeing with her own question. "And I thought that while we were on the subject of death, it probably would make sense to tell you all my plans for when I actually do die. I did mention that I don't plan on dying this weekend, right?"

"It was implied," I say. "Although, you did just mention that you like surprises."

"Well, death is nature's ultimate surprise, isn't it?" She chuckles, tapping the top of the hatbox. "Anyhoo, I want to tell you all what I want done with my body when I die."

"Do you want us to put you in the hatbox?" Miles asks, looking slightly uneasy at the conversation. "Because if that's how you want to go, I feel like we can get a better one."

"I don't want to be cremated." She opens the box. "It just doesn't seem sanitary. I can't wrap my head around how some guy making minimum wage is going to sweep all of the people bits out of that oven. I can never properly clean my oven, and neither can George. Isn't that right, George?"

George nods as if discussing oven cleaning and people bits is a normal topic of conversation. "It's very difficult, especially with an older oven."

"It's not actually an oven, Mom," I say. "Nobody is tossing corpses into a Maytag and calling it cremation."

"No cremation," Kat says, taking notes on her phone. "Got it."

"So you want to be buried?" Miles asks. "Maybe at Hollywood Forever Cemetery? That would be chic."

Leave it to my brother to find a chic cemetery.

"No. Burial makes me uncomfortable too." Mom shakes her head. "It's too much pressure."

"Like you're worried the casket would cave in?" Avery asks.

"No," Mom replies. "Figuring out what to wear and what to take. I'd drive myself mad just trying to come up with the perfect ensemble and carry-on."

Because being buried is exactly like going on a cruise ship.

"No burial," Kat says, slowly, before looking up from her phone. "Frozen maybe?"

"No, no." She shakes her head. "Now, I know it's in vogue for folks to be turned into trees or buried in bags of mushrooms to help replenish the earth and whatnot. I'm not interested in any of that. I also don't want to be turned into jewelry—not because I don't like the idea of spending eternity in a diamond, but because I just can't get over the oven part."

I'm starting to worry that we're running out of options here. Short of a Viking funeral, which I'm guessing is highly illegal, I don't know what other option Mom has come up with.

"Now, this right here is what I want." She takes what looks like a brochure out of her hatbox and passes it to Kat.

"I'm afraid to ask, but what is it?" Miles asks.

"She wants to be donated to science." Kat makes a face. "Really? That's what you want?"

Mom's eyes widen. "Oh no. No. Wrong brochure. You see, this is why we have meetings like this. One wrong pamphlet, and I'm being carved like a turkey by some kid in a lab coat."

"They also send back the body parts they don't use," Avery adds, garnering the attention of everyone at the table. "What? I saw a TikTok. This woman donated her body to science, and her daughter freaked out when they started sending her the parts they didn't use."

"How do they send it?" Miles gasps. "UPS?"

"Can we stay on topic?" Kat taps the top of the table. "Mom, we'll find the brochure later. Just tell us what you want."

Mom sits up a little taller in her seat and smiles proudly. "I want my body to become art. Now, before you try to talk me out of it, I've already applied to the program, and I'm happy to report that I've been accepted. It's a traveling show, like the circus. Just think about it, whenever the show is in town, you guys could come visit me. You could visit me anywhere! Paris. London. Kansas City. Wouldn't that be a hoot?"

That's what I flew a thousand miles to hear. My mom plans on running away to Kansas City to join the dead circus.

It occurs to me at this moment that my family is not normal. This is something I've always been acutely aware of on some level. Mom was an actress, Dad was a musician, I was a child actor, etc. But when did we become the kind of family who discussed death over cold cuts and tea?

"What if the show goes out of business?" Kat asks. "What if they file bankruptcy or something, and then we have to deal with the bank repossessing you?"

Mom pops a cheese cube into her mouth. "Honey, you can't assume a show is going to be a dud. Do you think Andrew Lloyd Webber thought a show about a bunch of cats would run for eighteen years and nearly eight thousand shows?"

"What else do you have in the box?" Miles asks. He takes the hatbox and picks out a brochure titled *H2O Cremation: The Way of the Future.* "Oh. Nice. Death by spin cycle."

"That one I don't mind, but it's not a widely available option yet," Mom says. "Something about the technology not quite catching up with the demand."

Miles folds the brochure and slips it into his pocket. "Just in case the show goes under before she does," he mutters under his breath. "Pass the salami."

Chapter 10

We watch the sunset from the poolside, just Kat, Miles, and me . . . and three bottles of cabernet. Hearing that your mother plans to join a traveling corpse circus is the sort of news that warrants drinking an entire bottle of wine without having to share. Avery goes to the guest room in the Big House early with a pile of Mom's magazines and pink sticky notes, and George stocks us with freshly baked sourdough bread and rosemary butter. We wrap ourselves in blankets like human burritos.

"We can all agree that was the weirdest thing we've ever done as a family, right?" Kat asks.

"Yup." Miles slathers a layer of rosemary butter on an end piece of sourdough. "And keep in mind, we had to witness an entire season of Mom on *Big Brother*."

"I just want to know why," I say, leaning back into the pool chair. "I don't mean I want to know why Mom wants her dead body turned into art. Oddly enough, that tracks for her in some twisted way. What doesn't track is why she's acting like it's happening tomorrow. Giving away all her things. Making all these plans. It's not normal for her. Why is she doing it now?"

"Because she's old." Kat tops off her plastic wineglass. "I have plenty of older clients, and they regularly make plans for when they die. They worry about what will happen to their assets once they pass."

"But why now?" I ask. "Something had to set this crazy train in motion."

"What if she has some terminal illness?" Miles muses. "What if six months ago, she got some terrible diagnosis, and she's just been waiting until she's closer to death to tell us? She did that with our dog. Remember? What was his name?"

"Domingo," Kat whines. "Oh, poor Domingo."

Domingo—named after the Spanish opera singer for god knows what reason—was a Dalmatian that Mom brought home from the pound one day after she and Dad divorced for the final time. I guess she thought that a dog would help take our minds off of the trauma of losing our father a second time, and maybe it would have if the dog were a puppy or at least in semigood health. Domingo was neither of those things. He was old and cranky, missing a leg, and needed insulin injections several times a day.

After a few months, Mom announced that it was Domingo's birthday. She threw a party for him that he clearly hated, because balloons, cake, and the sound of children's laughter terrified him. The day after the party, when the three of us came home from school, we noticed that Domingo wasn't at the door to nip at our ankles and bark. I asked Mom where he was, and she tried at first to tell me that she sent him to a special farm for old dogs. I would've bought the story because I wasn't overly invested in the dog's welfare, but Kat, being older, said that farms like that didn't exist.

Mom's never been very good at lying, and upon hearing Kat's doubt, she immediately confessed to having Domingo put down after the vet informed her that the dog had very low quality of life due to his ailments. This was a conclusion I could've come to the day we got Domingo. Mom told us she made up the birthday so we could have one last good memory of the cantankerous old mutt.

"You don't think she's going to put herself down like she did Domingo?" Kat fights back a laugh.

"I think that's illegal in this state," Miles says. "And I think she looks fine. She still has all her limbs, and as far as I can tell, she doesn't urinate on things to claim her territory."

"Do you not see what I see?" I stand up and motion toward the elephant and glitter balls, which actually are really cool solar lights. "She's marked all of this as hers."

"Mom didn't do this. Chauncey Hill did," Miles grumbles into his wine. "He's the sick dog peeing all over everything."

"What's your deal with him?" Kat asks.

"I don't have a deal with Chauncey Hill," Miles says. "He's a wretched, sniveling, pompous, arrogant—"

"You like him." Kat's eyes widen. "You're in love with him."

"I am not," he snaps. "And if you say that again, I'm pushing you into the pool."

Kat doesn't know about Miles and James. She's just teasing him the way siblings do, but knowing what I know about the status of Miles's marriage, I think Kat might be on to something. He did mention he was dating. I decide to file that bit of information away for another time.

"I want to be in love with someone." Kat sighs.

"What about the client with the helicopter?" I ask.

"He's not my type." Kat pours a little more wine into her glass. "But I do think he might like me a little. He keeps buying properties he doesn't even use. I think it might be his way of staying in touch with me."

I'm not sure I know what Kat's *type* is. She's always kept her love life close to the vest. I've met a few of the men she's seriously dated over the years, and they were a mixed bag of deadbeats and losers. It was almost like she was trying to find some version of our father so she could fix him.

"Why is he not your type?" I tighten my blanket around me, the effects of the wine starting to lull me to sleep. "He was willing to let you borrow a helicopter at a moment's notice. Hell, maybe he's my type."

Dad died when Avery was four. A guy that had two albums go platinum and three Grammys died alone in a trailer that he rented weekly. I wouldn't say that Dad's death was hard on me, or Miles for that matter.

Whatever emotions Mom felt about it, she drank away. But Kat was different. Maybe it's an oldest daughter thing, but Kat always wanted Dad's approval. She was the only one of us who would check in on Dad, which meant she was the one the manager at the trailer park notified when Dad didn't make his weekly rent payment. Sometimes, I think the reason Kat's never gotten serious with anyone is because she's never gotten over her first real love, which was Dad. He just also happened to be her first real heartbreak.

"He's older." She sighs. "A lot older."

"Are we talking Anna Nicole and J. Howard Marshall?" Miles yawns.

"Gross." Kat makes a face. "Not that old. He has kids that are in their early twenties, so he's kind of beyond the whole starting-a-family phase of life."

"Have you asked him?" I ask.

"If he wants to have a baby? No." There's a vulnerability in her tone. Like she's giving a voice to thoughts she's never dared speak aloud. "That's why I started looking into embryos. I thought that maybe I could just have my own baby, instead of trying to find someone. You've been able to raise a kid on your own. Why can't I?"

"Of course you could," I say. "But you could also maybe see if the person who keeps buying houses to spend time with you and lends you his helicopter when you're in a crisis might be interested in having a life with you."

"You should invite him to the funeral," Miles says.

"Oh, that would be fun," I say.

"And then you can invite Scotty," Miles adds.

Scotty.

Somehow, in the fever dream that's been the last twelve hours at the ranch, I managed to completely forget the fact that I sent my daughter's father a voice memo proclaiming my lust for him. God, I've managed to go an entire day without a phone. It's kind of glorious, this not being reachable and not having constant access to the whole world in a screen.

"That would not be fun," I say.

"Then time for bed." He takes his bottle of wine and blanket and heads to the Casita, looking like the sad, adult form of Linus from *Peanuts*. Kat and I follow him inside.

The Casita was added onto the property sometime in the eighties. It's a weird hodgepodge of Southwest-inspired pastel prints, black lacquer furniture, and fake plants. It's a little gawdy, but in the best possible way. There was a brief period after Avery was born that Scotty and I lived in the Casita. It's actually the only place in the world where the three of us ever lived together, which makes it feel kind of special.

It has only one bedroom, which I take. Miles will sleep on the pull-out couch. When we were deciding sleeping arrangements this morning, I didn't consider how strange it would feel being back in the room I once shared with the guy I thought I was going to marry. But standing in the doorway, looking at the little place where *my* family once existed, sends a swell of emotions roiling inside me.

"Sleepover?" I reach for Kat's hand. "Just for tonight? And maybe the next night too?"

She doesn't ask me any questions. She just nods and starts turning down the bed. I give her a spare pair of pajamas, and together we fall asleep.

I wake just before sunrise and slip on my running shoes. I don't think of myself as a runner. I've never done a race, and I've never come close to feeling a runner's high. It's a ritual for me. I like the way my body slowly comes to life with each stride. The way my joints and muscles loosen, releasing the tension that I always seem to be holding in my back. My brain feels sharper. Every problem feels a little more manageable. I don't even measure the distance I run. It's not important to me. I turn back when I'm ready to face the day.

In a perfectly serendipitous moment, I come across my old iPod, complete with charger and headphones, while looking for a hair tie. I charge it up while I stretch, giddy to hear what early 2000s musical treasure it holds. When I step outside into the crisp morning air and press play, Kelly Clarkson's *Since U Been Gone* is waiting for me.

This is going to be an epic run.

There are a dozen different trails on the ranch, but I stick to my favorite route, which runs along the back road into Day Ranch. It's near the road that Miles and Kat worried their cars and Miles's stomach wouldn't be able to handle. It's not nearly as smooth as the other trails that were once used for horseback riding, but that's what I like about it. At home, I have perfectly even pavement to run on. Here, I want something wild.

I turn up the music as loud as I can. I want Kelly Clarkson to sing her way into my soul and never leave. I start running. Slow at first, making sure to watch my foot placement, but as the beat picks up, I pay less attention and let the music take me over. I start to sing along, belting out the chorus, feeling stronger and surer of myself with every note.

I might run all day. I might never go back to the ranch. It'll just be me and Kelly for all eternity, which I suspect might be the best interpretation of eternity anyone has ever thought of. I round a corner on the path just as the song ends and the intro to Ashlee Simpson's *Pieces of Me* begins. I have died and gone to millennial heaven. And then seconds later, I nearly die for real when I slip on a patch of loose gravel and fall on my ass.

"Dammit!" I cry out.

The spill scares me more than anything. It catches me off guard, but I'm unscathed, minus a little road rash on my shins. My ego takes the worst of it. She's been through a lot lately. I start to pick myself up when I notice a black speck at the end of the trail. The low hum of a motor gradually becomes louder. It's a motorcycle.

Why is there a motorcycle on my road?

I consider the possible answers to this question, of which I can only come up with two. Serial killer looking for an easy murder to commit, or paparazzi. This is the first time I've ever hoped it was the paparazzi following me.

I reach for my phone, which of course I don't have because Miles drowned it in a glass of wine, so I guess if this is a serial killer, then he's really hit the jackpot.

The rumble of the motorcycle draws closer as it maneuvers easily through the uneven terrain. In my experience, paps aren't known for being great drivers. A shiver runs down my spine. I might need to actually defend myself, which is not my strong suit. Not unless I can deter the murderer with my teacher voice.

I look around for something that could be used as a weapon and pick up a heavy dirt clod just in case. I've never actually assaulted someone before, minus one scene on *Sunset Breeze*, but I did play softball one summer when I was six. There's probably some muscle memory still there. Hopefully.

The motorcycle slows as it approaches me. Sweat prickles at the back of my neck and on my palms. My mouth goes dry as my heart thumps like a drum against my chest so hard that for a moment I think I am still listening to music. Maybe I should run instead? Tear off into the groves. I've always been more of a flight than a fight kind of girl. Maybe now's the wrong time to deviate from this strategy. Of course, they're on a motorcycle, which would close in on me in seconds. I guess I could always play dead.

The rider slows to a crawl and eventually stops about twenty feet in front of me. I squeeze the dirt clod so tight the edges of it dig into my palm. The rider/murderer dismounts his bike and starts toward me. No wave or otherwise friendly gesture, and no camera. He just walks, his heavy boots making my heart race with each step. He lifts his hands over his head—to do what, I have no clue in hell, but something inside me takes this as confirmation that he does plan to kill me. So, I do the only thing that comes naturally to me. I scream and throw my dirt clod at him.

The clod sails through the air in what feels like slow motion. The rider must've started the process of removing his helmet around the same time I launched my attack, because the clod connects with his face so perfectly, it would be impossible to ever duplicate the same shot. He reaches for his face and lets out a yelp before falling to his knees.

I've done it! I've slayed the dragon. I've David and Goliathed it. I will not be on an episode of *Dateline*. I will—

"What the hell, Liza?"

My heart goes from racing to a full-out stop as my brain makes sense of the person kneeling on the ground. Sandy-brown hair peppered with white and gray along the side. California tan skin. A scar along the side of one hand—an old surfing injury from his youth—which happens to be clutching his cheek.

"Scotty?" I yelp. "Shit. Is that you?"

"Of course it's me," he groans.

"Why are you on my road?"

"In case you didn't notice, the entrance to the ranch looks like Coachella." He stands up, his hand still cupping his cheek. As I run toward him, the redness of his wound comes into view. "I came in the back way to avoid being harassed. Clearly that didn't pan out."

"Oh, that's going to leave a mark," I whisper.

"You could've blinded me." He winces.

"Well, I didn't know it was you," I say, defensively. "And I've been under a lot of stress lately. A lot of which is your fault, now that I think of it. I didn't want to end up on *Dateline*."

"You'd never end up on *Dateline*. All the victims on that show are always described as the kind of person who didn't have a mean bone in their body or the nicest person you could ever meet. Those are not phrases I would use to describe you right now."

I laugh for a moment, but then the adrenaline from the situation starts to wear off. Reality sets in, and I become aware that Scotty

Samson is at Day Ranch. Scotty Samson is at Day Ranch, and he knows I want to *lust him.*

"Are you here because of the voice memo thing?" I decide to rip the Band-Aid off. "Because if you are, then you should know that I didn't mean to send it. My phone was in my boobs, and I was feeling vulnerable. Also, those two things aren't necessarily related."

"Your boobs and vulnerability?"

"Obviously."

He laughs. "Good to know."

"So is that why you're here? Because I don't even think I meant a word of what I said. I was drinking, and it had been a long day of traveling. I don't even remember most of what I said."

"I could play it back for you." He reaches for his backpack.

"Don't!" I shout. "That would actually kill me."

"Relax." He pulls out the same envelope that was in my mailbox Tuesday morning. "I got Darla's invitation when I got back into town. I tried to talk to you about it, but you blocked me, I think."

"Not exactly," I say, sheepishly thinking about my phone in the glass of wine. "I kinda blocked the whole world. It's a long story."

"Well, I would love to hear it after I get something for this shiner."

It takes me longer than it should to realize he's waiting for me to invite him to the Big House to get his wound cleaned up. "Mom usually has a first-aid kit in the bathroom. Do you want to come see?"

"Probably a good idea." He hands me his helmet. "You still remember how to ride?"

"Oh, I'm fine walking," I say, taking a step back from the helmet like it's diseased. The thought of holding on to Scotty—my arms around his waist, my thighs rumbling next to his—terrifies me almost as much as being murdered. "I'll run and meet you."

He points to the road rash on my legs. "No offense, but I think I'd feel more confident in your ability to get there if you let me give you a lift."

"Really, I'll be fine."

"If you walk, then I'm walking too."

"Well, now you're just being ridiculous," I say.

"I don't think you get to insult someone after you've assaulted them." His lips curl into a crooked smile that makes me feel like I've just walked into a sauna. "Put on the helmet, and let's go, unless you're prepared to help me push this bike back to the house."

"Fine." I slide on the helmet. "But to be clear, I was acting in self-defense."

"I'll keep that in mind the next time I try to say *hi* to you."

Scotty peels off his leather jacket and drapes it over my shoulders. It's covered in his signature amber-musk cologne, which I love because I'm the one who first bought it for him. I can't believe he still wears it. He gets on the bike, and I cautiously place my hands on his waist. A surge of heat flashes across my skin, making every hair on my body stand at attention. I pull back, as if I've just touched a hot stove.

"You OK back there?"

The engine roars to life, catching me off guard. I clutch onto him instinctively, and this time I don't let go.

"I'm fine," I say.

But the truth is I'm dangerously far away from fine.

Chapter 11

Sunset Breeze, Season One
November Sweeps

We're getting canceled.

That was my first thought when I saw the script for Monday's episode. It's fall sweeps, which means shows everywhere are pulling out all the stops. Since soaps air every day of the week, we've got to work a little bit harder to nab viewership than the average sitcom or drama. *Sunset Breeze* has barely been hanging on by a thread, pulling in a fraction of the viewership for our time slot. By no means am I a writer, but as someone who's spent a decent enough time reading romance novels and watching rom-coms, I know a beach picnic isn't going to be enough to pull the kind of numbers we need to keep the show going.

"We need to get naked," I say to Scotty. I'm lying on the floor of his dressing room with Monday's script fanned out in front of me like a detective working a crime scene.

"Uh, excuse me?" Scotty's voice breaks a little.

"Ryan and Naomi need to get naked," I clarify. "We've been going on these stupid, cutesy dates for weeks now, and we haven't had a serious make-out session since the pilot episode. Nobody is going to tune in to watch us hold hands and eat hoagies when they could tune in to *Passions* and watch a love triangle between a witch, a doll that comes to life, and a supermodel."

"I don't think that's actually a current storyline on *Passions*," Scotty says, looking slightly relieved. "I think the love triangle is actually between—"

"You're missing the point." I cover my face with my hands. "The script is boring. The show is boring. It's weird, but it's boring. And do you know why it's so boring?"

"Because we don't have a doll that comes to life?"

"My mother." I sigh. "*She's* the reason it's so boring. She's trying to make the show not a soap opera. She's trying to turn it into something elevated and on par with the sorts of movies she did twenty years ago. Do you know what women and girls who are watching afternoon television during the week don't want? A show about a middle-aged woman performing brain surgery while hunting for KGB operatives."

"I mean, I'm not a woman, but I see your point. It does seem like the more cerebral the writers skew, the fewer people tune in."

Our highest-ranked episode was our pilot, when my character and Scotty's sucked face. Critics called our chemistry refreshing and electric. I'm not one to put a ton of stock into what critics have to say, but viewership doesn't lie. Viewership is made of cold, hard facts, and the unfortunate fact of the matter is that people aren't tuning in to *Sunset Breeze*. They're just not.

Darla Day and her daughter might've had an early appeal with older viewers, but the coveted age categories of women under forty aren't tuning in to see Mom, and nobody's tuning in to watch me fumble through medical dialogue. They didn't grow up with her movies, and they don't give a rip about the Day acting dynasty. If they don't tune in, advertisers don't spend money, which is what everything boils down to in television. No advertisers equals no show.

"Have you talked to Todd?" Scotty asks. "Or some of the writers?"

"Todd's too scared of my mom to listen to anything I have to say, and the writers couldn't care less what a teenager thinks of their ability to put together a script," I reply.

"What about your mom? She's invested in the show doing well, isn't she?"

No. Not even a little. But that's a truth I'm not willing to share with Scotty, or anyone else for that matter.

Mom hated the idea of doing a soap from the very beginning. It was a step down for her, career-wise, but it was the only step she was being offered. Part of me thought that the opportunity for the both of us to work on a project together might at least get her a little excited, but it seems like it's had the exact opposite effect. Now she just obsesses over how to reinvent the modern-day soap opera in between bottles of Jose Cuervo.

"She is," I lie. "But I've got a different idea. What if we go off script at the beach today?"

"What do you mean?" Scotty stares at me in the mirror. "We have a very finite amount of time to film on the beach. Sunsets don't allow for many second takes."

"Exactly," I reply.

"So that means if we screw it up, there's no being able to go back and fix it before it airs."

"Bingo." I hand Scotty a section of the revised script. "They'll have to air it, and since it's the first scene of the episode, people might actually watch it."

He skims the pages, biting his bottom lip the way he always does when he's mulling something over. It sends an electric current across my skin. The two of us have only been an official couple for a month, but in that short time, I've studied Scotty's body language like a scientist studying a new life form.

"You want us to skinny-dip?" Scotty's eyes widen. "There are still people out at the beach at sunset."

"We'll wear flesh-colored garments underneath, and we'll mostly be hidden under the waves," I say. "We're not going to do anything illegal. We're just going to get a little attention, which is exactly what we need if we want to keep the show going."

"They really won't be able to do a second shoot if our clothes are all wet." Scotty runs his hands through his hair. "You're kind of an evil genius."

"I like to think of myself as a genius for the greater good." I check my watch. "We have half an hour until wardrobe. Are you in or are you out?"

He reaches for my hand and pulls me into his hold. I drape my arms around his neck and kiss his forehead. Connecting with Scotty physically comes so easy. I've never been a touchy-feely person, but with him, I crave it. It's not just a sex thing. We haven't done that yet, and I don't think either of us are ready to move to that level. But being close to Scotty, whether we're holding hands or cuddled up together on a couch watching a movie, is like being wrapped up in warm sheets fresh from the dryer. I never want the feeling to end.

"I'm always in with you," he whispers.

~

When I came up with the idea to go fake skinny-dipping with Scotty, I didn't really take into account that it's November. It may always be sunny in Southern California, but that doesn't mean the ocean water is always warm. In fact, the Pacific Ocean is known for being chilly, and this evening feels like no exception.

"I wish this were summer sweeps," Scotty whispers, as we get into place. "I should've stuffed my undergarments." I give him a look. "Shrinkage. It's a thing."

"Hey, we just want people to watch. The reason why seems less important," I tease.

Someone from makeup comes over to add a little bronzer to my cheeks, while our skeleton crew of camera operators and sound guys set up around us. The scene as it is written is pretty straightforward. Ryan and Naomi are supposed to be on a date in between Naomi's schedule of evening surgeries and Ryan's last lifeguard shift. Dinner on the beach has kind of become their thing and is supposed to keep the viewers engaged in their budding romance—except the romance is currently about as hot as the Pacific. Other than hand-holding and a very G-rated kiss here and there, Ryan and Naomi act like they're involved in some sort of fundamentalist courtship.

Scotty and I are supposed to discuss a fight that my character had with Mom's character, Lana, during a routine brain surgery on Ryan's father. My character isn't supposed to know that Lana is also an FBI agent hell-bent on exposing the fact that Ryan's father is a secret KGB agent. It's all very confusing, and while it certainly has the potential to be interesting and entertaining, the show is never going to reach its potential without a little bit of heat.

The sound guy adjusts my mic one more time before giving us the OK to sit. One of the props assistants places the fake sandwiches and a bowl of chopped fruit on the picnic blanket in front of Scotty and me. All in all, it looks like a wholesome little scene. Scotty is dressed in a navy-blue pullover and his signature red board shorts, while I'm dressed in a pair of boring blue scrubs and white sneakers.

"You should probably take those off now." Scotty points at my shoes.

"OK," I reply, suddenly nervous. How the hell am I going to strip down to my bra and underwear if taking my sneakers off is making me nervous? "You're sure we should be doing this, right?"

"No." Scotty smirks. "But everything you said made sense to me. I trust your gut."

"Why?" I untie my shoes and slip them behind me, out of the shot. "You barely know me."

"How long you've known someone doesn't have anything to do with how well you can trust them," he says. "Sometimes you just trust people because something inside you knows they wouldn't lead you down the wrong path. It's like Jack and Rose. You jump, I jump."

"Jack ends up dying in the movie, you know." I snag a grape and pop it into my mouth, careful not to disturb my lip gloss.

"In an ocean, no less." Scotty nudges me.

"Alright, you two. Are we ready?" Todd shouts from his director's chair.

Scotty gives him a thumbs-up.

"Perfect. Action!"

The minute Todd says *action*, it's like a switch inside me activates. Whatever fears Liza had cease to exist as I become Naomi Parker. God, I'd give anything to feel an ounce of Naomi's confidence off-screen. To be able to walk into a room and command it. To have people listen and take what I have to say seriously without discounting me because of my age or my gender. That's the one thing the writers definitely got right when creating this character. Naomi has guts. She just needs to be a little less robotic and a little more human.

"How did the surgery go?" Scotty asks, slipping into Ryan mode. "Everything routine, or as routine as things can be when you're slicing into someone's brain?"

"Pretty routine craniotomy," I say. "Minimal swelling. We were even able to attach the bone flap. All in all, a nice little Thursday."

He kisses me, and per the script, it's not much more than a peck.

"That's amazing," he says. "I probably should've gotten you more than a sandwich for saving my dad's life."

"Sandwiches are perfect," I say, making my voice breathy. "Not too heavy but packed with enough protein to get me through my rounds tonight." I make eye contact with Scotty, checking to make sure he's still with me for the script change. He gives me a wink, sending a very unscripted flutter through my chest. "Did you bring any coffee by chance?"

"I didn't."

"Cut," Todd interjects. "Naomi doesn't ask Ryan for coffee. Let's take it back from the top."

I freeze, suddenly worried that my plan for subverting the script might not actually be as easy to pull off as I thought it would. If Todd's paying close enough attention to know that Naomi doesn't ask for coffee, how am I going to get a sunset dip in the ocean past him?

"Hold up." Scotty turns toward Todd. "I think it might be a good idea for Naomi to ask for coffee. I mean, she's working a twelve-hour shift doing back-to-back surgeries. Wouldn't asking for a little caffeine help humanize her?"

Todd taps his chin for a moment before finally nodding. "Somebody get us a thermos or a cup of coffee. Take five."

"We don't actually want coffee," I whisper to Scotty.

"It's fine." Scotty gets up. "I'm going to have a chat with Arlo really quick."

Arlo is one of the senior sound guys on staff. Scotty runs up to him and whispers something in his ear, making sure to cover his mic pack. I'm not sure what's said, but I do catch Scotty slip Arlo a couple of folded-up bills. A PA brings me a floral thermos filled with coffee, which probably actually belongs to her. I thank her just as Scotty comes back and sits on the picnic blanket with me.

"What was that?" I whisper.

"Don't worry," he replies. "You just stick to your script. OK? Just roll with it."

"Alright, thermos of coffee should be behind Ryan. Let's go back to Naomi asking about coffee," Todd announces. "Quiet on set and . . . action."

"Did you by chance bring any coffee?" I ask, my adrenaline pumping at full tilt.

"I did," Scotty says, in his signature low and gravelly voice. "You need something to help wake you up?"

It's not the exact way I wrote the line, but I can improv with it. "Sometimes I do."

"Can I ask you something, Naomi? When do you ever get to just be a regular eighteen-year-old? When do you ever just have fun?"

I can hear my pulse pounding in my brain, expecting Todd to say something. But he doesn't, and once again, Naomi takes over.

"I do plenty of things that normal eighteen-year-olds do," I say, defensively. "I'm having fun now. Aren't you?"

"Sure, but in forty minutes you're going to be scrubbing in for another surgery. Don't get me wrong, it's impressive. What you do is nothing short of a miracle, but don't you ever want to cut loose? Don't you ever want to be a little less responsible and a little more young?" He leans in close like he's going to kiss my cheek, but instead he whispers, "Arlo cut the sound from Todd's headset. If we're going to do this, we do it now. You jump, I jump."

I don't know that I've ever been the type to jump first in any situation, but right now seems like one of those *now or never, put your money where your mouth is* kind of moments. I give him a wink as I pull the claw clip out of my hair.

"Oh, I can be spontaneous, Mr. West," I say, standing up. "I can be young and wild and still make it in time for my second craniotomy of the day." The sea air whips through my long, dark locks, shielding me from Todd's line of sight just enough to keep my nerve. "Did you know that exposure to cold water can help increase blood flow to the brain, producing a feeling of alertness?"

"I love it when you speak doctor to me," he smirks, just as the sun starts to dip below the horizon. "But just to be sure I'm not misunderstanding, explain it to me like I'm just a regular, dumb guy."

"I'm saying I want to go skinny-dipping in the ocean with you." I grab the bottom of my scrub top and start to lift it. "Unless that's too young and free for you."

"I'm a lifeguard, Parker." He whips his pullover off in one swift motion, revealing the most gorgeous, tanned abs. "I was born to get naked in the water."

Together, we race toward the ocean, stripping down to our underwear. The adrenaline pulsing through my veins is so intense, I don't even notice the frigid cold of the water as it laps over my toes and climbs up my legs. When the water reaches our bellies, Scotty picks me up like a bride on her wedding day. His hot skin presses against mine, making every hair on my body stand at full attention.

"What's the plan?" he whispers to me. Nobody can hear us now that we're in the water without our sound packs. "The script said we run off together into the sunset, and that's it."

"This." I twist my body, wrapping my legs around his torso. "We kiss."

"I can do that."

He runs his fingers into my wet hair and kisses me long and hard. If our first kiss on-screen was electric, then this one is nuclear. It's all-consuming, and I allow myself to get lost in it.

When we finally break apart, I brace myself to face a pissed-off Todd, but to my surprise, he isn't scowling at the two of us. He's clapping.

Chapter 12

The Big House is silent when Scotty and I arrive, which is a bit of a relief. I have yet to process the fact that he's actually here. Trying to do that with my entire family present would be a bit like wrangling a goat rodeo.

I lead him into the guest bathroom to get cleaned up, being careful not to wake anyone. He sits on the edge of the seafoam-green tub, while I grab the first-aid kit, which thankfully doesn't look as old as the bathtub.

"This place hasn't changed a bit," he says.

"Well, there's a giant pink elephant by the pool, but other than that, it's same old, same old."

I crack one of those instant ice packs on the edge of the vanity and give it a shake before handing it to Scotty.

"So tell me more about you blocking the whole world." He holds the ice pack to his cheek.

I decide I'd rather not tell Scotty that I drowned my phone on purpose to avoid having to talk to him and go for a vaguer approach. "It broke."

"It broke?"

"Yup. I guess it wasn't that long of a story after all." I tear the corner of the antiseptic wrapper with my teeth and open it. "Oof. This smells like it's going to sting."

"I trust you, Dr. Parker."

Something about the way he says *Dr. Parker* makes a shiver snake down my spine. It's not the same melty sensation I got when he said *our daughter*, but it's still a dangerous feeling.

"Do not call me that," I whisper. "Not unless you want a lobotomy."

"Did you ever perform one of those? Because if you didn't, then that was a definite missed opportunity."

"Just sit still." I roll my eyes. "You were a much better patient when all your lines were scripted."

I carefully apply the cool, wet corner of the wipe against Scotty's skin. He winces, and I blow on his skin the way I used to blow on Avery's elbows or knees when she skinned them. It's not an open wound, just some small abrasions and swelling. It looks more like a bit of road rash on top of a black-and-blue hill.

"You're good at this," he whispers.

"Well, I did play a doctor on TV." I pull back. "All done."

"Oh, so you can bring up being a doctor but not me? I see how it is." He presses the ice pack against his cheek and points to scrapes on my shins from my fall. "Now it's your turn."

I glance down at my shins. They do look a little worse than what I originally thought. Maybe it's just the yellow lighting and the fact that we're in a bathroom that is the color of pistachio ice cream. He grabs a washcloth and runs it under the faucet and then pats the edge of the tub.

"Put her up."

The *her* he's referring to is my leg, I'm assuming. I was fine cleaning up Scotty's face, but him wiping up my leg feels way too personal.

"I'm fine," I say. "Really. It's not a big deal."

"You say that a lot."

"I say what?"

"'I'm fine.'" He says it in a mocking tone. "I'm starting not to believe it."

"Just because I don't want you to bathe my leg doesn't mean there's something wrong," I argue.

"Oh. Um." His eyebrows knit together like I've just told him a riddle. "I wasn't going to wipe down your leg. I was going to give you the washcloth to do it."

I can feel the heat rush into my cheeks like a hot summer wind. How is it possible that I can take an already awkward situation and somehow make it a million times worse?

"I knew that." I grab the washcloth and wipe away the dirt and grime from my shins, propping each leg one at a time on the edge of the tub next to him. I'm acutely aware of the fact that he's trying to hold back from laughing and failing miserably. I find it equal parts annoying and amusing. "You don't have to be so smug, OK? I've been under an inordinate amount of stress."

"Like what?" he asks.

"Well, for starters, I quit my job. I didn't really have a choice. The school was trying to get rid of me. Anyway, I don't want to talk about it. Everything is going to be fine. I just wanted to let you know."

I'm surprised at how easily I say it. He was the one person other than Avery who I dreaded telling. Scotty's always made more money than me—that much is obvious—and he's always made sure that Avery and I are more than well-cared for, but I've always maintained certain financial rules. For one, I pay the mortgage and my car payment with my paycheck. I cover almost all of the major bills, saving as much of Scotty's child support in Avery's college fund. I've never wanted to feel like I've needed to rely on someone else to take care of the two of us. I've never wanted anyone to worry about us or, worse, pity us.

Maybe it's the fact that he's got a black eye thanks to me, but suddenly, telling Scotty I'm newly unemployed doesn't seem nearly so intimidating. And it doesn't feel that way either. It is relieving.

"Did you get too old too?" Scotty deadpans. "Is that why they wanted you out?"

I laugh so hard that I lose my balance, my foot slipping off the tub's edge. Scotty reaches out to steady me, but his hand juts past my arm as I fall and connects directly with my cheekbone.

"You punched me," I yelp. "My face has a pulse."

"Oh my god." He cups my face with his hands. "I am so unbelievably sorry. I—" He pauses, and for one terrifying moment, I think he might kiss me. "I . . . uh . . . here." He places his ice pack on my cheek.

"Thanks," I say, taking a cautious step back. "I guess we're even now."

There's a knock on the door, and it startles us both so much we both jump a little.

"Liza," George says. "Is that you?"

"Yes," I squeak.

"I thought I heard a scream."

"Oh, I, uh . . . thought I saw a spider," I lie.

"Do you need me to kill it?"

"No, I'm fine, George. I'll be out in a few."

"Alright. I'm going to start on breakfast. Would you like some coffee?"

"Directly injected into my veins, George."

"I believe all we have is Folgers."

"That sounds great." I lean against the door and wait until George's footsteps grow faint before turning my attention back to Scotty. "You need to get out of the house, and then you can come back in."

"Why?" He looks at me like I've lost it, and honestly, maybe I have a little. "I have an invitation."

"You have an invitation to my mother's funeral, not her bathroom." I take the doorknob in my hand and give it a turn, but it just spins like a wheel in my hand. I adjust my grip and pull it this time, but the mechanism inside that allows the door to open and close won't catch. Like everything in this house, it's old. The hardware is rusted and clearly temperamental.

"Let me help you," Scotty says.

"No." I block him from the doorknob like a child protecting a valued toy. "I can get it."

I repeat the same process as before, only this time I add profanity. In my experience, cussing at an inanimate object may not fix anything, but it makes me feel better. I hike one foot on the wall and grab the knob with both hands, twisting it as slowly as I can.

"It's like the damn thing is stripped," I huff.

"Are you sure it's not locked?" Scotty asks.

"Of course I'm sure. I didn't lock it. Why would I want to be locked in a bathroom with you?"

"I can give you an entire voice memo worth of reasons why you might want to be locked in a bathroom with me."

A hot flash consumes me, but I refuse to give both it and Scotty any attention. "I meant none of that."

I tug as hard as I can until something inside the knob makes a snapping sound. I loosen my grip, and the knob hangs limp in my hand.

Scotty leans over me. "Can I look at it now, or do I have to wait until you break down the entire door?"

I raise my hands up in mock surrender and move to the back of the bathroom.

Scotty jiggles the handle in his hand and shakes his head. "I'm probably going to need to take this apart."

He raises his hand to knock on the door, but I stop him. "You're not here. You can't wake up the whole house."

"Really? We're going to keep hanging on to this thread of a lie because what? You're worried that George might think we were hooking up in the bathroom?"

"Ew." I scrunch my nose.

His eyes widen in surprise. "Ew?"

"I meant to the bathroom, not to you." I regret the words the second they leave my lips. "Not that I want to hook up with you, because I don't. I just don't want to hook up in a bathroom even more than I don't want to hook up with you. Does that make sense?"

"Not according to your voice note."

"If you mention that voice note one more time, I'm going to beat you over the head with this doorknob."

"Look," he chuckles. "Eventually, one of us is going to need to use this bathroom, and I'm willing to bet that's going to be awkward. Can we please get someone to help us?"

He has a point.

"Give me your cell phone." I hold my hand out. "I'll call my brother. He's in the Casita."

"And he won't think that we were hooking up?" He hands me his phone. "Unlike George, who apparently thinks you would hold me in here like a sex hostage."

I hate that he makes me smile this much. I hate that his stupid banter makes me feel like I'm sixteen again. It's intoxicating. I could get completely wasted on it, if I'm not careful. I dial Miles's number.

"This is Miles," he says, sounding half-asleep.

"I'm stuck in the bathroom," I whisper. I don't know why I'm whispering, but it feels like the right thing to do. "Come get me."

The call ends. I look at the phone screen to check the signal. I call again, only this time it goes straight to his voicemail. I shoot him a text instead. "I don't have anyone else's number memorized except for Avery's, and that would be weird for her. Why isn't he answering?"

"He probably thinks it's a prank," Scotty says. "That's what I would think if a random person called me this early and told me they were trapped in a bathroom. Give me the phone."

"Why?" I ask, staring at the screen for a reply.

"Because it's mine." Scotty grabs the phone from me. "And because I have your sister's number saved."

"Why would you have Kat's number saved?"

"Because she's helped me with some real-estate stuff in the past." He dials her number, and sure enough, Kat answers. Scotty explains the situation and hangs up. "She's on her way. Crisis averted."

Something tells me that there will be much bigger crises for Scotty and me to avert the longer we're in the same zip code.

Chapter 13

Scotty manages to slip out of the Big House just before Mom and Avery wake. He rings the doorbell, and I make a big production of being surprised by his arrival, which everyone seems to buy except for George.

"It's interesting," he says, as I pour myself a cup of coffee. "I thought I heard an engine rumbling earlier this morning, but when Scotty arrived just now, I didn't hear anything."

"It's probably a very quiet engine," I say. "European, most likely."

"Most likely." He raises an eyebrow. "Also, isn't it interesting that you both suffered facial injuries this morning?"

"Not really. Scotty is an action star, and I'm a little clumsy." I leave George to finish making breakfast before he can find any more coincidences to point out.

Everyone's gathered around the table, minus Miles, who's never been an early riser of his own accord. Mom dotes on Scotty like he's the prodigal son returned. The two of them have managed to get along the past few years, even when Mom and I couldn't. Avery sits in between them, her face lit up like it's her birthday and Christmas all rolled into one.

Kat nods in Scotty's direction. "I didn't expect to see him this morning."

"Neither did I." I sip my coffee. "But apparently, he's just one of many on Mom's mystery guest list."

"Can I ask what led to the bathroom fight club?"

"I thought he was going to murder me on my run."

"That's an interesting meet-cute."

"We are not meeting cute," I say.

"We'll see." Kat winks at me. "By the way, I invited the helicopter man to the funeral."

"Good for you." I rest my head on her shoulder. "Does the helicopter man have a name?"

"He goes by Rooster." She says it with such a straight face that I question whether she's the one who should've been an actress all along.

"Can't wait to meet him."

George puts the final touches on breakfast and serves it buffet style, or as he prefers to call it, *ranch style*. We pile up our plates with bacon and eggs and toast. My stomach growls just looking at all of it. It's amazing the appetite thinking you're going to be killed creates. I'm about to take my first bite of bacon when Miles comes barreling through the back door, out of breath.

"Mom, you'll never guess who I just got off the phone with." He leans over the counter to catch his breath. "Scotty?"

"Hey." Scotty waves.

"That's who you were on the phone with?" Mom asks.

"No." Miles shakes his head. "I just didn't expect to see Scotty in the kitchen."

"Well, he's family. Plus, I invited—"

Miles cuts her off. "Diane Sawyer!" he practically screams. "Well, not actually Diane Sawyer. Her people. Diane's people called me this morning, because she wants to do an interview with you. She actually wants to do a piece on the whole family. The Day Dynasty. Isn't that incredible?"

The whole room goes quiet, all eyes on Mom, waiting for her to squeal in delight. Mom has idolized Diane Sawyer for as long as I can remember. She's watched a million of her specials, if not all of them, and she used to make us kids sit and watch them with her too. It was Diane that she modeled herself after for her role in *Champagne After*

Midnight, where she played a hard-hitting journalist who falls in love with a politician running for president. The role got Mom her first Oscar nomination. She didn't win that go-around, but she always talked about the speech she prepared in case she did win.

Diane was the first person I was thanking after God, she'd say.

But Mom doesn't jump for joy or cheer. She doesn't get out of her seat and dance around the kitchen with Miles the way she used to whenever she got good news. She just sits there, silently.

"Mom?" Kat reaches for Mom's hand, which is still holding a fork. "Is everything OK?"

"Of course," she stammers, placing her fork back on the plate. "Everything is fine."

"So, I'm telling her yes, right?" Miles asks. "She says she'd like to set something up early next week. They can send out a crew tomorrow to film some B-roll of the funeral. What do you think?"

Mom reaches for her orange juice and sips it slowly, completely ignoring Miles's urgency. "The cake is going to arrive this morning. Soon, I believe. I know cake at a funeral seems odd, but Chauncey came up with the most brilliant idea. You're going to love it. It's a little macabre, but—"

"Mom." Miles pulls out the open seat next to me at the table. He has his phone cued up to his email. "Does next week work?"

"Work for what, dear?" She sighs.

"For what? For Diane Sawyer. What else have I been talking about? This is a big deal for you. It's a big deal for everyone."

"That's very nice, honey. Very exciting." She folds her napkin in a perfect triangle, her eyes never meeting his. "But I don't think next week works."

Miles looks as if Mom has just kicked him in his shin. Wounded doesn't begin to cover it. "What about the following week?"

"That might work." She pushes her chair away from the table and stands. "I think I'm going to check on the rabbits. George, will you come with me?"

"Might work?" Miles's mouth practically hangs open. "Mom, this is Diane Sawyer, not a reservation at the Olive Garden. What am I supposed to say to her people?"

"Oh, Miles." She kisses him on the cheek as she makes her way to the back door. "I can't commit to anything while in the midst of planning a funeral. I'm sure Diane will understand. Send her one of those edible-fruit bouquets. People love those."

She saunters out with George on her arm and every pair of eyes in the kitchen glued to her. With a look of utter defeat, Miles slumps back in his chair. "It doesn't make any sense. She was supposed to be happy."

"Maybe she's just overwhelmed," Kat offers. "She's got a lot going on."

"Or maybe she's nervous," Scotty adds. "You know, her last few interviews and interactions with the press weren't exactly favorable."

That's putting it mildly. They were downright cruel.

Sunset Breeze was supposed to pump some new life in Mom's career. After the second divorce, she tried to get parts, tried to reinvent her career, but Hollywood likes women best when they're shiny and new. *Sunset Breeze* was a step down and in the wrong direction as far as Mom could tell, but her agent was adamant that it would introduce her to a new generation. It would make her relevant again. Show her range as an actress. The reality was that it was Mom's only real offer, plus it was a chance for the two of us to work together.

That part excited me. I was used to having Mom as my manager on the small roles and commercials that I infrequently booked, but this would be different. This wouldn't be a little variety show performed in a club. This would be a chance for us to make something real together and to maybe, just maybe, let me step into my own. That hope was short-lived.

The tabloids and press immediately started going on about Mom's fall from grace. They came after her for her looks, her failed marriages to Dad, and of course, her inability to land a major role. Most of those she could brush off. Not that it was easy by any stretch, but she'd grown thick-enough skin over the years to handle a fair amount of vitriol. It was the way Miles was treated in the press that eventually put her over the edge.

When Mom adopted Miles, Grandma Vivian insisted they tell the press that she adopted Miles from a relative. I suppose she wanted to help Mom save face, especially in light of Eddie's infidelity. So that's what Mom did. She told the press she adopted Miles from a distant cousin who wished to remain anonymous, and Eddie agreed to be on the paperwork so that all three kids would have the same core family. I assume Miles's birth mother agreed to not say anything, and the story went off without a hitch. Things were different back then. Gossip blogs didn't exist. Investigative journalists didn't spend their time poking around in the daily life of celebrities.

But by the early 2000s, the mediascape was completely different. You had bloggers like Perez Hilton and TMZ posting hourly updates of celebrities doing everything from grocery shopping to driving down Rodeo Drive drunk out of their minds. Secrets and shame were what sold, and with a camera and internet on every phone, anybody could be a journalist. A person's whole life was one click away from absolute disaster.

That's all it took. One bored person looking to make a little money found Miles's birth mother's obituary and saw that Miles Edward Vance was listed as surviving family. A little more research made it easy to trace back Eddie's short-lived relationship with Miles's mother, Mindy, and it took no time at all for someone to do the math on Miles's conception. The humiliation nearly broke Mom. She started drinking one day and kept drinking until it took nearly everything from her.

We move on to other topics. Avery's volleyball team. Mom's menagerie of stressed-out rabbits. And, of course, Scotty's black eye, which he tells everyone is an injury from a rock flying out of nowhere while he was riding without a helmet. Avery gives him hell for not wearing a helmet, and I quite enjoy watching him on the receiving end of her lecture.

It's one of those slice-of-life little moments that I never allowed myself to dream about. Sitting around a table with my brother and sister and daughter and Scotty, talking about nothing and enjoying each other's company. What would life be like if this had been our norm? What kind of people would we be?

We clear away the dishes. Scotty has plans to check in to the Heavenly Motor Lodge, where he's booked a room for the weekend, and Avery wants to tag along.

"I'll take the back road," he says, standing in the driveway. "Keep us away from the cameras."

"And I'll make sure he wears a helmet," Avery adds. She's sitting on the back of his bike, looking so grown up it hurts.

"Just try to be back around lunchtime," I say. "Mom wants us to try on our outfits for tomorrow night."

"Ah, yes, the Night of a Thousand Darlas." He slides his helmet on. "I hope nobody wears my outfit."

"Which one is that?"

"Ryan West. Obviously, I've got to represent *Sunset Breeze*." He makes the hang-loose sign with his hand, a Ryan West trademark. "I'm bringing back the board shorts and puka shells. What about you?"

"Haven't decided yet."

"You should be Naomi, Mom," Avery says.

"Oh, I don't know about that," I say. "I've seen more than enough of myself as Naomi Parker over the past few days than I care to for the rest of my life. Plus, the idea is to dress up like Mom, not me."

"Good point," Scotty says. "Unfortunately, I don't think I packed a pair of pumps."

"Pumps? How old are you? I don't even think Mom would call a pair of high heels *pumps*."

"C'mon, guys," Avery pleads. "It'll be cute. Please, Mom? At least think about it."

Maybe I'm hard up for some positive attention from her, but part of me wants to agree just to make Avery happy.

"I'll think about it," I say.

"Ryomi forever." Scotty winks.

He gets on the bike, and I watch the two of them drive off, and something inside me whispers, *There goes my whole world.* It's something I used to say each time Scotty took Avery. I stand in the airport, watching them go on their next big adventure, while my life comes screeching to a halt.

I'd enjoy the first few days alone. Take hot baths. Watch all the TV I wanted. Read until I couldn't keep my eyes open. Eventually, though, the quiet would sneak in. There were no toys to pick up or messes to clean. My house was like a movie stuck on pause, waiting for someone to hit play and bring it back to life.

That's the thing about being a mother. It's easy to get lost in the role. Easy to forget to build a life outside of it, and even easier to judge your own success and happiness based on your kid's.

What's going to happen when this weekend is over? What's it going to be like watching Avery go to the school I'm no longer employed at? If she was ditching class while I was on campus, what's she going to do when I'm not there at all?

I head back to the Casita to charge my iPod all the way. I have a feeling I'm going to need to go on another run.

Chapter 14

When I enter the Casita, I find Kat and Miles in different states of panic. Both have decided that the combination of Mom blowing off Diane Sawyer and treating all her earthly belongings as a *take a penny, leave a penny* cup at a gas station are signs that something is epically not OK.

"She's dying," Miles moans from the unmade sofa bed. Next to him, there's a bottle of orange juice that looks mostly untouched and a bottle of prosecco that looks like it's nearly empty. "I knew it. She's Domingo-ing us."

"We're not being Domingo-ed," I say, sitting next to Kat at the kitchen counter. "I think what Scotty said at breakfast about Mom being leery of press makes a lot of sense."

"Diane is not simply press, Liza," Miles says. "She doesn't do tawdry stories about cheap celebrity bullshit. She makes hard-hitting, beautifully poetic pieces that inspire people. She shines a light on overlooked people. Remember that special she did about the Amish who were addicted to Mountain Dew? That was riveting."

"It wasn't the Amish that she covered," Kat says, tapping away on her laptop. "It was the people of rural Appalachia living in poverty."

"The point is still the same. The Day Dynasty," he says wistfully. "It was going to be magic."

He covers his face with a pillow and lets out a half-hearted scream. I lean over Kat's shoulder and glance at what she's been furiously typing.

"What's that?" I ask.

"I'm emailing a commercial real-estate broker I connected Mom with," she says, biting her bottom lip, deep in thought. "A few months ago, Mom was asking me to look up the deeds to the ranch. She told me she lost them and wanted them for her records. I printed out what I could find and mailed them over. Then last month, she asked me if I could help her get an appraisal for the ranch. She said she just wanted to know the value of the property, since she'd never had one done. I don't do commercial real estate, and honestly, I didn't feel like dealing with the million questions Mom would ask about the property, so I connected her with a friend of mine. That's who I'm emailing."

I've bought exactly one home in my life. My knowledge of the inner workings of real estate is limited to that one experience and whatever I've watched on HGTV. "OK, and why are you emailing this person?"

"I want to see if Mom talked about selling the ranch." Kat hits the "return" button on her keyboard with finality. "Sent."

Now, it's my turn to start to panic. "Kat, this is a big deal. When were you going to say something?"

"Yeah." Miles's voice is muffled under the pillow. "What the hell?"

"Look, you two aren't around her as much as I am." Kat lets out a slow exhale. "Not to say that we're close at all, but I'm usually the person Mom calls when she needs something. A toaster. An opinion on whether a mole looks suspicious. Access to information about important documents. That's what she calls me for. Mom wanting to know how much the ranch is worth didn't seem all that different from her wanting to know if I thought the birthmark on her hip looked like it might be cancerous, OK? I did what I always do and connected her with someone she can ask all the questions she's willing to pay for. This morning, when I sobered up, it occurred to me that she might be getting rid of her memorabilia because she's planning on downsizing."

I know it's not logical and that it probably makes me sound like a cold, deplorable human, but somehow, hearing that Mom might sell Day Ranch actually bothers me just as much as the thought of her being sick. Day Ranch is where all my good childhood memories were made. It's the place I felt the safest when the rest of the world and my life felt scary and unpredictable. It's where I brought Avery home with Scotty. Mom may have lived here longer than any of us, but Day Ranch was never her first choice. It was mostly her only choice or last resort.

She can't just get rid of it. Selling Day Ranch would be like selling a piece of my childhood. It's a member of our family. In some ways, it's the most dependable Day there ever was or will be.

"I could be wrong." Kat closes her laptop. "But if I'm not, I'd rather we know now."

"And if she is planning on selling it?" My stomach churns. "Is there any way we can stop her?"

"Everything is in her name. It's her ranch." Kat glances out the window overlooking the pool, where an army of florists are constructing a flower wall. "She can do whatever she wants with it."

"This is the most depressing funeral I've ever been to." Miles sits up and cuddles the pillow against his chest. "And nobody's even dead yet."

"I'm going to rinse off in the Big House," Kat says. "I'll let you know if I hear something."

Miles and I make his bed back into a couch so we can sit on it and contemplate in silence how our lives are falling apart. He offers me some of his prosecco, but I turn it down and instead eat a sleeve of Ritz crackers that are probably left over from when I last lived here with Avery.

I was doing so good at disassociating from all my real-life problems since coming to the ranch. Avery and I had enough space between us to not be at each other's throats. No phone meant no constant reminder that I no longer had a job, and I was actually starting to warm up to the idea of spending a little bit of time around Scotty. But now that there's even the slightest possibility that Mom might be selling Day Ranch, I am faced with a problem I can't ignore.

"Can I tell you something?" Miles grunts.

"Only if it's not going to make me sad," I say.

"I almost slept with him."

"Scotty?" My neck turns so fast in Miles's direction that it pops. "You almost slept with Scotty?"

"No." Miles makes a face. "I mean, he's hot, but the last thing I ever want to do is sleep with someone who can say to me, *That's not how your sister did it.*"

"Ew."

"Chauncey." Miles sighs. "I almost slept with Chauncey."

"Oh."

I take in the gravity of what this admission means. For Miles to be able to almost sleep with someone other than James must mean that he really, really thinks the two of them are done. I don't even think I believed Miles when he said he was dating, because Miles isn't someone who dates, or at least he wasn't. Unlike Kat, who self-sabotages relationships, Miles is a serial monogamist and is damn good at picking out quality partners. Miles almost sleeping with some guy he met on an app while still not actually divorced doesn't sound like him.

"How do you feel about that?" I manage to ask.

"Don't shrink me." He grabs my box of ancient crackers. "I've already paid for someone to do that, and it didn't do a damn thing but make me lose an hour of my life that I'll never get back. Because I'm old. Do you know that? We're old."

"Old for what? And also, I don't think your age has anything to do with a shitty therapy session."

"Oh, but it does." He stands and begins pacing the room. "Because if I wasn't old, I wouldn't be in therapy, crying over the worst one-night stand of my whole life."

"It was that bad?"

"You have no idea."

Miles proceeds to tell me in more detail than I would've ever possibly wanted about his evening with Chauncey Hill. The two met at a party in West Hollywood for some influencer whose name I forget as soon as I hear it. According to Miles, he and Chauncey hit it off immediately. They spent hours talking about old Hollywood starlets and scandals and whether new Hollywood would ever find a feud as compelling as Bette Davis's and Joan Crawford's. Chauncey invited Miles over for a nightcap, a.k.a. a hookup. It had been six weeks since he and James had spoken a single word to one another.

"I thought I was ready." He alternates bites of Ritz crackers with gulps of prosecco straight from the bottle. "But apparently not all of me was." He looks downward, which says more than enough for me to know what he means. "It was awful. The worst humiliation I've ever felt in my life."

"Did he make fun of you?" I ask. "Because if he did, I'll kill him. Seriously. You saw what I did to Scotty, and I only had one dirt clod."

"He didn't make fun of me." Miles sits. "I mean, not directly at least."

"I don't understand."

"He said I was old," Miles says. "He said I had nothing to be embarrassed about. He said he'd been with men my age before, and he understood that this was something that just happened when they got older and were a little out of shape."

"I'll go get the dirt clods," I growl. "You know, Scotty said the same thing. I mean, not exactly, but he just got dropped from the Brock Lucas franchise for being old, and here's the thing. We're not even remotely close to being old. We're young. We're in our prime."

"He thought I was forty-six." Miles clears his throat. "Not thirty-six, which I thought I clearly enunciated when we were comparing our birth charts at the party."

"That's still not old," I say. "Is it?"

"It's not just the age reference or not being in great shape. It's the fact that I couldn't actually be intimate with someone else, because the truth is I don't want to be. I want to still be married to James. I want to have the life we had together again. I love that life."

"Have you told him that?" I ask.

"No. I've been waiting for him to reach out to me. I don't want to risk being the only one who feels this way." He rakes his messy curls with his hand. "If I knew there was no hope of James missing me the way I miss him, I don't know if I could get out of bed in the morning."

I wrap him in a big hug and let him sob on my shoulder for all of two minutes, which is an emotional record for Miles. We're not a family of criers—not unless we're being paid to cry on TV—but I appreciate the opportunity to be there for Miles.

"So when Chauncey shows up today, do we hate him?" I ask.

"No." Miles reaches for his phone and pulls up Chauncey's Instagram account. "He's going to make tomorrow night absolutely breathtaking for Mom."

Chauncey's Instagram is one of those perfectly manufactured grids of complementary tones and artistic lighting. I scroll through the photos of his events. A divorce party on a yacht in Malibu titled *Murder Before Matrimony* catches my eye. The first photo is of a group of women in beautiful white gowns. The second shows them gathering around a five-tier wedding cake. The next is a picture of the women carving into the red velvet cake with butcher knives. The last photos in the series are of an epic food fight, ending with all the women covered in red cake. Avery would describe an event like this as *iconic*.

"He's really good," I say, as I continue to scroll. "How do you think Mom found him?"

"I gave him her number when I was drunk." Miles rolls his eyes. "I think it was my way of showing off. I told him about the ranch and about what a cool property it is. I told him he could call Mom up whenever he wanted, and he and I could go look around at the place. Get some inspiration for his next event."

"You pimped out our mom. Nice. Why didn't you tell Kat or me about this connection sooner?"

"Look, do you enjoy reliving stories about your sexual dysfunction to your family members?"

"I think I'd have to be having sex in order for it to be dysfunctional," I say. "But I see your point."

We take turns showering and slowly morphing into adult humans rather than the giant toddler personas we've donned while eating crackers and drinking juice on the couch. I drank the juice. Miles finished off the prosecco, which I think might technically be juice. We're about to head to the Big House when Avery bustles through the front door with Scotty not far behind. She's smiley in a way I haven't seen in months. There's a glow about her, as if the few hours she spent with her father has righted every wrong in her life. Maybe it has. I wouldn't know. I can only remember counting the minutes down each time I was forced to spend time with my dad.

After the second divorce, Dad basically disappeared from our lives. His music wasn't as popular as it once was. Hair bands weren't as much in demand in the nineties as they were in the eighties. He moved from one shitty apartment to another. Eventually, he landed in the first of what would be many, many mobile-home parks. This one was for people over fifty-five. He wasn't fifty-five, but the woman he was shacking up with must've been.

The three of us went to visit him once. Mom's hair was done up, and she was wearing a short dress with tall boots. I remember her driving us in Grandpa's old Cadillac. She walked us up the porch and pounded on the door until Dad finally answered it. Smoke poured out of the trailer like it was on fire. The pungent odor of weed and cigarettes made my stomach queasy. I remember reaching for Mom's hand, something I rarely did. I wanted to tether myself to her like a life raft. Dad held the door open for us and coughed something about it being too damn early. It was after lunch, but time never seemed to be relevant to Dad.

Well, come on inside, he muttered, lighting a cigarette. *Kathy doesn't like to run up the air-conditioning bill.*

None of us budged. I'd never met Kathy, but in my childlike brain, she was a nasty swamp witch who ate children when she wasn't puffing like a chimney.

Well, see. You've turned them against me, Dad said. *How the hell am I supposed to watch them for you if you fill their heads with a bunch of lies about me?*

Mom doesn't talk bad about you, Miles said. He was always her defender. *We just don't like sitting and doing nothing all day while you sleep.*

She's not even your real mother, kid, Dad growled.

I don't remember what words were exchanged between Mom and Dad after that. I just remember there being yelling and cursing and eventually the slamming of doors and the purr of the Cadillac's engine as Mom threw it into gear. She didn't leave us with Dad that day, and she never took us back there again.

"Mom," Avery says, leaning her head on Scotty's shoulder. "Can I stay with Dad at the motor lodge? It's really cool, and it has Wi-Fi that actually works."

Cool isn't the way I would describe the Heavenly Motor Lodge. Condemnable, maybe, but not cool. Then again, I've never actually stayed there. I didn't realize anyone stayed there until I saw it on Mom's invitation.

I'm about to tell Avery that I'd rather have her stay at the ranch when there's a knock on the Casita door, which is peculiar because I don't think anyone has ever knocked on that door. Scotty's the closest to it, so he opens it, revealing a very confused-looking delivery driver carrying an ice chest.

"Is this where the walk-in is?" he asks.

"The walk-in what?" I ask, now looking presumably just as confused as the driver. "Are you talking about a freezer?"

"Yeah, I have the cake," he says, nodding toward the red cooler. "It's just the pieces, but Frankie will be by tomorrow to do the assembly with the pieces."

Pieces? Does he mean tiers? Like a wedding cake sort of thing?

"We don't have a walk-in," I say. "Is that important?"

Scotty takes the ice chest from him because it seems like somebody needs to do it, and that's when we realize what the delivery driver / baker actually means by cake parts. There's a piece of duct tape stuck to the side of the ice chest, which reads: *Left Torso*.

"I don't know. I just drive the cakes. I don't make 'em." The driver wipes a bit of sweat from his brow before heading back to his truck.

"Was your mom ever in a Mafia movie?" Scotty asks.

"Not that I remember," I say.

"Uh, little help out here," the driver calls from his truck. "I got eleven more of those things."

Of course he does. I sigh. "Avery, come help me bring in Grandma."

Chapter 15

"We're supposed to eat Grandma?" Avery asks.

It's like one of those phrases English teachers use to teach children the importance of commas. One forgotten comma, and now Grandma is the main course—or, in this case, dessert—instead of an innocent participant in a conversation. However, there isn't a missing comma. Avery is quite literally questioning whether we're supposed to eat a cake modeled to look like my mother.

"I don't think I can do it," Avery adds.

"That's because it has a face," Scotty says, closing the lid on one of the twelve ice chests that are now arranged in the Casita living room. "A very lifelike one at that."

"And cleavage." I motion to ice chest number seven. "I think he accidentally gave us Dolly Parton's bust instead of Mom's."

"Are we supposed to put it together?" Kat asks. "I can't even put IKEA furniture together."

She showed up seconds after the last box of mom-cake was delivered, which is good, because this is the sort of thing you've really got to see in person in order to appreciate. Maybe *appreciate* is the wrong word. *Believe*, maybe.

"Is it here?" Mom barrels into the Casita like a kid given free range into a candy store. "Let me see it. Let me see it."

"Maybe you should sit down, Mom," I say. "It's a little unnerving."

She ignores me, kneeling over the ice chest containing a fondant wig and looking at it the way a mother might look at a newborn. "It's breathtaking," she gasps. "Chauncey was right going with the Marie Antoinette. I almost forgot I played her off-Broadway when I was still a teenager. He really knows how to make an impression, doesn't he?"

"So do serial killers," Miles deadpans.

"You don't like it?" Mom looks up at us like a young child desperately seeking approval for an art project that looks unintentionally abstract. "You can tell me if you don't."

That's a lie. I mean, sure we could tell her we think a giant cake made in her likeness as an ill-fated French queen for her funeral is a little off-putting, if not completely unhinged. But that wouldn't change the fact that I'm going to have to spend the night with chunks of my mother in cake form scattered throughout the living room.

"It's kind of morbid, Grandma," Avery says, eyeing the ice chest marked *Right Foot* uneasily.

"Oh, honey, the only part that's actually cake is the gown, which has yet to be assembled. The rest is mostly fondant and modeling chocolate. It's art."

The phone in the kitchen rings, and my siblings and I take turns looking at one another to figure out who is supposed to answer it. Mom eventually gets up to take it.

"I thought they only had those things in hotels," Avery says, pointing to *that thing*, which happens to be a cordless phone.

"Remember when you said we weren't old?" Miles whispers. "We're dinosaurs."

Mom hurries through the call with a few *OK*s and one *Be right there* before hanging up and announcing that it is now time to meet the man behind the pink elephants and the mom-cake himself. Chauncey Hill is here.

Kat and Miles go ahead with Mom, while Scotty, Avery, and I hang back to make sure the ice chests are all properly sealed. We also crank down the air-conditioning to a temperature that is just above freezing.

I don't know if this will make a difference, but I'd hate to see some of the more delicately constructed features, like her face, melting.

The three of us walk together to the Big House, with Avery walking in between Scotty and me.

She's almost my height now, but something about the three of us walking together in a line takes me back to when she was little. Scotty would fly into town for a night for her recitals or promotions when he could, and afterward, we'd take Avery out for a cheeseburger and fries. On the way into the restaurant, Avery would grab both our hands and beg us to swing her as high as our arms would allow. She'd cackle with laughter and beg us to do it over and over until our arms wore out. It was one of the few times I'd wonder if people thought we were a regular, happy little family when they saw us.

"I think there's something wrong with Grandma," Avery says, out of the blue. "She was being weird last night."

"The woman has a cake that looks like her for everyone to eat at her fake funeral tomorrow," I say. "She's weird in the daytime too."

"That's not what I mean," Avery replies. "Last night, I couldn't sleep. I went to the kitchen to get a snack, and I saw that the back door was open. It was late, and it made me nervous. I went to go wake up George, but he wasn't in his room and Grandma wasn't in hers. Aunt Kat's room was empty too. I was scared that something happened, and I was going to go to the Casita to tell you, but that's when I saw Grandma and George outside, walking."

"What time was it?" I ask.

"I don't know." Avery shrugs. "Late? Definitely after midnight."

"That doesn't sound so weird," Scotty says. "Maybe she couldn't sleep. She's got a lot going on, after all."

"I thought that too," Avery continues. "But Grandma was yelling at George."

This hits me like a brick wall. Mom doesn't yell at George. She doesn't really yell at anyone, unless she's been drinking, but especially not to George. George can do no wrong in Mom's eyes. George could burn down the ranch and lose every one of her rabbits, and Mom would find a way to prove that it wasn't George's fault.

"What do you mean, 'yelling'?" Scotty asks.

Avery stops walking. A serious expression casts across her face. We're about twenty feet away from the Big House, and through the living room window, I can see Kat and Miles. I also see wild hand gesturing just above Kat's and Miles's heads, which I assume belongs to Chauncey Hill. Miles mouths, *Help me,* and I hold up my finger and mouth, *Wait a minute.*

"She was talking about Eddie, or Grandpa, I guess." Avery only saw my father once, when she was a toddler. We've never referred to him as Grandpa. We've barely mentioned him at all. Hearing her say his name seems so out of place. "She kept asking why he hadn't RSVP'd. She wanted to know why he wasn't on the list of guests. She said she kept calling, but he wasn't picking up."

It feels like someone's just sucked all the breath from my lungs. The ground feels unstable, and my head feels like it's trying to float away from my body. "Are you sure that's what you heard?"

"Maybe it's a different Eddie?" Scotty offers.

"Yes. I mean no." She shakes her head. "Yes, I'm sure I heard their conversation correctly, and no, I don't think she was talking about another Eddie. She kept saying that the least he could do after all the hell he put her through was RSVP."

"What was George saying?" Scotty asks. "How was he reacting?"

"Did he tell her Eddie was dead?" I ask.

"I couldn't hear everything he said," Avery says. "I think he was just trying to get her to go back inside, and he did, eventually. He got her back into the house and locked up."

"Did you talk to him?" Scotty asks.

She shakes her head. "I don't know why, but it didn't feel right to say anything. Plus, he seemed so exhausted. I just wanted to let him sleep."

It's as if I'm being transported back in time. I remember standing in hallways late at night, while someone tried to coax a very drunk Darla into her room. She'd talk nonsense. Argue with people who weren't in the room. It was like she was fighting and arguing with all her ghosts at once. The only way to get her to stop was to get her to sleep, which was an almost impossible task. George would do it when we lived in the Big House, and then when we moved out on our own, it was up to one of us kids.

"Thanks for telling me, sweetie," I say. "I'm sorry you had to see that. It must've been uncomfortable."

"I'm fine," she says. "I just want her to be OK."

"I'm sure she is," I lie.

"Hey, kid, can you give me and your mom a minute?" Scotty pats her back.

"Sure." She nods.

We wait until Avery walks up the steps of the porch, her long, dark ponytail swinging back and forth, before we say anything. A surge of anger floods over me, thinking about what she must've felt like last night. I should've been there with her. She shouldn't have had to go through that alone. It's terrifying seeing an adult you love out of control, especially when you don't understand why.

"Do you think she's drinking again?" Scotty asks.

"She has to be," I say. "Why else would she be arguing with George in the middle of the night? Hell, why else would she be doing any of this?" I motion to the pink-and-magenta flower walls that the florists completed earlier this morning. "This is what somebody who isn't in their right mind does, isn't it?"

"Maybe," Scotty says. "But maybe not. I remember what Darla is like when she's drinking, and she didn't seem that way to me."

"Well, maybe she's just gotten better at hiding it," I huff.

"OK. What do you need from me?"

"I want you to take Avery back to the motor lodge," I say. "I don't want her to be around to see if things go sideways with Mom."

"And what about you?" he asks. "I can take care of Avery, obviously, but what do you need from me?"

"A phone," I say.

"A phone?" He quirks his brow. "I was thinking more along the lines of some type of moral or emotional support. What's wrong with your phone?"

"I told you, it broke."

"How?"

"Is that really relevant right now?" I ask.

"No." Scotty nods. "It's not. You need a phone, and I will get you one. I'll take Avery with me too. It'll be great."

I don't think *great* is how I would describe any of this, but I appreciate Scotty's acting nonetheless.

Chapter 16

When Scotty and I enter the Big House, I've mentally prepared myself for an intervention. I've never actually taken part in one, but in my head, it involves getting everyone together in one room to tell Mom to cut the bullshit and come clean. As luck would have it, everyone is already in the living room, including Mom. Step one of Liza's *How to Stage an Intervention* tutorial is off to a solid start. What I fail to remember is that my family and Scotty aren't the only people in the room. It's all of us plus a man who resembles the human embodiment of a peacock.

Chauncey Hill.

"Naomi Parker!" The man in a floral linen suit with patent-leather shoes points his finger at me and smiles. "And Ryan West! I've been waiting my whole life to meet Ryomi!" The man stands up from his spot next to Mom and hugs me like an anaconda squeezing the life out of a mouse. He moves on to Scotty, hugging him with just as much enthusiasm. "I'm Chauncey Hill. I'm the man in charge of planning your mother's big day."

I'm stunned into silence, but thankfully, Scotty is not. "Thanks. Nice to meet you."

"Wait a minute!" Chauncey points at Scotty and me and then at Avery. "This is your daughter, isn't it? Oh my god, this is Baby Ryomi!"

Avery grips my arm. She holds on to me like a kitten in a pet store being eyed by an overzealous toddler.

"We call her Avery," Scotty says, calmly.

"You know"—Chauncey turns to Avery—"you're kind of like an urban legend. The baby with no pictures. I think that's what they called you for a while. Your dad famously attacked a pap who was—"

"I don't think we need to put all this attention on Avery or really anyone other than Darla," Scotty says, firmly.

He positions himself between Chauncey and the rest of us. He's gone from the soft, gentle giant of a man that I'm used to seeing to the Brock Lucas action star who pummels bad guys with a broken tailpipe.

It's kinda hot.

"So sorry. You just have to understand that I watched *Sunset Breeze* obsessively as a teenager. My grandmother recorded every episode. You were both my crushes at different points. Actually, you were both my crushes at the same point during that ocean scene in season one." Chauncey fans himself. "Is it really true that you two ad-libbed that whole scene? *I* needed to run into the ocean after that episode, if you know what I mean."

I am struggling to understand how the genius behind these incredible concept parties has the maturity and social awareness of a Great Dane puppy. I scan my siblings' faces, looking for confirmation that I am not the only one thoroughly convinced we are part of an elaborate prank, but Kat looks like she's trying to keep from crying from laughing so hard, and Miles won't make eye contact with me at all. He must've been very, very drunk to have found this guy even remotely charming.

"Well, that's a mental image, isn't it?" Scotty motions for me to take a seat next to Avery on the couch opposite Chauncey. "Alright, let's get this show on the road. What's the game plan, guys?"

I'm not sure I've ever seen Scotty take charge of a situation like this before. Not that he and I have ever been in a situation like this before. I'm just used to him holding back more. He's a leading man on-screen, but in real life, he's always played more of a supporting character in our lives. I make the plans, and he goes with the flow, which I thought I liked. But I could get used to someone else taking the reins every now and then.

"Chauncey was just about to share with us his vision for tomorrow," Mom says. "He's very good at this sort of thing. I've been to a lot of parties in my day, and his work looks top shelf."

Top shelf. I feel my brain start to slowly come back into focus after the jump scare that is Chauncey Hill. I reach for my phone to drop a text in the sibling group chat when I realize that I don't actually have a phone.

"I need your phone," I whisper to Scotty.

"I thought you needed me to buy you one," he whispers back.

"Just give it to me." I hold my hand out. "I need to text Miles and Kat. Oh, and also set up a group chat with Miles and Kat."

Letting Scotty take the reins might need to wait until I have a phone of my own. He sets up a group chat and hands his cell to me.

Scotty: We need to talk. Immediately.
Scotty: Also, this is Liza.

Chauncey moves in front of the old slate fireplace, which now has a white screen affixed to the mantel. The warm glow of a projector casts his shadow onto the screen, as he paces like a big cat. A big, floral, peacock cat.

An old-timey vaudeville jingle starts to play. "The final curtain call." Chauncey holds his arms out dramatically. "A single moment in time. An acknowledgment of a job well done. Farewell. The show is done."

Scotty's phone buzzes.

Kat: About what?
Scotty: Mom.

The sound of a throat clearing draws my attention away from the phone. It's Chauncey, which is no surprise. He strikes me as the kind of guy who isn't used to not having all eyes on him. He wouldn't last a day as a teacher.

"As I was saying"—Chauncey continues his melodramatic presentation—"while a funeral is normally the last course in the grand banquet of life, this event is an amuse-bouche to Darla's fascinating life—past, present, and future. All the world is a stage, and tomorrow, Darla will be the showrunner."

I realize that this presentation could go on endlessly. At some point, this Willy Wonka of a party planner could take to just saying random nouns. *Turkey leg. Idaho. Gout.* We'd all just be expected to continue to sit here and listen as if the man were reciting Shakespeare. Thank god Miles didn't sleep with him.

When he turns away to get something from his briefcase, I fire off another text.

Scotty: Make an excuse to stop the meeting.

I look up, waiting for either one of them to check their phones, but they don't. Maybe they silenced them after I was chastised by Professor Peacock. I nudge Scotty with my foot and mouth, *Make him stop,* while glaring at him. Something must get lost in translation, because Scotty does nothing.

"Tomorrow's event isn't just a funeral. It's a . . ." He pauses for suspense or possibly for time to think of a more long-winded way to say the party's theme. "Well, before I tell you, I want to make sure you can clearly see my vision. I want it to be as if you were inside me."

"Ew," Avery whispers. "How do we make this stop?"

"How do you make a teacher stop talking in class?" I mutter.

"Like this." Avery raises her hand.

Chauncey smiles eagerly. "Yes. Please share your thoughts. Your questions. Ideas."

"I need to use the bathroom," she says.

There are times when I've often wondered if Avery had gotten anything from my gene pool other than physical appearance, but this moment right here removes any doubt. She used the *shit your pants* exit, and I didn't even have to coach her on it. She also said it so much more eloquently than I ever could have.

"Can we take five or something?" Avery asks.

"That sounds like a great idea," I interject. "I think I need to use the bathroom too. Avery, why don't you use the hallway bathroom, and I'll take the one in the foyer." I stand up and point with my head toward the front door, now the unofficial bathroom coordinator. "Miles, Kat, you two need to go, don't you?"

"Uh, yes." Kat nods. "We do."

Miles, who still apparently hasn't seen the group text, looks thoroughly confused. "I think I'm good."

"No." Kat stands and lifts Miles by his arm. "You're not."

"What about me?" Scotty asks. "Should I go?"

"What on earth is going on?" Mom asks. "How is it possible that all of you need to take a bathroom break at the same time? Did you all eat something that upset your stomach?"

George's eyes widen in horror, most likely at the thought of his breakfast poisoning our entire family. "I promise everything was prepared correctly."

Well, now I feel like a terrible human.

"George, your food was excellent," I say. "My stomach isn't upset."

"Mine either, Papa George," Avery says, apologetically.

"Well, if nobody's dying of a stomach virus, can we all kindly allow Chauncey to finish his presentation?" Mom says, sternly. "There's a lot to be done, and I'm sure he has other things to attend to. You're almost done, Chauncey. Right?"

The look on Chauncey's face tells me he most certainly is nowhere close to done, but he quickly recovers with a smile. "Drumroll, please." He presses a button on the projector remote and a canned applause plays. "Tomorrow, the Darla Day we all know and love will cease to exist . . ."

"This is starting to sound a lot like a human sacrifice," Scotty mutters under his breath. "You want me to tackle him?"

"You're on standby," I whisper.

Chauncey steps away from the fireplace as NIGHT OF A THOUSAND DARLAS appears on the screen in an old-Hollywood script font.

A slideshow plays. Pictures of Mom throughout her career flash across the screen. Mom as a child actress dressed in a little suit and tie, tap dancing with Grandpa on a stage. Grandma holding Mom next to a poster of the Darling Baby Food logo with her face in the center. As each image fades into the next, I feel myself being sucked into another place in time. Suddenly, the urgency of Mom's health takes a back seat for the moment, along with my general disbelief in Chauncey Hill's ability to produce something truly magnificent in her honor.

An old home movie begins. Grandma Viv is holding the camera shakily, and Mom is sitting on the diving board, her legs hanging long in the water, just like Avery had when we first arrived yesterday. It's hard to tell if Mom knows she's being recorded beneath her broad-brimmed hat and sunglasses. She's singing something—the audio is too old to make out the words—but it doesn't matter. She looks so peaceful and content.

I feel my throat tighten with emotion unexpectedly.

A photo of Mom on the set of *Summertime Madness* pops up. Her hair is pulled back in a ponytail, and she's wearing a white linen button-down, exactly like the one Avery has on. I reach for her hand and squeeze it. She doesn't pull away. Her hand squeezes mine back.

I wish I got to know that version of Mom. I wish I could go back in time and talk to her. I'd warn her about what was to come. Stay away from booze. Stay away from guys like Eddie Vance. Stay away from acting altogether.

Then there's a clip of Mom with a man I don't immediately recognize, standing on a balcony in Paris. A glass of wine in one hand and a cigarette in the other. Her head tilts back in laughter, and the man smiles at her like she's the most beautiful creature in the world. In that moment, she is.

"Who is that?" Avery whispers. "Is that Grandpa?"

"Mack Houston," Scotty says, softly. "He did a movie with your grandma."

"He's hot," Avery adds.

"He married my best friend, Debbie," Mom says. "She and I did a couple of movies together. You'll meet her this weekend."

The show continues for a few minutes longer, finally ending with a cast photo from the first season of *Sunset Breeze*. My heart swells at the sight of young Liza and young Scotty. We were just babies. I remember thinking we were so grown up and that I knew exactly what my life was going to look like—*Sunset Breeze* for a few seasons and then I'd break into a sitcom or maybe a one-hour family drama. I didn't really care what my next project was. I just knew that I wanted to keep acting, because that's when I felt the most at peace. Life was predictable on a set, and I wanted more of that.

When the slideshow ends, everyone is a little choked up. Miles is dabbing the corners of his eyes with one hand and holding Mom's hand with the other. Even Kat looks a little glassy-eyed. It's George, though, who shows the biggest emotion. I realize he's the only one in the room other than Mom who knew all those different versions of her. He's seen her best and worst, and everything in between.

"Tomorrow, we will honor the woman Darla was and welcome the woman she is to become in this realm and the next. I've created a lookbook of Darla's styles throughout the years," Chauncey says, tapping a black binder. "There's more here than what's on Darla's website for the other guests. I assume the family will want to dress as authentically Darla as possible. After all, you're the people who know her best."

I can't help but think that nobody other than Mom and possibly George has ever really known who Darla Day actually is.

Chapter 17

Sunset Breeze, Season Two Premiere
Fall 2005

"A ghost? That's your solution?" I shove next week's script back across Todd's desk. "We've got to figure something else out. What if Darla's character goes on vacation?"

"We're open to a coma," Maggie, one of the senior *Sunset Breeze* writers, offers. "A coma could easily buy us a few weeks. A month, if we stretch it. Do you think your mother might . . . uh . . . be feeling better . . . or uh . . . back to normal, maybe in a month?"

I want to say yes, but the truth is, I don't know how long it will take to get Mom sober. The last time she went on a bender like this was when I was younger, and Kat shielded Miles and me from so much. I don't remember how long it lasted, and I don't know how long it took for her to get better. I just know that she was able to without rehab, and if she can do it once, surely she can do it again. Right?

"My offer still stands for Emerald Springs," Todd says. "We both know she's got the money to afford it. I'm willing to do whatever I can to help get her admitted."

"She doesn't need rehab," I say, defensively. "She's just having a hard time. She's been like this before, and she was able to get back on track. We just need a little time. That's it."

"Then I think the ghost angle is the best one we've got." Todd runs his fingers through his thinning blond hair. "She can keep her lead credit, and if she gets better, we can work her into the script. It beats the alternative."

"Which is what?"

"Killing her off." Maggie makes a face. "Or I guess I should say permanently killing her off. Technically, she has to die to become a ghost."

"Honestly, it's good for the plot, Liza." Todd sighs. "We've been trying to figure out what to do with Darla's character for months now, and it seems like every attempt we've made only adds to her frustration. Maybe she'll see this as an opportunity."

"An opportunity?" I scoff. "Since when does being killed off a series ever feel like an opportunity?"

Todd and Maggie give me the same apathetic stare. I get it. They're over dealing with a drunk actress. I'm over it too, but she's still my mom. What kind of a daughter would I be if I didn't at least fight for her a little?

"Give me this week," I say. "If I can get her back on track and cleaned up enough this week, then I know I can do it the next week, and the week after that. Just give me this shot. Please?"

They look at one another, neither of them saying anything in words but both saying plenty with their expressions. Todd's desk feels as big as a football field, and I feel about as small as a fly on a goalpost. I wish I wasn't doing this by myself right now. I wish I had Kat and Miles.

Kat's been gone ever since she turned eighteen. She got her real-estate license and started managing a little apartment complex in La Jolla. Miles managed to graduate high school early and got an internship working with a publicity firm based out of New York. He's been living in a two-bedroom apartment with three other roommates for the last three months. He says he's having the time of his life. They both say that, and they both think I'm doing the same. God, I wish that were true.

"One week," Todd finally says. "After that, she's dead to the show. Got it?"

"Got it," I say, before heading to Mom's dressing room.

I don't bother knocking. I storm into the pitch-black room and am immediately met with the stench of cigarettes and alcohol. It takes a moment for my eyes to adjust, and once they do, I peel back the curtains and open the window to let some fresh air in. Her dressing room looks like an abandoned frat house. Empty bottles and overflowing ashtrays litter every surface.

"Get up," I say, with zero empathy in my voice. I used up all my empathy at the end of our first season when Mom's drinking started. "C'mon. You have to get into hair and makeup. Where's your script?"

She mutters something from the couch, underneath the robe she has draped over her face like a blanket. I tiptoe across the room, careful not to step on any stray cigarette butts or fast-food bags, and yank the robe off of her. She recoils, covering her face with her hands, as if the mere existence of natural light is too painful for her to bear.

"What's wrong with you?" she hisses. "I never woke you up so cruelly when you were a child."

"You do realize that I'm technically still a child, right?" I force a bottle of water into her hands. "I just spent the last hour working on your behalf to make sure you still have a job. Does that sound like the sort of thing most kids have to do for their parents?"

She sips the water begrudgingly, looking at me with just one eye open. The shift in our relationship has grown painfully evident, especially since Scotty and I pulled the beach stunt during November sweeps, which changed the entire direction of the show. It also changed the power dynamic between Todd and Mom. He lost all interest in trying to make her elevated-soap-opera idea work, and she seemed to lose all interest in anything that didn't come in a bottle of booze.

"Do you know your lines?" I pick up her script from underneath the couch. "We can probably run through them a few times. The medical jargon is pretty light this episode, so at least—"

"Don't talk to me like that." She sits up, her bones cracking in protest.

"What do you mean?" I kneel on the floor and start piling up empty bottles of liquor. "I'm just making sure you're ready."

"Stop that." She knocks over the collection of bottles I've accumulated. "I don't need you to mother me, Liza. I've been doing this job a hell of a lot longer than you."

This—this anger and resentment—is the newest development in our now daily routine. Up until recently, Mom would be pretty subdued when I'd come into her dressing room to get her. Sometimes, she'd even be apologetic about the state she was in. But once we started preparing for the premiere of our second season, her entire demeanor changed.

It started when she realized how much less screen time her character would be getting. After sweeps, the show moved away from focusing on Mom's character, Dr. Lana Parker, in favor of Naomi and Ryan's storyline, as well as some of the other younger cast members. That was a hard pill for Mom to swallow, but she was still getting decent screen time. The writers were still looking for ways to keep her character relevant, even with the new change in direction. But when Mom started drinking more and generally being more difficult to work with, her character slowly started to disappear from the page.

We're shooting the premiere today, and she barely has ten minutes of total screen time. It'll be a miracle if I can get her on set to shoot any of it.

"I'm not trying to mother you." I sigh. "Do you think I like coming in here and seeing you like this?"

"Sometimes, I think if I weren't like this, you wouldn't even see me at all. You're never home. You're always out with that boy, doing god knows what."

That boy is Scotty, whom my mother has grown to despise with every fiber of her being. She says he reminds her of Dad, but I think she just says that to get under my skin. Scotty isn't anything like my father. He doesn't party. He doesn't screw around and flirt with other girls. He's just a normal, decent guy. Part of me wonders sometimes if she's jealous of what we have.

Mom waited so long to settle down, get married, and have a family. She dated actor Mack Houston for years. He proposed to her twice, or at least that's what the tabloids printed, and she turned him down. I have no idea why, because everything I've ever read about the man makes him sound like a great guy. But then again, I think you could compare just about anyone to Dad, and they'd look better.

When Dad came around, Mom was experiencing her first career slump of what would be many. Hollywood is as fickle as a toddler. What it wants one day, it couldn't care less about the next. Dad was carefree, and like most rock musicians, he wasn't interested in conforming to what anybody thought he should be. He lived his life the way she wanted to live hers, and for a while, I suppose they did. It wasn't until they decided to have a family that Mom realized Dad wouldn't be conforming to any of the conventional rules and expectations of marriage or parenthood.

"He'll break your heart." She takes another sip of water. "They always do."

"Thanks for the advice, Mom."

"I-I'm serious," she stammers. "Men in this industry will always choose what suits their needs first and foremost. He's a better actor than you are. He's going to go places."

I ignore her and search for a bag to collect the trash scattered across the room. I check under the sink, where most of the cleaning supplies are kept in the dressing rooms. As soon as I open the cabinet door, more bottles tumble out from underneath.

There's a knock on the door, followed by Scotty poking his head in. "Everything OK in here?"

He knows everything is the opposite of OK. I don't think there's a single person working on *Sunset Breeze* who isn't aware of how not OK things are with Darla. Scotty also knows that the last thing I want is for him to be anywhere near Mom when she's in a state like this.

"It's fine," I lie. "We'll be in wardrobe and makeup in just a few."

"Scotty, does my daughter do this to you too?" Mom motions toward the piles of clutter I've gathered. "Does she clean up your messes like this?"

"Mom, knock it off." I temper the anger in my voice. "Scotty, just go. I'll be out soon."

He starts to close the door, just as Mom lets out a dry laugh that turns into a coughing fit. His eyes meet mine, and I can tell he doesn't want to leave. I haven't told Scotty about how mean she can get. I don't know why, but I feel a certain need to protect Mom, even if she doesn't always deserve it. This isn't who she really is. She's just in a bad place—a place that I had a hand in putting her in, as Mom would never have done a soap if I hadn't pushed her because we needed the money—and she'll get out of this place. She has to, and when she does, I don't want Scotty's impression of her to be tainted.

"Let me help," he says.

"No." I shake my head. "I've almost got everything picked up. I'm just going to get a little food in her and some more water. She'll be fine."

"I may be drunk, but I can still hear perfectly fine." Mom walks across the room and plops herself down in front of the vanity. "Scotty, if you want to help, be a lamb and go find me a very dirty martini."

"You can't drink anymore, Mom," I say.

"I can do whatever I want," she snarls, pounding a fist on the vanity surface. "I have an Oscar. I've been on red carpets since I was a baby. I've got more talent in my pinky finger than anyone on this whole damn show."

"I don't think she's going to be able to work today, Liza." Scotty lowers his voice just above a whisper.

"She'll be fine." My voice shakes slightly. "She only has one scene today, and she's shooting with me the whole time. I'll carry her through it."

"You think you're going to carry me?" Mom chuckles. "I'm the one that gave you your name. I made sure you were more a Day than a Vance, because Days are winners. Without me, you'd be nobody."

"That's enough," Scotty says. "Liza, let's go."

My body freezes in place, but my mind travels back in time. I'm ten years old again, standing in the hallway of the Big House with Miles and Kat. Dad was gone again, this time for good, and Mom was self-medicating with Jose Cuervo. The three of us were listening to Mom and Grandma Viv scream at one another. Mom had slept through the morning and into the afternoon, which wasn't unusual at this point, and once again, she'd forgotten to take us to school.

Grandma Viv would usually take us when this happened, but that day, she refused. I thought she was mad at the three of us. I thought we'd done something wrong. Everyone seemed happier when Mom wasn't around, even if it was because she was drunk. George made sure we were fed, and Grandma would drive us to school, pick us up, and help with homework. It was almost like old times, I thought. Mom would eventually get herself back together, and then it would be like Dad never happened to us. Like their second marriage never existed. But things weren't the same. Grandma Viv was different. She'd always grumble under her breath that she wasn't the one who was supposed to be raising us, and that she'd raised our mother better than how she behaved.

That day, Grandma Viv and Mom were screaming at one another because Grandma was tired of Mom being *a lazy drunk*. Grandma told Mom that if she didn't get some help, she'd call child protective services on her. Grandma had already set something up at a facility for Mom to go to for thirty days, but Mom was adamant that she couldn't go get help because she had us kids to take care of. That's when Grandma asked her to sign some papers that would give her guardianship of the three of us. I remember Grandma saying it would only be temporary until she got better, but Mom lost it. She became completely unhinged, screaming that she wasn't about to allow us to be raised by someone who would use her kids for a paycheck, the same way she'd been used when she was a child.

It was the first time I'd ever heard Mom talk about her childhood that way. It was the first time I ever got a glimpse into what her life as a child actor was like. She never talked about those early years, the years before the big movies. Those were the years, I would later learn, that she didn't have a say in whether she worked. She worked because that's what her father demanded from her, and she hated him for it.

That was the last day we all lived at Day Ranch as a family. Mom moved us out, and slowly but surely, she got sober, or at least sober enough to function. There were rough patches, but she got better.

Why isn't she doing that now? Why can't I fix her the way Kat and Miles and I were able to fix her last time?

"Liza, trash can." The panic in Mom's voice snaps me back to the present. She's dry heaving, and I'm still somehow too frozen in space and time to be able to move. "Liza!"

Scotty rushes a trash can into Mom's arms seconds before she vomits. She retches a few times. Scotty stays with her the entire time. He rubs her back and tells her everything will be OK. He even helps get her back on the couch when she's done.

Mom doesn't fight him. I don't know if it's because she's too drunk or too weak to push back. Whatever the reason, I'm grateful she accepts his help. I'm even more grateful he's willing to offer it.

We get her settled on the couch. She falls asleep almost instantly. Somehow, Scotty manages to get Todd to push back the filming of Mom's scenes until later this evening. It might be enough time for her to sober up, and even if it's not, it gives me enough time to recover from the ordeal.

"My uncle was an alcoholic," Scotty whispers. We're sitting on the beach, waiting for our next scene to start. "I know what you're going through, Liza. You can't do it on your own."

"I'm not." I force a smile. "I've got Miles and Kat. They're just busy right now. I don't want to bother them."

"Darla needs to get into rehab. She needs professional help."

"She won't go, and I can't make her."

He kisses my cheek. "Maybe you need to consider the idea that it's not your job to fix Darla. It's hers."

I feel myself tremble. "What if she can't?"

"What if she can?"

I don't go back to Mom's dressing room after Scotty and I finish filming. Instead, I wait for her on set, and to my absolute shock, she shows up. She looks a little worse for wear, but that doesn't take away from the fact that she's here now. And maybe, just maybe, she can fix this without me.

Chapter 18

Scotty and Avery leave to find me a phone shortly after Chauncey finishes his presentation. Mom, who hasn't had nearly enough time with the man who never stops talking, takes Chauncey out to the Casita to show him the mom-cake parts. I take the opportunity to debrief Kat and Miles on Mom's possible relapse, and the three of us decide there's only one thing to be done.

The scene in the kitchen looks like something out of *Goodfellas*. George has his sleeves rolled up and is grating fresh Parmesan for lunch, while Miles and Kat pace behind him like a pair of Mafia enforcers trying to get him to crack. Kat focuses her line of questioning on whether Mom's drinking again, while Miles has a slightly more dramatic angle.

"What do you mean, you don't know where she's hiding the good stuff?" Miles throws his hands in the air. "I will drink it. All of it. Problem solved."

"I actually think that's just creating a new problem," I say.

"Well, excuse me for wanting to get Mom back off the wagon," Miles fires back.

"I thought the phrase was *on the wagon*." I tap my finger to my chin. "Don't people say someone has fallen off the wagon when they're drinking again?"

"You're really going to argue semantics with me right now?" Miles asks. "You teach drama. Not English."

"Well, excuse me—"

"Will you two cut it out?" Kat glares at Miles and me. "George, if Mom's drinking again, you have to tell us. I know she's your friend, but—"

"Your mother isn't drinking." George lets out an exasperated sigh. "I can assure you that she's not. Now please, let me work on making lunch."

I don't think George has ever lied to me, or anyone for that matter, which makes this moment all the more crushing.

"Is she asking you to cover for her, George?" I ask.

"Where is all this coming from?" He drops the block of cheese onto the floor. "Darn it."

"It's fine. I'll get it," Kat says. "We're not trying to stress you out, George."

"Avery saw you last night," I say. "She saw you and Mom arguing."

"We weren't arguing." He takes the cheese from Kat and slowly eases into a chair at the table. He cuts the top layers off with a paring knife before he begins grating again. "Your mother and I don't argue, at least not when she's in her right frame of mind."

"So she is drinking?" Kat asks.

A hush falls over the table. Only the sound of a pot of water finally reaching its boiling point disrupts the silence.

"The pasta needs to go in the water," George says. He doesn't get up, though. He just stares at the center of the table for what seems like forever until he finally breaks his silence. "Go make sure the back door is locked. I don't want to risk your mother or anyone else interrupting what I'm about to say."

Miles gets up to lock the door, and Kat pours the fettuccine into the pot on the stove. I get up and fill a kettle to boil for tea, because George would never allow anyone to share something important without a warm beverage. Then, the three of us siblings settle back in and brace ourselves.

"Your mother isn't drinking," George says, slowly. "I would hope that you all know me well enough to know that if that were the case,

I would never cover for her. Not again. She wouldn't ask me to do so either."

A sense of relief washes over me. She's not drinking. We don't have to fight that battle again. No trying to convince her to go to a facility. No figuring out how to pay for it all. This is good.

"Was she having a night terror?" Kat asks. "I remember Mom having those when I was younger."

A night terror would make sense. I think I might even remember her having one or two when I was little. Avery has night terrors, and she used to sleepwalk. Sleepwalking we can deal with. Sleepwalking is easy.

"That's what I thought was happening at first." George looks up for the first time. Tears glisten in his eyes. "Once or twice a month, maybe, I'd find her bed empty in the middle of the night. I've always been a light sleeper. She'd usually just sit on the back porch. I'd bring her back inside and fix her a little tea. She'd go back to bed, and that would be that. But then, I realized there were other symptoms."

"What do you mean, 'symptoms'?" Miles asks.

The kettle whistles. I start to get up, but George stops me. "Let me do it."

"I don't mind," I say. "I want you to be able to relax."

"Then let me do it. Staying busy is the only way I relax anymore."

George serves us green tea with wedges of lemon and honey. While he pours and fixes each of our cups exactly the way we like them, from memory, he explains what the last eight months with Mom have been like.

"At first, she would forget little things. Things people don't pay much attention to," he says. "Remembering to turn off the oven or leaving all the lights on after going to bed. But progressively, those little things became bigger and happened more frequently. She'd leave the water running in the tub and forget that she was drawing a bath. She'd stare at the TV remote for long periods of time, unable to remember how to change the channel. These things concerned me, but it wasn't until she got lost trying to drive into town that I realized something was very much wrong with your mother."

Mom doesn't drive at all now. She was in a car accident once while filming in Paris, and after that, she only drove when there was no other option. The thought of her voluntarily getting behind the wheel now, at her age, is as wild as the possibility of her flying to the moon. It's just not like her.

"How far did she get?" Kat asks.

"Just down the dirt road," George says. "But I didn't realize the car was missing until late afternoon. By the time I'd figured out what had happened and where she was, it was after dark. She was so scared and confused. I'd never seen Darla like that before."

"Why didn't you tell us?" I try my best to temper my tone. "This sounds serious and not just scary for Mom, but for you too."

"Talking about someone's health is a complicated matter, especially as people get older. After the car incident, I told her either she needed to go see a doctor, or I was going to tell you all what was going on. She agreed, and that's when she received the diagnosis. Darla has dementia."

"'Dementia'?"

The word prickles my tongue, like a million little cactus needles. It feels wrong, like it doesn't belong there, especially not alongside Mom's name. Suddenly, the idea of her drinking doesn't sound so awful. Alcohol is a devil, but it's one we know. We understand how to fight it and what the battle will look like. But dementia—I don't even know where to begin.

I glance at the little stack of sticky notes from yesterday. Mine, Kat's, and Miles's are lined up on the counter. Is this why she's getting rid of everything? Is she ridding her home of memories before her mind ends up purging them against her will?

I realize that while I've retreated into my own thoughts, Kat is getting her bearings with Mom's diagnosis. She's asking questions about stages of dementia, medical trials, and different therapies available to

Mom. I glance over at Miles. He's frozen, eyes glued to his cup of tea. I reach across the table and give his hand a squeeze.

"She's been declining," George says. "The wandering at night happens multiple times a week now. The meds she's been on keep her pretty stable during the day, but nights are hard."

"I don't understand why we're throwing a party instead of trying to fix her," Kat says. "We're wasting time. She should be at a university hospital, getting the best care available."

"This weekend isn't a waste of time for her," George says. "She wanted to try to create one last big memory. The planning has actually been good for her. It's given her brain a task to focus on. She knows that once the funeral is done, life will have to change for her here."

George's words unlock something in my brain. It's like he's given me the missing piece to a puzzle I've been struggling with for days, and now I can see the full picture. She wants to say goodbye to people while she's still her. She doesn't want to wait until everyone's names are fuzzy and faces are unrecognizable. She hasn't told us about what she's been going through, because she doesn't want our pity. This—the three of us and George, sad and trying to figure out how to fix everything—is the exact opposite of what she wants. At her core, Mom is a performer. She loves to put on a show, and this is her last one.

"She is Domingo-ing us," Miles says, softly.

"No, she's not," I say. "Mom isn't dying tomorrow or the next day. She's not going off to a farm somewhere. Next week, she'll still be here with the rabbits and George."

"That's not exactly true—" George starts to say something more, but there's a knock at the back door. It's a landscaper hired to trim the hedges into swans and flamingos. George excuses himself to help the guy figure out which bushes should be which birds, and we offer to finish up making lunch.

Miles picks up the cheese and starts to grate again, while Kat stirs the noodles. I go to the fridge and take out a head of butter lettuce and carrots to start a salad. The idea of sitting idle at the table with my thoughts, wondering what the hell George meant by *That's not exactly true*, makes my skin crawl.

We work together in silence for a beat. It's been a long time since the three of us cooked together. Sometimes, the three of us would have trouble sleeping, and we'd sneak into the kitchen and make a midnight snack. Usually, it was something pretty basic. Hamburger Helper or Easy Mac. The actual food wasn't as important as just knowing that the three of us weren't alone. We had each other then. We have each other now.

"I don't want to do this," Miles says. He stands up and wipes his hands on a tea towel. "I refuse to do it."

"You don't want to grate the cheese?" I ask.

"No." Miles shakes his head. "The cheese is fine, and I've already grated it. I'm talking about Mom. I don't want to deal with Mom being sick."

"Do you think any of us want to do this?" Kat snaps. She rests one hand on her hip while the other stirs the pasta. "This isn't the sort of thing that we get a say in."

Kat's tone catches me off guard. She's the calm one. She's the *we'll figure all of this out and everything will be fine* one. Our group dynamic needs her to be that way, because if she's not calm, then there's nothing to keep me or Miles from spiraling into an epic meltdown.

"Well, I refuse." He starts to exit the kitchen. "I'm going home."

"What? You can't go home," I say. "You can't just leave us when things get hard."

"You did," Miles says. "You left. Why can't I?"

"What are you talking about?" I ask.

"You left," he says, his tone sharp. "You got pregnant, had a baby, and left all of us."

His words hit deep below the belt, piercing me like a knife. "I had a child to take care of, Miles. I had a baby who needed a normal life. What was I supposed to do?"

"Y-you wanted to leave," he stammers. "You wanted to get as far away from Mom as possible, and Avery was your reason. You can say it was the paparazzi or being an actress or whatever you want to tell yourself, but the truth is you left here to get away from Mom."

I mull over his words, each one slicing into a piece of what I thought was my heart, but it might actually be my ego. I don't think he's completely right or wrong. I did want to give Avery a normal life, but I also knew that the only way to parent my daughter the way I wanted to meant no longer parenting Mom.

Working on *Sunset Breeze* was one of the best and worst experiences of my entire life, and every part of it that I hated had to do with her. Actually, maybe that's not fair. It was her drinking that I hated having to deal with, not her. I was just too young and too vulnerable to understand the distinction.

"Miles, this isn't helping," Kat says. "Liza had just had a baby. She wasn't in any sort of condition to take care of Mom."

"Well, I'm not either." His voice breaks with emotion. "I've already watched the love of my life leave me this year. I'm not about to watch Mom slip away too." He backs out of the kitchen, tears streaming down his face.

Kat tries to stop him, but I pull her back. I fill her in on James leaving. It's heavy talk, but we cook through it the entire time. She works on gathering ingredients for the sauce, while I round up more vegetables for the salad. I take my feelings out on the lettuce, chopping it so thinly it ends up looking like coleslaw, and Kat melts down some butter until it starts to burn.

"What are we going to do, Kat?" I crush a piece of garlic with the knife blade. "What's the plan?"

She doesn't answer me. She doesn't even acknowledge that she heard my question. I clear my throat and ask again. Nothing. I finally turn around and see Kat crouched down, leaning against the cabinets, tears spilling down her cheeks.

"Oh, Kat."

"Don't hug me." She holds her hand out. "If you hug me, I will sob, and if I sob, I won't be able to get back up."

"What if I just sit next to you?"

"I need you to put the Parmesan into the roux. That's what I need right now."

"OK, but you know I'm awful when it comes to—"

"Liza, I need you to make the sauce," Kat whines. My sister never whines. Up until a few seconds ago, I didn't even know she was capable of it. "I keep burning the roux, and you can't make Alfredo with a burnt roux."

I nod, despite having zero clue what a *roux* is or how it eventually becomes an *Alfredo*. Since when did we start giving human names to food? I walk over to the kitchen table and collect the Parmesan. "I just dump it in the pot?"

"No!" she sobs. "You have to start it over."

"OK. No problem. I'll just dump this brown sludge into the sink." I reach for the pot handle, not realizing that it's partly positioned over the flame. "Shit!"

I drop the pot onto the tile floor, sending piping-hot brown goo flying across the kitchen. My mom instincts kick in, and I throw myself on top of Kat to protect her from the burning ick, accidentally banging her head against the cupboard and my knee on the stove. I reach for the counter to pull myself off of Kat, but my fingers catch the cutting board full of cheese. It tumbles down, baptizing the both of us in Parmesan.

"What is wrong with you?" Kat snorts, dusting cheese from her face.

"I was trying to save you from Ruby or Alfredo or whatever that muck you made is called." I wheeze with laughter. "It's thanks to me that your face isn't on fire right now."

"No, thanks to you, it looks like I have the worst case of dandruff anyone has ever seen." She grabs a handful from her head and throws it in my direction, just missing me.

"Hey! Don't do that."

"But"—she grabs a second handful from the floor, squeezing the dry cheese into a loose ball—"it's making me feel better." She chucks it at me, connecting beautifully with my neck. Little wisps of cheese fall down the front of my shirt.

"Kat, I'm serious. You're making a mess." I stand up and dust off my jeans. Another cheese ball bounces off my backside. "Katherine Emilie Day! This is your last warning. Hit me again, and I am going to show you no mercy."

She gets to her feet, eyeing my freshly peeled carrots. She grabs one and tosses it in the air to herself like it's a tennis ball.

"Put the carrot down. You could poke my eye out." I head toward the closet to get a mop. The carrot sails past my head. "That's it. It's on."

I reach down and grab a handful of the now-cold brown goo. I turn on my heels and send it sailing across the kitchen. It lands with a satisfying plop on the center of her flannel shirt. She lets out a yelp before reaching for the bowl of lettuce to use as ammunition. I take cover behind the sink, then quickly realize I can use the detachable faucet as a water gun.

Something happens in the madness of it all. We turn back into kids, laughing and screaming, living fully in the present moment. The threat of consequence or of tomorrow doesn't exist. It's just me and my sister and thirty-something years of pent-up emotion finally being uncorked.

"What the hell is going on!" Miles's voice pierces through the din. "I come back here to tell you guys I'm sorry for leaving like a child, and you two are—" Before he can finish, a blob of brown goo flies out of Kat's hand and connects with Miles's cheek. A look of absolute disgust and horror takes shape on his face, but it slowly morphs into a smile. Then a chuckle. And then an all-out belly laugh. "I play in a gay softball league on Sundays. It's over for you losers."

We play, the three of us, like nobody is watching. We play as if our world isn't changing once again without our consent. We play in a chaos of our own creation, where we determine the rules of the game.

We play until we're exhausted. Cheeks aching from smiling. Tears of laughter staining our faces.

Heads finally clear enough to face the chaos we can't control.

"What do we do?" I ask.

The three of us sit on the floor, leaning against the kitchen cabinets.

"We probably need to figure out lunch." Miles sticks a Parmesan flake in his mouth. "Do you think anyone delivers out here?"

"I could ask Scotty to bring something," I say.

"You're going to sleep with him this weekend, right?" Kat asks. "If you don't sleep with him, then I might consider asking him for his sperm. Think about it: Avery could have a cousin *slash* sister if he knocks me up."

"You will *not* give my daughter a cousin *slash* sister." I elbow her. "What is wrong with you?"

"Probably a lot," Kat says.

"What happens after lunch?" Miles asks, his voice once again serious. "What do we do then?"

We grow silent, each of us trying to think of something to say to bring calm to the others, despite needing our own comfort.

"We dress up in Mom drag," I say, softly. "And go to her funeral tomorrow."

"After that?" Kat squeezes my hand. "What happens next?"

"We figure it out together," I say. "We do this together, so nobody has to feel alone."

Chapter 19

It takes the three of us a solid hour to clean up the remnants of our collective mental breakdown, which seems like a record, if you ask me. Scotty saves the day by picking up the absolute worst bucket of fried chicken I have ever seen. To his credit, it was from a gas station, where his only other option was a bucket of corn dogs. My new phone is also from the gas station, or possibly a secret time portal back to the early 2000s. It has prepaid minutes, and I'm pretty sure the only smart option on it is the preloaded game of solitaire.

"The corn dogs really looked that bad, huh?" I ask, taking a sad drumstick from the bucket and plopping it on a paper plate. The plate bends under the weight of the chicken, but I manage to catch the drumstick before it rolls onto the floor.

"You have no idea." He scoops what's supposed to be coleslaw but looks more like cabbage and mayonnaise soup onto his plate.

We make our way through the buffet line that George has arranged in the dining room. George has never yelled at my siblings and me before, but the look on his face when he saw what had become of his Alfredo was the equivalent of a horror-movie scream. Then, in true George fashion, he pivoted effortlessly and still managed to whip up a batch of fresh mashed potatoes and gravy.

At the table, it's just family. Chauncey and his crew are hard at work transforming the pool deck. Well, from what I was able to glean through the window, the crew is hard at work. Chauncey appears to be spending most of his time vacillating between downward dog and child's pose.

"He's an old soul. I can feel it. Creativity like his can only take shape after having lived multiple lives." Mom picks up her chicken breast and wrinkles her nose. "Are we sure this is chicken and not squab?"

"What's squab?" Avery asks, holding her piece of chicken to her lips.

"Pigeon," Mom says. "I ate quite a bit of it when I was overseas. It didn't taste bad, but there was a certain ick factor I couldn't get over. You know, pigeons make milk for their young."

"Does that mean pigeons have nipples?"

Miles makes a horking sound and pushes his plate away.

"No, don't be silly. Only mammals have nipples," Mom clarifies.

"Could we possibly stop saying *nipples*?" Kat pinches the bridge of her nose. "Just until we finish eating this roadkill."

"Oh, grow up, Kat," Mom chides. "Pigeons don't have nipples. They secrete a milklike substance from their undigested food that they ferment in their craw, then regurgitate it to feed their young."

"And I'm done." Kat sets her fork down next to her plate.

Scotty and Avery follow suit. I'm just as put off by our lunch conversation as they are, but I'm also impressed by how knowledgeable Mom is on the topic. I doubt that pigeons are a typical conversation point between Mom and George. Could a person with worsening dementia rattle off so many facts this easily?

"How do you know so much about pigeons, Mom?" I ask.

"I considered purchasing a flock before I settled on Angora rabbits." Mom takes a bite of her coleslaw soup. "I thought I might try my hand at pigeon wrangling. Pigeons are incredibly smart creatures."

"Why did you go with rabbits instead?" I ask.

"Because your brother is terrified of birds." Mom points at Miles. "He'd never come see me again if I had a house full of pigeons. Do you remember that time we were at the zoo and those peacocks chased him?"

And there it is. A tiny glimpse of the newest monster living inside her.

"Mom, I'm not afraid of birds," Miles says, nonchalantly. "I own a bird. Liza doesn't like birds. She was the one chased by the peacocks. Remember?"

Mom's brows knit together. The tiniest hint of uncertainty crosses her face, but she recovers quickly. "Oh, you two were basically twins. What scared one of you usually scared the other. Kat was the bravest of the group."

"After lunch, we should have the girls pick out their outfits for tomorrow," George interjects, taking back the reins on the conversation. "Your mother's clothing collection could rival Imelda Marcos's."

"Well, I don't know what Imelda's dress collection looks like, but I'm sure she has me beat with shoes," Mom says. "The woman had over three thousand pairs. Who needs three thousand of anything other than dollars and maybe diamonds?"

It's funny how the human brain works. Watching Mom recollect obscure facts with ease but then falter over moments she lived—moments we lived together—makes me wonder which memories her brain will hold on to and which it will cast aside.

We finish up lunch and disperse throughout the ranch. Miles and Kat insist on watching *Summertime Madness* with Avery because, according to Miles, the Darla Day experience is best when started at the very beginning of her career. Mom needs a nap, and George needs to prepare for tomorrow night's hors d'oeuvres—which he makes clear will require no help whatsoever from my siblings and me.

He does, however, need help feeding Mom's rabbits. George salvages as much of my poorly executed salad as possible and tasks Scotty and me with the chore. We take a walk down to the pond, where Mom's amateur rabbit farm has taken up residence. I take the opportunity to fill Scotty in on Mom's diagnosis.

"I'm glad she's not drinking again." Scotty tosses a handful of lettuce into the rabbit pen. "My grandmother on my dad's side had

Alzheimer's. I don't remember a ton about her before she got sick. I just remember visiting her in the nursing home."

A nursing home? How could Mom go from living out here with her rabbits and the land and the home her own mother so carefully curated to something as sterile as a nursing home? Then, like a flash of lightning, I remember what George started to say in the kitchen before we were interrupted by the landscaper. I said Mom would still be here after the funeral, and he made it seem like that wasn't guaranteed.

What if Mom's not thinking of selling the house to downsize but instead is getting rid of everything because she thinks a nursing home is in her future?

"Did you visit her much?" I ask.

"A couple times a month," he says. "My mom insisted on doing her laundry. She didn't want Grandma to end up with lice or scabies. It wasn't a great facility. It was run by the state, but it was the best my family could do."

I focus my attention on feeding Benny a carrot, unable to bring myself to ask more questions, even though I have many. Scotty must sense the shift in my energy. He takes me by the hand and holds my gaze. "Darla's not going to end up in a place like that. She's got money, and if by some crazy circumstance she runs out, I've got plenty to cover her."

"You wouldn't need to do that," I say. "My siblings and I will figure this out."

"What if I want to?"

"Want to what?" I ask.

"Want to help take care of our daughter's grandmother."

There it is again. That hot and tingly and melty all over feeling that is now becoming as automatic as blinking whenever he says *our daughter*. What is it about those two words and the way he says them? Is there some Pavlovian sexual response connected to hearing the person with whom you conceived a child acknowledge that this child only exists because, one night, your bodies connected, and the rest is history?

"What are you doing?" he asks.

Suddenly, I realize that I'm just staring at Scotty like he's a nice piece of artwork on a wall in a museum.

"I was just thinking," I stammer, pulling my hands away. "I was thinking that you better get back to the hotel with Avery. She sounded like she was excited to stay there with you."

"You mean motor lodge. Calling it a hotel would be a very generous and completely false description. I also think the Wi-Fi and having her own room might've been what she was more excited about instead of staying somewhere with me." He points toward Lake Vivian. "You and I went skinny-dipping in that lake on the Fourth of July, didn't we?"

"Uh, yeah. I guess. Why?"

He points to his front tooth, and all of a sudden, I remember that Fourth of July with perfect clarity. Not because of the skinny-dipping, though that was fun and memorable in its own right. What I remember most about that day was Scotty slipping on a rock and knocking his front tooth out. "Do you think it's still out there?"

"Only one way to find out." He smirks.

"If you think I'm going in that lake naked with you, then you're—"

"I wasn't suggesting anybody get naked," he interjects. "Everything always turns to sex with you. Your voice memos. Patching me up in the bathroom, and now my tooth."

"I hate you." I smack his arm playfully. "You promised not to bring up the voice memo."

"I feel like you only threatened me if I did, but I wouldn't say I made a promise," he says. We walk back toward the Big House together. "But if I could ask just one question about that memo, then I promise I'll drop it. Maybe not forever, but at least for the next twenty-four hours."

"I'm listening," I say, as we pass a group of workers putting up a giant white tent by the pool. "You got one question."

"It's not really a question. It's more of a comment."

"You better hurry up with it," I tell him. "Once we get to the back patio, I go back to making threats."

He reaches for my arm, his fingers delicately grasping my wrist and sending a thousand little sparks of electricity up and down my body. "You know that thing you said about wanting someone?" I nod, completely tongue-tied. "Well, I know what that feeling is like too. I've felt it every time I ever picked Avery up or dropped her off. It's not something as simple as liking someone, and loving you has always been a given. It's this in-between feeling. It's not lust. It's knowing."

"What do you mean, 'knowing'?" My voice is suddenly thick. "What does that mean?"

"It means that a part of me has always known that my happiest place in this whole world—the place I feel most at home and most like me—isn't a physical location. It's people. It's Avery, and it's you. Together. I know that's where I'm supposed to be."

There's a sudden crash from across the pool. A worker carrying a crate of wineglasses trips and sends the crate careening onto the deck. It startles me, and I jump a little into Scotty's arms. I glance up at him, and for a second, I wonder what would happen if we kissed. That second passes when a flurry of expletives erupts from another worker, who accidentally steps on the broken glass and slides into the pool.

"Do you want to stay here tonight?" I ask. "Unless you have your heart set on the Heavenly Motor Lodge."

"I mean, the Heavenly Motor Lodge does have HBO," Scotty replies. "But all kidding aside, are you sure it's alright? I'd understand if you wanted some space."

"No space," I say. "At least not from you or Avery."

"Sounds good to me."

~

I lean my ear against Avery's door, a habit I picked up after she started staying on her phone late, talking to boys. All I can hear is the quiet hum of the little space heater inside. I knock twice before opening the door.

She's sprawled across the little daybed with headphones on. There's something nostalgic about the scene. I can imagine Mom at her age, in the same room, listening to old vinyls. She flicks her gaze in my direction for half a beat but doesn't say anything. She holds out an earbud to me, and I plop down on the bed next to her. We stare at the ceiling together, both of us humming along to the music. I tilt my head against hers, and she doesn't pull away. Instead, she leans into me, and for a moment, I consider that maybe we've somehow reached a truce. Maybe all we needed to get back to us was to get out of our own way. A change of scenery. A change of routine. A change in the roles we've been playing since this summer.

It occurs to me that having Scotty stay the night at the ranch might add another complication to my relationship with Avery, which, despite this placid moment, is hanging on by a thread. As much as I would like to explore what Scotty meant by this *knowing*, I can't let it affect her negatively. Even at sixteen, it's easy to build up false hope. She's lived her whole life with parents who, as far as she can remember, never slept under one roof. She's lived her whole life with parents who never once let on that there might be an ember of a relationship to stoke between them. Maybe it's not fair to change the rules sixteen years into the game.

"Are you OK with Dad staying at the ranch with us tonight instead of the motor lodge?" I ask her, softly. "Miles says there's paparazzi at the motor lodge, now that more people have arrived for tomorrow. I'm fine with it, but if you're not, then—"

"Why wouldn't I be?"

"I don't know." I shrug. "Maybe it's weird?"

"A cake of Grandma parts is weird, Mom."

"Good point."

"Uncle Miles thinks you're into Dad." She lies on her side, resting her head on my chest. "Aunt Kat does too." I make a mental note to give both of them a dead leg when they least expect it. "I think he might be into you a little too."

"What? Why?"

"You and Dad never marrying other people after all this time, and now he's here, and you two are making googly eyes at each other."

"Nobody is making googly eyes, Avery."

"Fine," she scoffs. "Then explain why neither of you ever got married. Huh? I mean we live in the sticks, and the prospects for available men are slim to none outside of Bass Pro Shops and that one weird teacher who follows you on Instagram. But Dad has had plenty of opportunities. He's surrounded by gorgeous actresses, and yet, he's never gotten serious with any of them."

I decide to ignore the fact that she thinks the only opportunities I've had for love are with members of the Clampett family.

"Back to the point." I roll my eyes dramatically, the way she does when she's over our conversation. "You're OK with Dad spending the night. In his own room, of course."

"Of course." She mimics my tone. "I would hate to leave my grandma's funeral with a baby sister or brother."

"That reminds me of a conversation I need to have with your aunt." I giggle.

"Can I show you something first?" She sits up and slides off the bed. "I found these." She's holding up an old VHS tape labeled "Sunset Breeze: *Season 1, Episodes 1–3.*"

I kneel on the floor next to her. Underneath the bed is an old cardboard box filled with videos. I know Miles joked about Mom possibly having the DVDs, but VHS tapes were not on my trip-down-memory-lane bingo card.

"I've never seen these," she says. "And I thought it might be kinda fun to watch them together as a family."

"You want to watch our old show together?" I hold the VHS tape in my hands. "Why?"

"Everyone else at school is." She shrugs. "Would that be weird for us to do?"

There's no way I can watch every episode of *Sunset Breeze* with Avery without something eventually getting a little weird. I do have very fake vanilla sex in the second season, according to Melinda Martinez.

"I think it's cool you want to spend time with us," I say. "It's not weird. Not for me, anyway." The door creaks open softly, and a chunky white rabbit waddles its way in. "This is weird, though."

"Alice," Avery coos.

"Her name is not Alice," I argue. "She is not your rabbit."

Avery grabs a pink sticky note off the desk and puts it on Alice's back again. "Yes, she is."

"Is there a party going on in here?" Scotty pokes his head in the room. "Hey, what's all that?"

"Mom's old shows," Avery says. "Yours too."

He sits on the floor in between Avery and me. It's funny seeing him, this tall action movie star, sitting like a kid getting ready for story time.

He picks up one of the VHS tapes labeled *Season 2, Halloween episode* and smiles. "You remember this one?" He chuckles. "They stuck me in that stupid metal knight costume for hours. Every time I moved, it felt like a can opener was slicing into me."

"You think you had it bad," I say. "I had to wear that pleather catsuit. It was a sauna in that thing."

"We should watch it," Avery says.

"I guess we could stream it," Scotty says.

"Nope." I shake my head. "Mom doesn't have a smart TV. She barely has working Wi-Fi."

"We don't need that," Avery says. "Grandma has one of those vintage movie-player things in the living room."

"Did she really just call it a 'vintage movie-player thing'? Is she being sarcastic?" Scotty cocks an eyebrow at me. "I blame you for this."

"It's called a VCR, honey," I say, giving Scotty a little shove. "Not a vintage movie player."

"Well, excuse me for not being born back in the 1900s." She takes Scotty by the hand and attempts to help him stand. "C'mon. Let's go watch. Family movie night. We've never done that before."

Scotty and I look at one another, as if we're asking for permission. He nods and gives me a wink. "Family movie night."

"Why don't you go set up the VCR, and I'll put together a girl dinner?" I brush the dust and stray bunny hair from my pants. "I could invite everyone. Uncle Miles mentioned wanting to revisit *Sunset Breeze*. Of course, he assumed we'd have DVDs instead of these fossils."

"No," Avery snaps. It's not an angry snap. It's more of a reactionary response, which she quickly realizes. "I don't want to be rude, but I thought it would be nice if it could be just the three of us. Our family. Is that OK?"

Our family. Hearing her say it hits different. It's a good different.

"Yes," I say. "You two go set up. I'll get the girl dinner."

"Somebody is going to need to tell me what a girl dinner is first," Scotty says.

"How do you feel about Pop-Tarts and salami?" I ask. "Or cheese cubes and chocolate chips?"

"Sounds weird." Scotty nods. "But I'm into this."

Me too. I think I'm into whatever *this* is too.

Chapter 20

George doesn't believe in girl dinners. He's more of a traditionalist when it comes to meals, but he warms to the idea once he sees how much I enjoy putting them together.

"I would've never thought to pair pickles with s'mores," he says, holding a speared marshmallow over the flame on the stove. "I suppose you learn something new every day."

"I don't know if I'd say we're pairing them together so much as we're inviting them to the same party." I sprinkle a handful of shredded coconut over a Jell-O cup. "There aren't any hard-and-fast rules, other than whatever is on the tray has to be edible."

I scan the cupboards for items I would consider girl-dinner staples, but George keeps the house stocked with what I'm sure 90 percent of the population considers to be actual pantry staples.

"Ooh, score!" I grab a can of Vienna sausages. "George, do we have any green olives in the fridge?"

"I'm on it."

"What are we cooking?" Miles asks, closing the door to the back patio behind him. He leans over my shoulder to look at the tray and makes a face. "I don't think we can call this cooking. It looks more like foraging. Feral cat foraging in a dumpster, to be exact."

"Well, you're not invited to our feral-cat dumpster party." I pop the lid off the jar of olives George hands me. "Scotty, Avery, and I are having a little family movie night."

"Cute. Love it." His eyes glimmer. "Tell me more."

"We're watching an old episode of *Sunset Breeze*. Avery found a whole collection of old VHS tapes under her bed that Mom must've saved. How is she, by the way?"

"Tired," Miles says. "She's currently in bed, attempting to brush the rabbits and harvest their hair to knit. Wait, do the rabbits have hair or fur?"

"I believe the hare has fur," I tease.

"Great, now we've got dad jokes." Miles rolls his eyes. "I thought not having to listen to dad jokes was one of the perks of having an absentee father."

"Where exactly will Scotty be sleeping tonight?" George asks. "I would like to make a bed up for him before I turn in tonight."

"Yes, do tell." Miles grins from ear to ear. "Are we using scrunchie code? Because if we are, I don't have a scrunchie handy."

"What are you talking about, Miles?" I ask, genuinely confused. "The couch, George. He'll be sleeping on the couch. We'll take care of it. No need for you to worry."

"OK." George heads toward the living room but stops just short. "And I believe if a scrunchie isn't available, a sock will work in a pinch."

I turn to Miles. "A sock? A scrunchie? Are we setting house elves free or something?"

"You know." He gives me a look. "If there's a scrunchie on the doorknob, that means you're getting it on. How do you not know that?"

"No scrunchies and no socks," I say.

"And how exactly do you think the two of you ended up as family?"

"Teenage hormones."

"Whatever. Go have your movie night. Just don't end up making any movies after Avery goes to bed." He takes the bag of leftover marshmallows and tucks it under his arm. "Kat and I are going to hang with Mom tonight."

A wave of guilt washes over me. I think back to our argument in the kitchen. Miles feeling like I abandoned him and Kat and Mom.

"I'll join you guys," I say. "Let me just—"

"No." Miles rests his hands on my shoulders. "You be with your family tonight. Tomorrow is all about Mom. Tonight should be about the three of you. OK?"

"OK." I nod.

I head into the living room to find that Scotty has rearranged the furniture setup to be more suitable for movie watching. The main sofa is facing the old box TV that Mom keeps in a curio cabinet, and next to it, there's a slipper chair in a bold mod print. Avery's perched in the middle of the couch with a blanket wrapped around her like a burrito. I elect to sit on the floor, next to the coffee table full of food.

"Is there anything I should know about the show before we start?" Avery asks, eagerly. "I've googled it before, but to be honest, the Wikipedia page was really hard to follow."

"You should've tried following the script," Scotty teases.

"The beauty of soaps is that you don't really need to know anything about them in order to appreciate how completely ridiculous they are." I pop a cheese cube into my mouth. "You can just jump in wherever, and it will make the same amount of sense as if you'd been watching from the very first episode."

"This sounds terrible." Avery grabs a s'more and takes a bite. "I can't wait."

Scotty pushes play, and slowly but surely, the screen comes to life. He turns off the lights just as the intro begins and takes a spot on the floor across from me. It's one of those Enya-inspired melodies—the kind that had an absolute choke hold on the early 2000s. Goose bumps prickle across my arms, and my heart begins to flutter as the cast is introduced.

"Mom," Avery says, pointing at the screen. I'm in a pair of low-rise jeans and a bubble gum–pink halter top, with some of the most offensive, chunky, blonde highlights known to mankind throughout my chestnut-brown hair. "You were a total babe."

"Stop." I roll my eyes.

"She's right," Scotty says softly, holding my gaze. "Total babe."

Heat flushes across my cheeks, and I'm thankful for the low lighting to help hide it.

"Dad." Avery points at Scotty's picture on the screen. "Your hair. It looks like plastic."

The hair and makeup team used to go through a tub of LA Looks gel every week to get his hair perfectly spiked. Objectively, I can say it now looks hideous, but back then, I was enchanted by Scotty's whole look. Frosted tips included.

"Your dad regularly got mistaken for random singers in boy bands," I say. "Once, when we were out on a date, a girl asked for his autograph because she thought he was JC Chasez."

"Who?" Avery eyes Scotty and then me. We both let out a collective heavy sigh. "Well, excuse me for not knowing every member of the Backstreet Boys."

Scotty and I just look at each other and shake our heads, neither of us having the heart to tell her JC Chasez was not a Backstreet Boy. It wouldn't matter anyway. The early 2000s seem as foreign to Avery as the seventies felt to me growing up.

I turn my attention back to the show. All holiday episodes of *Sunset Breeze* were stretched over a week. Filming a soap opera was grueling, but I always enjoyed the holidays the most. Episodes were usually filmed in real time, which meant I rarely had a traditional Halloween, Thanksgiving, or even Christmas experience, but that was OK with me. Filming at least provided consistency.

"Pardon me." George cuts through the living room, holding a tray with two stemless wineglasses next to a bottle of cabernet and a glass of Dr Pepper for Avery. "I assume a girl dinner isn't complete without beverages."

"Thanks, Papa George," Avery chimes, her attention focused on the screen.

George gives me a wink before disappearing down the hall.

"So, Mom," Avery says, "you played a surgeon on the show, right?"

"That was the idea." I cringe, watching my teen self on camera in a pleather bodysuit and flip-flops. "It wasn't always a very well-executed idea."

"And Dad was a lifeguard?" she asks.

"That's right." Scotty nods. "I also played the occasional surgical assistant."

In this particular scene, Scotty is assisting me with an emergency baby delivery that is taking place on the beach. He's dressed like a knight because our director loved the idea of trying to make everything symbolic. Apparently, Scotty was a symbol for a hero, and I was just a symbol for Catwoman.

Scotty takes the bottle of wine and realizes it's still corked. He scans the tray for an opener, but there isn't one.

"I'll open it," I say, taking the bottle from him. "You two keep watching. If I remember correctly, that pregnant surfer has twins."

"Spoiler alert," Avery mutters.

It takes me longer than expected to find the wine opener. I search drawer after drawer but keep coming up short. I'm about to give up and head back into the living room when Mom shuffles into the kitchen, holding a toothbrush. She doesn't acknowledge me. Maybe it's the dim lighting in the kitchen, or maybe she's just too focused on whatever it is she's trying to do.

She turns on the sink and lets the water run over her toothbrush. I'm about to say something, but instead I decide to just watch. She turns off the water and puts the toothbrush in her mouth for a second before pulling it out. Her hand fumbles for the drawer next to the sink, where George keeps the silverware. She opens it and just stares at the drawer, as if she's unsure what all the silverware is doing in a drawer that should have her toothpaste and toiletries.

"Hey, Mom." I gently touch her shoulder before flicking the light over the sink on. "What are you doing?"

"Huh?" She flinches at my touch, as if the light and my voice are too much for her to process all at once. "Oh, Liza. What are you doing in here?"

I hold up the wine bottle. "Looking for a way to break into this."

Mom studies the bottle for a moment before her eyes slowly shift to the rest of the kitchen, taking in the surroundings. She glances at the wet toothbrush in her hand and then at me, like she's trying to gauge whether I've realized her mistake. The corners of her lips fall slightly. "I think I got a little confused." Her voice is uncertain. "I needed to brush my teeth, but I guess I got distracted."

She reminds me of a lost child in a grocery store, one who's stepped too far away from their parent and now isn't sure how to get back to safety.

"That's OK, Mom." I swallow the lump forming in my throat. "It happens."

"I guess so." She nods.

"Do you need some help getting pointed in the right direction?" I ask.

"No, of course not." She forces a smile.

We both stand in the kitchen, just staring at one another for a few beats, neither of us sure what to do next, the both of us ignoring the growing elephant in the room. I prefer the giant pink elephant outside so much more. I wish I had Kat or Miles with me. They're better with Mom than I am. They always have been. They're the ones who came together to finally get Mom into rehab after the show ended. They're responsible for getting her settled at the ranch again. The two of them get Mom in a way I've never been able to.

I lean against the counter, clinking the bottle of wine against the stone countertop. It's as if I've just struck a bell.

Mom glances down at the bottle and snaps her fingers. "George keeps the wine opener in the pantry. I've never understood why, but that's his system." Mom motions for me to follow her, and sure enough, inside the pantry in a small wicker tray is a hand-cranked wine opener. A look of pure joy spreads across her face. "There it is."

"Thanks, Mom," I say, taking it from the basket. "I never would've thought to look in here."

Out of nowhere, Mom hugs me tight and long, like she's holding on to a life raft in the middle of a choppy sea. Maybe that's what life with dementia feels like—like you're navigating an ocean alone, trying to keep your head above water while searching for a life preserver.

"You get some sleep." She lets me out of her embrace, now just holding me by my shoulders. "It's my big day tomorrow."

"I love you, Mom."

It's the first time I've said those words to her in years. We've never had that sort of *I love you* relationship. I never doubted that she loves me, and I hope she's never doubted that I love her. We just didn't say it. Maybe life was too busy, or maybe sometimes our relationship just felt too hard to speak life into those words. Regardless, I want her to hear those words from me now. I want her to feel them, and maybe if I'm lucky, I want her to remember them for as long as she possibly can.

"Me too, honey," she says. "I love you too."

~

When I return to the living room, I find that Scotty's moved from his spot on the floor to the couch next to Avery. I pour us each a glass, setting the bottle of wine on the coffee table, and hand Scotty his before taking a seat in the slipper chair.

"Sit next to me, Mom." Avery pats the open couch space. "There's plenty of room," she insists, patting the open space again. "We can share the blanket."

"Are you sure?" I ask. "I don't want to squish you."

"We've got room." Scotty smiles.

I settle on the opposite end of the couch, tucking my feet under the blanket next to Avery. We're a little smushed together, but it's nice.

I sip my wine, and Scotty sips his. The three of us laugh at the horrible plotline and ridiculous costumes. Scotty pauses the episode periodically to tell a funny story about the scene or an actor. He remembers so much more than I do. In a way, it makes me a little jealous. He enjoyed this time of his life in a way that I didn't get to. He still got to be a kid, while I was forced into being an adult and looking after Mom.

The episode wraps up just as my eyes start to grow too heavy to keep open. Avery offers her bed to Scotty, and she takes the couch. She looks more tired than the both of us. Her eyes close the second we turn the TV off.

"I needed this," Scotty whispers, staring at her. "I missed out on so much, didn't I?"

"You're here now," I say. "That's what matters."

"But after this weekend, then what?"

"We could look for jobs together." I stand up and stretch. "I'll give you a good reference if you give me one."

"Would you ever act again?"

His question catches me by surprise. "I don't think so."

"You could move here," he says. "I mean, if you wanted to."

"I think right now the only thing I want to do is go to bed." I bend forward and give Avery a kiss on the cheek.

"Do you want company?"

Every inch of my body screams *yes*. The only problem is my mouth isn't quite brave enough to say it . . . yet.

"Maybe another time," I tell him.

Chapter 21

I wish I could run.

Not to get away but to clear my head. I want to listen to Kelly Clarkson while my shoes pad against the trail like they did this morning. That's what I really want. I want to be able to go back to this morning, when my problems seemed small and manageable and the only scary thing was Scotty on a motorcycle riding toward me. Instead, I'm stuck in the Casita alone—not counting the mom-cake—with every teeny, little memory I can eke out of Scotty and Avery and me living here.

I remember putting her crib next to my side of the bed. I *had* a side of the bed. It's the only time I've ever had one, not unless you count the times I shared a bed with Avery, which I don't, because sleeping in a bed with her was a lot like sleeping with a drunk octopus. I kept her clothes in a little white chest of drawers in the closet, which are probably still there if I dared to look. But I won't look. Not now when Scotty is just a hop, skip, and a giant pink elephant away from me.

I decide to rinse off to help calm my nerves. Showering is the next best thing to running. I turn on the old shower, crossing my fingers the whole time. The old pipes sputter to life, and thankfully they produce hot water. I slip out of my pajamas and let the hot water sting my skin. I lather myself in lavender soap and close my eyes, letting the water run until it starts to get cold. When I turn off the faucet, I can actually feel myself getting sleepy. In fact, I wouldn't be surprised if I fell asleep with my hair still wet in a towel.

A towel. *Dammit.* It's the one thing I didn't grab before showering. The Casita bathroom doesn't have a linen closet inside it. Some genius architect thought it would make much more sense to put that in the tiny hallway, because you know what people often think as they walk down the hallway? *I could really use a towel right now.* I pull back the curtain to see if by chance there's even a hand towel by the sink. There isn't.

I let out a sigh of frustration before hopping out of the clawfoot tub and sprinting into the hallway naked. I whip open the closet door and grab a peach-colored towel. I start to unfold it, but out of the corner of my eye, I realize there's a figure at the other end of the hallway. I scream, dropping my towel, as I make a dash for the bedroom. My feet fly out from under me in the puddle my naked body has made, and in a matter of seconds, I'm face up, on my back, completely naked.

"Oh, crap! Liza!"

It's a man's voice. That much I am able to catch over my own screaming and the subsequent ringing in my ears.

My eyes are glued shut, because in my experience, the best way to deal with humiliation is with your eyes closed. On the one hand, it's comforting to know that whoever is in the Casita with me knows my name and isn't some random worker who got lost when Chauncey's crew called it a night. On the other hand, there aren't any men who know my name that I'm currently OK with seeing me naked in this exact state.

"Don't move!" he shouts. "Let me help you."

It's Scotty. Of course it's Scotty. Why wouldn't it be Scotty?

"Look away!" I yelp. I try to turn on my side to shield what little dignity I have left, but it feels like a hippo has just tap-danced all over my body. It's no use. "Please leave."

"I can't leave you like this." His footsteps stop next to my head. Part of me wishes he'd just kick me and knock me straight out. Put me out of my misery. "Here." He places a blanket over me. "I'm going to scoop you up and move you to the bed."

"You are not!" My eyes fly open. "I'm naked under this blanket!"

"I'm aware," he replies, sheepishly. "But you're also soaking wet and probably in a little bit of pain. Not a good combination on a tile floor."

He's not wrong, but it doesn't change the fact that I don't want him to move me. I want him to leave and go back to the Big House, where he's supposed to be. Why isn't he there now?

"You're not supposed to be here," I say, suddenly feeling a little weepy. My body has this habit of completely coming unglued after experiencing pain. I was not a fun woman to be in the same room with during labor. Some people get angry during contractions and scream and cuss. I cry like I've just seen somebody kick a kitten. "You're not even supposed to be in here, let alone staring at my naked body like it's roadkill."

"You're not naked roadkill," he says, gently. "And for the record, I wasn't staring at you. You had your eyes closed, but if you didn't, you would've seen that I only looked at you when it was absolutely necessary."

"Well, that's kind of rude when you put it like that."

"You'd rather me gawk at you?"

"No," I sob.

"I feel like anything I say right now will be wrong, so whatever the right thing is that you want me to say, just pretend that I did, OK?" I nod in agreement. "Can you roll to your side a tiny bit so I can push the blanket underneath you?"

"Probably." I make an attempt.

He pushes the blanket underneath me on one side before repeating the process on the other.

"You still"—I sniffle—"haven't told me why you're here."

"You invited me to stay at the ranch. Did you hit your head?" He frowns.

"No, I know that," I whine, impatiently. "Why are you in the Casita?"

"Oh. I couldn't sleep." He lifts me so carefully and effortlessly that it almost makes me forget I'm naked and in pain. "I thought maybe you couldn't either."

"Well, you were right," I groan.

"I guess I could've showered. Didn't think about that."

Scotty gingerly places me on the bed. It creaks and moans so obscenely loudly under the weight of both of us that it's almost rude. He props my head up on a pillow and then leaves just long enough to turn off the shower that's still running.

"Why are you crying?" Scotty says. "Is it because of the naked thing? I've seen you naked before, and for what it's worth, I'm still a fan."

"Thanks, I think." I use the corner of the blanket to wipe my tears and then snot. There is no place for dignity in this bed. "I'm not crying just because I'm naked or because you scared me half to death and probably gave me a concussion in the process."

"Well, you did give me a black eye. I know you're going to say I hit you too, but you don't have a mark." He rubs his shiner, which has now turned a beautifully hideous shade of violet-green. "We make quite a pair."

There are too many comments swirling in my head, competing with one another to be spoken aloud. And I don't think any of them can accurately explain the surge of emotion that's gripping me. A week ago, my life made perfect sense. I was a teacher, a mother to a teenage girl who kinda hated me a little but mostly loved me, and my biggest problem was figuring out what my *thing* was going to be. I need a hobby. That is my main issue. I need something to keep me distracted from the fact that I don't have a lot going on in my life, and now there is so much going on that I literally just want to cry.

"Do you have a hobby?" I ask Scotty.

"What?" He places his hand on my wet forehead like he's checking for a fever. "You must've really knocked yourself out."

"Do you?" I press.

"Uh, I don't know. I used to golf sometimes." He tilts his head back, like he's deep in thought. "But I hated it. Mark Twain was right. It's a walk ruined. I have some succulents. Oh, and I have a penis cactus."

"I'm sorry, what?"

"It's a cactus that looks like . . . well you get it. I have plants. There. That's my hobby. How about you?"

I consider debating whether a cactus counts as a hobby, but I let it go.

"No." I shake my head. "I've been trying to find one, and everything I try feels wrong. My last hobby was a book club, and I sucked at it. Royally."

"What did you guys read?"

"*The Vagina Monologues*, which I know is technically a play, and that should've gotten me at least a little excited, but it didn't."

"Of course it didn't. You're an actress, Liza. You don't want to read a play. You want to be in it. That's how you are. That's how we both are."

Scotty wraps his arms around me, careful to make sure the blanket fully covers me. I don't stop him because I don't want him to stop. Instead, I focus on how good it feels to have him with me. This—his warm and tight embrace—feels like rain after years of drought. I've been hugged and comforted by other men, but never have I felt as completely at peace as I have with Scotty. He feels like going home. Now that I remember the way it feels, I don't know if I can forget it.

I don't know that I want to.

"Can you stay with me tonight?" I whisper.

"Sure." He pushes a lock of my hair away from my face. "I don't know how Miles is going to feel about sharing a bed with me when he gets back, but—"

"No. That's not what I meant." I pull him toward me, lacing my fingers together behind his neck. "Can you stay in this bed with me tonight?"

"Can I tell you something?" His lips brush against my ear. "I was hoping that's what you meant."

Our lips find one another's, carefully and slowly at first, like we're relearning the steps to an old dance, trying not to step on each other's toes. But once we find our rhythm together, the choreography doesn't matter. Our bodies crash into one another full force the way a wave meets its rocky shore. It's completely unscripted, and when it's over, my body aches in all the best ways a body can.

He's gone when I wake up in the morning. There's a note on the pillow in his scratchy writing.

Didn't want Avery or someone to know we spent the night together, so I snuck into the Big House after you fell asleep.
Scotty

P.S. Best sleepover I've had in about seventeen years.

I tuck the note underneath my pillow and fall back asleep, relishing the way my skin smells like him. Kat or Miles will come and get me when they need me. They can be in charge and tell me the day's agenda. Right now, I just want to soak in this memory for as long as humanly possible before rejoining reality.

Kat and I have very different taste in fashion. Her wardrobe is color-coded and divided into seasons. She owns clothes in colors like chartreuse and vermillion, which to me sound more like salad dressings than shades of green and red. By comparison, my closet looks more like one of those Spirit Halloween stores. Everything is black or gray, and if you look way in the back, you'll probably find cobwebs.

"What about this?" I yawn while holding up my tried-and-true little black dress. I got in a solid extra hour of sleep before my siblings and Avery came barging in, demanding to see my outfit for tonight. "Mom's worn black before."

"So has Darth Vader," Miles deadpans.

He and Kat sit perched on my bed in the Casita, Chauncey's look-book situated between them, while Avery helps me rummage through my suitcase.

"I really think we should consider wearing Grandma's clothes," Avery says. "She says she's got plenty for us to choose from."

"I think what we brought is fine," I reply. "Nobody's going to care what I'm wearing."

"Grandma does," Avery argues. "And what about you and Dad dressing up like Naomi and Ryan? It would be cute."

"I don't have anything that looks remotely like what a teenager in the early 2000s would wear."

"For what it's worth, it looks like you don't own anything anyone other than a nun would wear," Miles adds. "I refuse to allow you to embarrass my only niece with your dumpy wardrobe."

"First, I am not a dumpy anything." I place my hand on my hip. "And second, what are you wearing that's so superior to what I brought?"

"This." Miles points to a picture in Chauncey's look-book of Mom in an off-Broadway performance of *Bye Bye Birdie*. "I'm wearing a light-blue linen shirt. It's got tiny white daisies on it, or maybe they're tiny white rabbits? Anyway, I'm wearing that with a pair of white slacks and white loafers."

"I thought you weren't supposed to wear white after Labor Day," I tease.

"These are Versace," Miles says, defensively. "There's never a wrong time to wear them."

"Fine." I turn to Kat. "What about you? Are you wearing Mom's clothes?"

"I am." Kat smiles. "I asked George to put aside the canary-yellow dress she wore in *Florence and Camille*."

"What if I wear this instead?" I hold up a black button-up shirt and a pair of black wide-leg trousers. "It kind of looks like that picture of Mom in *Summertime Madness*, you know, when she's the bank teller.

I've got some black ballet flats too. I could do a fun winged eyeliner. It would really pull the look together, don't you think?"

"Are you planning on working the dinner shift at Red Lobster when you're done?" Miles wrinkles his nose in disgust. "This isn't working."

"What isn't? The black?"

"That among other things." Miles picks up a black cardigan from the bed and casts it aside. He repeats the process until all my clothes are on the floor. "Avery, does your wardrobe look like this?"

"Absolutely not." She shakes her head. "Silverton isn't exactly a fashion haven, but we definitely have more than just Chico's."

"My clothes are nice," I say, defensively. I reach for my black button-up on the floor. "This top is from Anthropologie, I'll have you know. That means I paid five times what a shirt like this is probably actually worth. Doesn't that count for something?"

"No," all three say in unison.

"It's not that your clothes are bad." Kat takes a sip of her coffee. "You always look very nice and put together. It's just . . . uh . . . How do I explain it?"

"Sad." Miles stands up and smacks the top of my suitcase closed. "Your clothes look sad."

"They do not!" I give Miles a shove. "Black isn't a sad color. It's professional. It's elegant and timeless. Steve Jobs wore a black turtleneck every day, and I bet nobody told him he looked sad."

"Now that you mention it, he did look a little sad to me," Kat says.

"Bad example." I toss my hands in the air. "Look, maybe my clothes look sad because they're being compared to the circus clothes you two plan on wearing. Lace, chiffon, and bunnies? What are you guys, toddlers dressing for an Anne Geddes portrait?"

"I'm almost positive that they're daisies, but that's beside the point. C'mon." Miles grabs my hand. "I've got a solution."

"A solution to what? I don't have a problem."

"Oh, yes you do. This is supposed to be fun, Liza." He leads me outside the Casita and around the white tents that have popped up on the pool deck. "You can't have fun wearing sad clothes."

"I can't afford the kind of clothes you wear. And don't act like Mom has always been this fashion guru. My clothes might be sad, but at least they don't look like something Little Edie would've worn."

"Little Edie was a fashion icon. You'd be lucky to look half as chic as she did with a safety pin and a scarf." Miles pushes through the back door of the Big House and leads me through the living room and down the hallway toward Mom's room. Avery and Kat follow us like we're part of some fashion-shaming processional. "Step aside. Fashion emergency coming through."

"You know, it's times like this that I wish I had a nice butch lesbian for a brother," I grumble.

"You and me both, babe." Miles taps on Mom's door before opening it. "You and me both."

Mom's dressed in a champagne-colored silk robe, with her hair done up in pink sponge curlers—the type she used to force me to wear when I was eleven or twelve. I was in that weird phase that some kid actors find themselves in—too young-looking to play a teenager, too much acne to play a younger kid. Mom thought that giving me ringlets like Shirley Temple and dressing me in frilly frocks would fix everything.

"Mom, I need to look at your wardrobe." Miles breezes past her and makes a beeline for the closet. "Liza doesn't have anything to wear, and I refuse to allow my sister to look like a candidate for *Queer Eye*."

"Liza, you're supposed to wear one of my gowns. You and Avery both."

"I just thought I'd save you the trouble of having to find something." I sigh. "Plus, I'm more comfortable in my own clothes."

"*Comfortable* is a good word to describe what I saw in your suitcase," Miles snarks, before turning back to Mom. "She only brought black. A whole suitcase full of black."

"It's not that bad," Kat says, coming to my defense. "It's just not right. It's depressing."

"It's a funeral, people!" I huff.

Mom eases herself off the bed, shaking her head. "Black is what you wear when you sit down with Oprah to talk about a cheating husband. Trust me, I know this sort of thing from experience. The assignment is to dress up like me, and that's what you're going to do. Follow me."

Mom leads us across the hall from her bedroom. This wing of the house is more cluttered than the rest. Boxes with labels ranging from *Taxes 1980s* to *Misc exercise equipment* line the walls of the hallway. The carpet runner has a path worn down the center. I think if George tried to vacuum it, the entire thing would dissolve into sand.

She takes us to the old primary suite that once belonged to my grandparents and then later just Grandma Viv. Mom opens the bedroom door. The light flickers a few times before finally coming to life, and when it does, it reveals nothing short of a Hollywood shrine. Gowns from Mom's movies and stage shows stand at attention on dress forms along the wall. Across from them is a rack of top hats. Grandpa loved his top hats, and he was known to collect them from other Golden Age actors. A glass cabinet that looks like something straight out of the Royal Vault glitters with costume jewelry in every color of the rainbow.

"This is stunning, Mom," I say. "I can't believe you've kept all of this."

That's not exactly what I mean. The woman has a box in the hall with her old Jane Fonda workout tapes. If those puppies were worth preserving, surely Dean Martin's top hat is too. What I actually mean is that I can't believe I didn't know all this history existed.

"Did you know this room was like this?" I whisper to Miles and Kat.

"No." Kat shakes her head. "And so help me, if you get to wear the dress she wore to the '87 Academy Awards, I will end you."

"I thought you were happy with your canary dress," I tease.

"That was the first year she wore Bob Mackie," Kat breathes. "It makes the canary dress look like sweatpants."

"It was the *second* year she wore Bob Mackie," Miles says, gently stroking a peacock feather boa. "And for the record, if I knew this room existed, I would never have allowed either of you to come in here."

I run my fingertip over a velvet Dior peacoat. "Mom, this stuff is too fancy for me to wear. What if I spill something on it?"

"Come here." She waves me over to the closet. "The silver dress bag in the back. Grab that one, and open it for me."

I do as I'm told, and Miles holds the bag while I unzip it. Inside is a pair of bell-bottom jeans and a white halter top. A woven leather belt is looped around the neck of the hanger, along with a turquoise-and-gold belly chain. I run my finger along the trim of the silky halter. This is Daisy's outfit from *Summertime Madness*. I'd recognize it anywhere.

"You'll be comfortable in this," Mom insists. "I'm pretty sure I have a pair of brown wedges to go with it. What do you think?"

It's not a formal gown, but it's still breathtaking in its own right. I think about the pictures of Mom in the magazine in this same outfit. The way her dark hair hung long down her back and the way her feathered bangs framed her face. She looked like the kind of girl musicians write songs about or that poets craft the saddest of sad sonnets for.

"This is so cool," Avery breathes, gingerly touching the delicate gold chain. "You've got to wear this, Mom."

A pang of guilt hits me out of nowhere. As I watch Avery inspect the details of the outfit—the hand-stitched flower on the back pocket of the jeans and the dainty lace fringe at the bottom of the halter—I realize that she would've loved getting to dress up in Mom's clothes as a little girl. She would've worn every frilly dress and satin bow under the sun, and she would've asked for more. Begged for it.

"Why don't you wear it?" I hold the dry-cleaning bag up to Avery. "It suits you. I'll wear Billie's dress from *Champagne After Midnight*."

"Are you sure?" She can barely contain her excitement.

"As long as Grandma's OK with it," I reply.

"That actually works out better," Mom says. "George just steamed Tom's tuxedo from the movie so Scotty can wear it."

"Who's Tom?"

"The love interest in *Champagne After Midnight* played by Mack Houston," Mom says, with a twinkle in her eye. "Won't that be nice to have a Billie and a Tom? What a happy coincidence—a match made in heaven."

More like a match crafted by a mastermind.

Chapter 22

I get ready in Grandma Viv's old room in the Big House with Mom and Kat and Avery. Miles and Scotty take the Casita. George keeps us hydrated and fed, popping in and out with trays of fruit and crackers and carafes of hot water for tea. Kat puts herself in charge of hair, while Avery is dubbed the unofficial makeup artist of the evening. There's an easy camaraderie that flows between the three generations of Day women, with each of us having our part and contribution. Mom tells little anecdotes about each of the different costumes we're wearing, and I try my best to keep us on schedule. To an outsider, it may look like this is the sort of thing the four of us do all the time. It actually feels that way too. Effortless. The way a family is supposed to be.

"FYI," Kat whispers, as we peruse Grandma Viv's costume jewelry, "the agent I referred Mom to about the property appraisal got back to me. She said Mom never talked about selling."

"Good."

Relief floods over me like a warm bath. *She's not selling.* I may not know what's going to happen next week or, hell, even tomorrow with Mom, but at least I know she'll have Day Ranch.

"Liza, look." Kat holds up a chunky sapphire-diamond necklace. "It's the Heart of the Ocean."

To say that this necklace was just a part of Grandma's costume collection would be like saying the Grand Canyon is just a big hole in the ground. This necklace, with its white-gold chain and teardrop-shaped sapphire, was the single most coveted item in Grandma Viv's collection. Coincidentally, it was also the number one source of all fights between Kat and me. We were obsessed with *Titanic* when it came out, and we'd literally pull each other's hair out fighting for the chance to play Rose and drop the necklace into the swimming pool.

Grandma Viv would have killed us had she seen us doing this. Thankfully, George always turned the other way and taught us how to properly clean the piece so it wouldn't be ruined.

"You should wear it tonight." Kat holds it out for me. "I would, but it doesn't go with the yellow. It'll look amazing with your blue dress."

"I don't know." I hold the necklace in my hand and admire it. "Don't get me wrong, I love it, but isn't it a little gaudy?"

"There's no such thing as gaudy, only people who are uncomfortable standing out," Mom says. "Remember, you're me tonight. Not Liza. What would Darla do? She'd wear that necklace."

It's the opposite of Coco Chanel's famous advice of taking one thing off before leaving the house. I think I like Mom's better, not just in this situation but in life. Stand out. Wear the damn necklace.

"I'll help you, Mom." Avery fastens the clasp. "It's so cool that you have all of this, Grandma."

"Well, get out your sticky notes," Mom says, pinning a French comb in place in her hair. "Claim what you want, so George can make sure to mail it to you. Otherwise, it's liable to end up in an estate sale when I die."

"Mom, you can't keep talking like that," I say. "You're going to freak Avery out."

"She looks fine to me." Mom points at Avery as my daughter claims a pair of gold hoops in Grandma Viv's case with a sticky note. "Avery, have I freaked you out or damaged you psychologically in any way?"

"Nope." She smirks.

"See? She's got a good head on her shoulders," Mom says. "Avery, how's school going this year? Are you still getting good grades? Your mother and aunt always had excellent grades. Your uncle, not so much, but in my defense, I had nothing to do with his genetic makeup."

"My grades are good," Avery replies. "Mostly As and always a B in math."

"Math isn't important." Mom sprays a cloud of Aqua Net on her head. I didn't even realize that brand still existed. Now the whole room smells like the eighties. "We Days are creative types. We don't need math."

"I use a decent amount of math in my work," Kat says. "Maybe don't write off the entire subject just yet."

"Yes, but Katherine, you're not an actress. You never wanted anything to do with show business. The thought of someone telling you what or how to do anything incensed you from an early age. You rely on a completely different part of your brain than Liza and I do. You see the world in black and white"—Mom motions to Avery, not me—"while Liza and I see a rainbow of possibilities. Isn't that right, honey?"

"Grandma, I'm Avery," she says.

"Of course you are," Mom replies, without skipping a beat. "Don't you think I know my only granddaughter's name?"

"You were calling her Liza, Mom." Kat treads lightly. "You were talking about Liza, but you were pointing to Avery."

A blank gaze casts across Mom's face. Her eyes scan Avery and then me, as if she's trying to get her bearings. I expect her to recover the way she did at lunch yesterday. But she doesn't do that this time. I can see her trying to make sense of things, but it's like her brain is stuck in the wrong gear. Each time she tries to shift, it stalls out. She needs help.

"Avery and I look a lot alike, don't we?" I get up from my spot in front of the mirror and place my hand on Mom's shoulder. "We could be twins, couldn't we?"

She nods, but she doesn't say anything. Mom just smiles and holds my hand. I can tell she's frightened. I can see it in her eyes and body language. She's hunched over more than usual, as if she's actively trying to make herself smaller. She used to do something similar after a night of heavy drinking. She'd crouch next to the toilet, taking up as little space as humanly possible. I'd try to squeeze in next to her. I'd rub her back and make sure she drank water.

"Avery, can you come over here and do my eyebrows the way you do yours?" Kat says, drawing the focus of the room away from Mom. "I know eyebrows are never identical twins, but right now mine don't even look like cousins."

"Sure," Avery replies.

"You girls today don't know how lucky you have it with YouTube and TikTok. Back in my day, the only beauty advice available was at the makeup counter at a department store." Kat sighs. "And don't even get me started on eyebrow trends from the early 2000s. One word: sperm."

"Here we go again with the sperm." Avery shakes her head.

"What's that now?" Mom chuckles.

"Aunt Kat is obsessed with sperm," Avery replies. "Eggs too. It's like being in health class."

For a moment, I worry that Avery might've said too much. Kat's not exactly made her desire to procreate in a petri dish a secret, but I don't know that she's brought it up with Mom just yet. But Mom can't conceal her reaction. She's genuinely tickled by the shift in conversation. I look at her and then to Kat, who also seems to appreciate Mom's sudden case of the giggles.

"Katherine, explain yourself," Mom insists.

I hold my breath, suddenly nervous for my sister. Talking about wanting a baby with Miles and Avery and me is one thing, but saying it to Mom escalates the situation. Saying it to her makes it a little more real.

"It's nothing. I'm just thinking about having a baby, Mom." Kat rolls her eyes. "And before you ask, no, I am not looking for a husband. I'm going to do it the way I do everything—by myself and likely through the mail. Don't make a big deal out of it. OK?"

"Well, there is a guy." I lift my brow. "He has a helicopter and he's older. He'll be here tonight too, won't he?"

"Yes, but—"

"I think that you will be an excellent mother, Katherine," Mom whispers, completely ignoring me. "Really, I do."

Kat glances at Mom for just a second before looking away. "I hope so."

"I know so," Mom adds. "And if this gentleman caller of yours doesn't see it, then you have your baby in the mail."

It might not seem like a lot, but for someone like Kat, there was a lot of emotion and vulnerability in that simple exchange.

"I think so too," I say.

"You've got a wonderful resource in your sister." Mom pats my hand softly. "She's the kind of mother I always hoped to be."

My heart swells in my chest. It might be the single best compliment Mom's ever given me. "Thanks, Mom."

"You know, rabbits are terrible mothers." Mom clears her throat. "They abandon their young almost instantly. They're basically the polar opposite of pigeons. Pigeons coparent and take excellent care of their young. Just another fact I remember from my research."

The three of us look at Mom and then each other, all of us in varying degrees of bewilderment.

"You are a much better mother than a rabbit," I say, trying my best to keep a straight face.

"Oh, that I know, honey." Mom squeezes my hand. "Rabbit mothers only feed their young twice a day. You were latched onto my breast like it was an oxygen mask until you were two."

The four of us laugh until we're in tears, and Kat has to make an emergency run to the bathroom to keep from wetting herself.

We finish our hair and makeup before retreating to our rooms to put on our outfits for the evening. When I arrive at the Casita, Miles is decked out in his full *Bye Bye Birdie* regalia. Pastel-blue button-down with little white bunnies—not daisies—and sharp white pants with matching loafers. His hair is slicked back, and he's wearing a pair of thick, black-framed glasses. He looks like he just stepped out of the early sixties, but he also looks exactly like our father.

"You just missed Scotty," he says. "He's back at the Big House, getting suited up with George."

"That's OK," I say. "It'll be a big reveal for the both of us."

"What do you think?" he asks, doing a little twirl.

"You want the truth?" I ask.

"Only if it makes me feel good."

"You look amazing," I say. "You also look just like—"

"Dad." He nods. "Yup. Thought the exact same thing."

"But you're nothing like him." I wrap him in a tight hug. "Nothing at all."

"Thanks." He offers a weak smile. "He might've been a shit dad, but the guy did have style."

"No." I shake my head. "*You* have style, Miles. Dad might've known how to pull together an outfit, but you have style."

"Thanks, Liza." He squeezes me once more before leaving me alone to get dressed. "You've got style too. Of course, none of it was in your suitcase, but you get the idea, right?"

"I do."

I check my watch. The party starts in forty-five minutes. Guests will begin arriving soon.

I head to the bedroom, where George has hung my gown on the back of the door. It's breathtaking. Cornflower-blue silk with a deep V in the front and back. A trail of Swarovski crystals pours down the back like a waterfall of shimmering ice.

I sit down on the edge of the bed and take it all in. I try to imagine what Mom looked like in it. What it must've felt like to wear something so beautiful and precious. The only time I've ever worn a formal gown was in the middle of *Sunset Breeze*'s third season. The show finally received a Daytime Emmy nod. Scotty received one too. He didn't win, and neither did the show, but the night was still memorable.

It's the night we found out I was pregnant.

Chapter 23

Sunset Breeze, Season Three, June 2007
Daytime Emmys

I'm going to puke on television.

The camera is going to pan to Scotty when they announce the nominees for Outstanding Supporting Actor in a Drama Series, and I just know in my gut that that's when it will happen. That's the moment this stomach bug I've been fighting for a week is going to end me. I wouldn't have bothered coming if it weren't for the show's nomination. Scotty couldn't care less if I were here to see him possibly get an Emmy Award. But the show being nominated is different.

It's the first time *Sunset Breeze* has gotten recognition from the Academy. Todd wants our table filled with all the major players, especially since Mom refused to show up after being snubbed in the Lead Actress category. I assumed I'd be over this bug by tonight, but clearly that was a mistake on my part. I'm just hoping my assumption about what's causing my 24/7 nausea is in fact a virus and not something more permanent.

"You doing OK?" Kat whispers. She's my plus-one for the evening. "You're looking a little pale, but that could just be the lighting."

My stomach churns. "I don't think it's the lighting."

Jazz music starts to play. An actress from a soap in a competing time slot glides across the stage, holding the envelope with the winner for Scotty's category. I miss the announcer calling her name over the speaker, but I clap and smile all the same. She's one of those beautiful blondes who has a face that looks like at least two or three other daytime actresses. A perk of being one of the few brunettes on a soap is that I'm usually fairly recognizable. If I end up being the actress who pukes during an award ceremony, I'm willing to bet nobody will forget my name.

The blonde actress begins her little monologue, but all I focus on is the sound of the actor behind me smacking his gum like his mouth is a musical instrument. I've never been particularly sensitive to smells or sounds, but right now, it's as if his spearmint gum has wheedled its way into my skull like a parasite.

Saliva starts to pool in my mouth. I take a deep breath and close my eyes.

"Octavian on *The Light and the Shadows*: Carlos Delfino." The announcer's voice booms across the speakers. "Edgar on *If Tomorrow Never Comes*: Rex Mayers."

"I'm next," Scotty whispers.

He takes my hand, and I blink back any hint of visible discomfort.

"Ryan on *Sunset Breeze*: Scotty Samson."

Our table whoops it up a little louder than the others. I manage to clap and cheer the way a doting girlfriend should. The camera pans to Scotty. He looks like he just stepped off the cover of *GQ* in the black Armani suit he bought with me a few weeks ago when he was nominated. It's the most expensive piece of clothing I've ever had a part in shopping for. He almost didn't buy it. He thought it would be more prudent and practical to rent something, but I pushed him into going through with the purchase.

You're going to need to wear something like this more than once in your life, I told him. *You know this is just the beginning for you.*

As for me, I'm in a rental gown. Unlike Scotty, I think this might be closer to the end of my career. It's not that I don't like the work. I enjoy acting. I enjoy getting to be Naomi Parker even more. It's the attention off-screen that I'm struggling with.

Last season, Scotty did an article with an online fitness magazine, and he casually mentioned that we had moved in together. Within a few hours of it being posted, paparazzi started driving past our little apartment. A couple of days later, we were asked by the management company to cancel our lease because of the distraction we were causing to the other residents. I've worked really hard to feel in control of my life. I've worked equally hard to distance myself from feeling responsible for Mom's life. And yet all that control slipped through my fingers the moment a blog or website decided they'd pay money for a photo of me and Scotty.

"Langston on *The Society Papers*: Ethan Scavo."

The spotlight finds its way back to the blonde actress just as my stomach begins to somersault. "And the Emmy goes to . . ."

"I think I'm going to be sick." I grab Kat's wrist. "Give me your purse."

"Oh my god. Really?"

"Give it!" I yelp.

I heave into her red satin purse just as the winner is announced, a winner who thankfully is not Scotty. Kat shields me out of view as the camera pans to the table adjacent to us. I finish vomiting and stuff the purse back under the table, wiping my mouth with the edge of the tablecloth.

"Air," I whisper. "I need fresh air."

We wait until Carlos Delfino is finished with his speech before we make a break for it. I can't get outside fast enough, but Kat guides me toward the back of the venue. She doesn't want me to inadvertently cause another paparazzi photo opportunity. She kicks open a metal exit door like she's a club bouncer. I'm pretty sure it would've opened with a regular shove, but I don't question Kat's protective instincts.

The moment the night air touches my face, I feel lighter. I lean against the brick wall of the theater, allowing the adrenaline to slowly seep out of my veins.

"Sorry about your purse," I say, once I've caught my breath. "I'll pay for it."

"No need." Kat holds up her black leather purse. "Wasn't mine."

"What do you mean?"

"I mean I wasn't going to give you my purse to yack in."

"Whose purse did you give me?"

"Not really sure." She riffles through her bag and pulls out a white paper sack. "You need this."

"It's a little late for a puke bag, Kat."

"It's what's inside that you need." She pulls off the bag, revealing a pink box. "It's a pregnancy test."

My heart stills in my chest. I suddenly feel nauseated all over again. She shoves the box into my hand. I can barely bring myself to look at it.

"I'm not pregnant," I say.

"And I'm not a doctor," Kat insists. "But I also know that you can't keep anything down and you're late."

She makes a valid point. It's a point I don't like, but it's still valid, nonetheless.

"You want me to take a pregnancy test here and now?" I scoff. "Do you know how crazy that sounds?"

"I know that I've been begging you to take one for the last week, and you've ignored me. I'm not leaving until you take it." She folds her arms across her chest, standing her ground. The overhead light casts a yellow glow on her red dress, making her look a little like a devil, which seems fitting, given her demand. "In three minutes, you can know whether you've got the stomach flu or a stomach fetus."

"That's not where babies grow." I make a face. "Please don't ever say that again."

"Take the test, Liza."

We walk back into the venue, my test securely hidden in Kat's purse. The hallway is still mostly empty. Everybody's clamoring for a little screen time to show off their gowns and tuxes. With how much time goes into getting ready for an event like this, I can't say that I blame them.

We duck into the bathroom, which is semiprivate. There are two stalls and a vanity in a cherrywood finish. The lighting is low except for around the vanity mirror, and there's a nice selection of hand lotions and body spray. It's actually pretty decent, as far as public restrooms are concerned. The smaller of the two stalls is occupied. I take the larger and insist that Kat come inside with me.

"I don't want to be in here," Kat whispers. "This isn't a team sport."

"It is today."

I task Kat with opening the test while I hike up my long, tiered gown. The woman in the stall next to us makes a heaving noise. The distinct scent of margarita wafts through the air. At least I'm in the right place if I have anything left inside of me to puke up.

"Hold the tip down," Kat says, reading the back of the box. "You have to pee a little first and then stop. Then you pee on the stick."

"Why do I have to stop first?" I ask, suddenly a little panicked. "I don't know if I can do that."

"What do you mean, you don't know? You just make yourself stop."

"I don't like being under pressure," I reply, defensively. "Are you sure that's a crucial step?"

"I'm not here to question the science. Just do it." She yanks the lid off the test and shoves the stick in my hand. "Go on."

I place the stick between my legs and lean over a little. I've drunk so much ginger ale that I know I have to pee, but right now I have stage fright.

"It's too quiet," I whisper.

Kat looks at me like I have three heads. "What do you want me to do? Sing? Do a little spoken word?"

The woman in the stall next to us upchucks again, this time while flushing the toilet. It's all the encouragement my bladder needs. I manage to start and stop like a champ. I hand the test back to Kat. She pops the lid on it.

"We need a flat surface to put it on." She starts to open the stall door.

"What are you doing?" I hiss, struggling with my underwear.

"I'm just going to set it on the vanity. There's nobody in here but us and"—Kat nods toward the other stall—"our neighbor. I can lock the main door."

"No. Just put it on top of the tank."

"That doesn't seem sanitary." Kat makes a face.

"It's a test, not a baby."

"Fine." She places the test on the toilet tank delicately. "One line means a virus. Two lines means—"

"Not a virus," I say. "That's what we're calling it. How many minutes do we wait?"

"Three."

"Set a timer."

She looks back in her purse. "I don't have my phone."

"Seriously?"

"You don't have yours either."

I'm not even prepared enough to take a test to see whether or not I'm pregnant. How in the world am I supposed to take care of another human?

"Let's count," Kat says. "We'll count to sixty. Twice."

"I thought you said we had to wait three minutes."

"I did."

"Well, then wouldn't we have to count to sixty three times? This doesn't sound very scientific."

"For the love of god, Liza," Kat huffs. "We just have to track the time. We're not actually conducting the test."

"Fine." I groan. "One, two . . ."

"Yup." Kat leans over the toilet. "There's two."

"Two what?" I breathe, clinging to my sister's arm.

"Two lines." Kat holds up the test. "Not a virus."

I take the test from her, holding it up to the dim light. It's undeniable. Two pink lines are looking me straight in the face. "But we just started counting." I swallow. "It can't make up its mind before we've finished. That's not fair."

Kat looks at me, her face now as pale as mine. "You're pregnant, Liza. You're really pregnant."

She touches my belly, and I instantly recoil.

"I don't know how to be pregnant." I kneel down against the stall door. "I barely know how to be an adult."

Kat stares at the test before slipping it back in her purse. The main bathroom door opens, followed by a gaggle of footsteps and laughter. There must be an intermission, or maybe the whole show is over. Someone knocks on the door of the stall.

"Just a minute," Kat says. She squats down next to me. "You don't need to decide anything right now. Right now, you just have to get up and wash your hands."

"What do I do after that?"

"Get out of the bathroom. Maybe tell Scotty. Maybe don't. It's up to you." She pushes back a curl from my face. "Whatever you decide, I'll be with you."

"Promise?"

"Promise."

Chapter 24

It's a perfect night for a funeral, if ever there were such a thing.

Chauncey's crew ushers all the guests, family included, onto the pool deck through an arch of purple calla lilies and red roses. Tea lights float atop lily pads in the pool, which has been lit a decadent shade of eggplant, giving the space a whimsical, gothic feel. Waiters dressed in oxblood jackets and matching slacks carry trays of caviar and shrimp cocktails, while waitresses dressed as cigarette girls pass out champagne, sparkling cider, and cigars. A small jazz band plays a blend of show tunes and old commercial jingles. It's like taking a step into Mom's imagination, and it's absolutely magnificent.

There are dozens among dozens of attendees dressed in Darla garb. It makes it a little difficult to recognize who's who, but I don't mind getting lost in the chaos. I take a flute of champagne and browse a portrait display of Mom. Unlike the slideshow we saw yesterday, these are candid photos of Mom off-screen. Mom pushing Kat on a swing at the apartment she and Dad moved into after they were married. Mom kneeling next to Miles while he blows out the candles on his fourth birthday cake. He hadn't even lived with us a full year, and yet Mom already loved him like he was her own.

My photo with Mom makes me smile and chuckle. It's Mom and me sitting on the edge of the pool with our legs hanging in the water. My arms stick out, my body in a T formation, thanks to the very-well-inflated water wings I'm sporting. Mom is sticking her tongue out at the camera, and I'm doing the same. *Forever her little shadow.* It comes to me like a whisper of a memory. That's what she used to call me. I was her little shadow, and she felt like the sun.

The last photo chokes me up unexpectedly. It's a picture of Avery and me at the indoor swimming pool at the Silverton rec center. She's holding a little ribbon that the teachers give kids when they graduate from one swimming group to the next. Avery was terrified of the water. She went weeks without putting her head under. The instructor asked if I would go in the water with her to calm her nerves. That's the day this photo was taken. All it took for Avery to get comfortable in the water was to know that I was in it with her. She was once my little shadow too.

I remember being so exhausted when Avery was that age. I was finishing up my teaching degree and drowning in single motherhood. Scotty was in a serious relationship, or at least I thought it was serious. Meanwhile, I doubted that I would ever love anyone again. As big as my smile is in that picture, there was an equally big empty space inside of me.

I glance at the photo of Mom and me again, and for the first time, I see myself in her. Not in appearance, but as a mother. We were both women struggling to keep from drowning while trying to make sure our babies never doubted that everything was OK.

A hand taps my shoulder, resting on it for a beat. Without turning around, I know who it is, and my heart skips a beat.

"She was so tiny," I say, still staring at the photo of Avery and me. "She was an absolute pistol, but a little one at that."

He doesn't say anything, and for a moment, I wonder if my spidey senses are off. I turn around, and sure enough, it's Scotty, dressed in a classic black tuxedo that looks like it was tailor-made for him.

"You look like you just stepped out of a movie," Scotty says. His eyes take me in, and he motions for me to do a little spin. I roll my eyes, but I oblige him. "You just made my whole night."

Heat flushes across my cheeks and spreads down my neck, settling into my chest. Now I'm the one a little speechless. "You clean up pretty nice too."

"Check out the eye." He points to the spot where his shiner was just a few hours ago. "Avery's makeup skills are pretty damn impressive."

I shorten the gap between us to get a better look at her handiwork and give a nod of approval. "I guess if a pap gets a picture of you, you won't have to tell everyone your ex assaulted you with a dirt clod."

"I think you mean *baby mama*." He can't even keep a straight face as he says it. "God, that sounds weird."

"Agreed. But calling me your ex-girlfriend makes me sound like I'm still sixteen. 'Ex' sounds mature."

"'Ex.'" He grabs a glass of champagne from a waiter as he passes by and takes a sip, considering the suggestion for a moment. "That term never sits well with me. Makes the other person seem like a mistake."

"Sometimes people are." I shrug.

"You weren't a mistake for me. Was I one for you?"

"Not a chance."

"What about last night?" He leans in close. "Was that a mistake?"

Every nerve in my body tingles with heat. I shake my head. "Not a chance."

"Good. I wanted to talk about that with you. Actually, there's a lot I want to talk—"

"Mom!" Avery waves from beneath the archway. "Dad!"

She's the spitting image of Mom. The halter top and bell-bottoms fit her like a glove, and I'm so thoroughly happy she's wearing the outfit instead of me. I'm beyond the point of wanting to bare my midriff. I've survived the low-rise-jeans fiasco of the early aughts and am officially in my high-waisted-jeans era. But Avery—she looks absolutely timeless.

There's an older woman following Avery. I don't recognize her, and it has nothing to do with the fact that she's dressed like Mom circa her *Sunset Breeze* days. The best way to categorize that period of Mom's fashion is *coastal grandma trollop*.

"Do you know who that is?" I mutter under my breath.

"I can't tell," he replies. "It's too hard to see with the lighting and the costume."

"Liza Day and Scotty Samson," the woman says. "Boy, you two make a beautiful pair." She holds out her hand for me to shake. "I'm Kimberly Glass."

"Hi," I say, shaking her hand. "Have we met?"

"No," she says, shaking Scotty's hand next. "Well, not directly. Your mother reached out to me two days ago. I guess it must've been when you got into town. Anyway, she mentioned Avery here."

"Oh?" I glance at Avery. "What for?"

"I'm an agent with Wilder Talent Group," she says. "I'm still not sure how your mother got my information, but I'm glad she did. She told me that Avery is interested in getting into the family business."

I look up at Scotty to see if he's as put off by this interaction as I am, but he's got his poker face on, which is not the face I was hoping for. I want the Brock Lucas version of Scotty to leap into action and get this bloodsucking agent the hell away from my kid.

"Well, I apologize for the confusion," I say, wrapping an arm around Avery's waist. "My daughter is still in school. She's not looking for representation right now."

"Mom." Avery gives me one of those incredulous looks that girls give their mothers when they think they're being absurd. "You haven't even heard what she has to say."

"I don't need to," I say. "You're not an actress, and that's what she's looking for. You don't even live in the state. What's left to discuss?"

"Dad," Avery whines. "Do something. Please."

She and I both eye Scotty, waiting for him to do or say *something*. Anything would be great at this point, but he's basically a statue.

Kimberly smiles, seemingly unaffected by my comment. "I don't want to upset your family or anyone tonight, so I'm going to get straight to the point." She hands both Scotty and me a business card, which I begrudgingly accept. "When your daughter is ready to act, I want to be the first call she makes."

Scotty skims the card, but I don't bother looking at it.

"Thank you," he says. "We'll be in touch."

We'll be in touch? What does that even mean? We don't know anything about this woman. I doubt Mom in her current state knows anything about her. She was probably just trying to do something sweet to bond with Avery, and now here's this agent, climbing out of the woodwork to latch on to Mom's surge of popularity.

"I could see you next week," Avery says, the desperation so clear in her voice. "Just tell me when and where, and my dad will take me."

"Excuse me?" I gasp. "We won't even be here next week. You've got school, and I've got work."

"Yeah. Sure," she scoffs. "One of those comments is true."

A pit forms in my stomach. I haven't told Avery a word about my job status. When we left, I told her I had taken the time off, and that the school board and Principal Long never indicated that they would announce anything right away. What private school wants to let a bunch of parents know they don't have someone lined up after firing a teacher who for all intents and purposes was well-liked by her students and school?

"What are you talking about?" I manage to ask.

"I know you got fired, Mom, or you quit or whatever." Avery's bottom lip trembles. "Matt told me. He also told me you hit him with your car."

"You hit someone with your car?" Scotty asks, now suddenly coming to life.

"I barely tapped him."

Part of me realizes that Kimberly Glass has no idea what she's just walked into, and that none of this is really her fault, but the fact that she's just standing there, watching my family's drama unfold, sets me over the edge.

"Can you leave, please?" I snap. "Clearly, you can see that we're not in need of your services, and if my mother contacts you again, you are not to speak with her. She's not—"

Scotty takes my hand and gives it a quick squeeze. It catches me off guard. It's the equivalent of being kicked under the table. He shakes his head, and suddenly I realize I was about to tell this complete stranger about Mom's health—something Mom hasn't even disclosed to us yet.

Kimberly apologizes profusely, to the point where I feel like an even bigger ass than I ever imagined possible, and disappears into the crowd of guests. A crowd that now looks to be double the size it was a few minutes ago.

"I can't believe you." Avery takes the card and pushes me away. "You humiliated me for no reason."

"I humiliated you?" I scoff. "Avery, you just told a complete stranger about my private life. Do you realize that if she wanted to, she could take that information and tweet it or X it or whatever the hell you call the damn thing?"

"Why do you always think about yourself first?" she fires back. "You know when you asked me what changed between us, Mom? You thought it was because you kept me from seeing Dad, which makes sense, because you think everything in my life somehow has to be connected to yours."

"Avery," Scotty warns. "Please calm down."

There's a small group of guests that have taken notice of our argument, and suddenly, I feel like I'm on display like a circus animal.

"Let's do this another time," he says.

"No." Tears spill over her high cheekbones. "I have to say this, because if I don't now, then I might not ever. Mom, what changed was that I realized you're only happy when I do everything exactly the way you want me to. We stopped being best buddies once I finally decided to stand my ground and have an opinion on what I want my life to look like."

"You're only sixteen, honey." I soften my voice and try my best to put myself in her shoes. "As much as you think you're all grown up, you're still a kid. I don't want you to have to grow up so fast, like I did."

"Because you had me," she says. "I'm the reason you had to grow up fast. I'm the reason you ended up with a job you hate in a city where, after all this time, you still don't really know anybody."

Her words cut me like a knife to the bone, and all I want to do is wrap her in my arms, take her into the Casita, and hold her like I did when she was a baby. I want to rock her until the crying stops and she's safe and fast asleep next to me.

"Avery, that's not true at all." Scotty clears his throat. "Your mom leaving here was the right choice."

"But Dad." Avery's voice trembles. "You said you would talk to her. You said you would back me up. You promised."

"Back you up?" I ask. "You promised her what? An agent?"

"Of course not." Scotty shakes his head. "Avery, I didn't promise you anything. I said I would talk to your mom for you."

"Why would my daughter need you to talk to me on her behalf?" I fold my arms over my chest. "Furthermore, why wouldn't you encourage her to come talk to me on her own?"

"Because you don't listen, Mom!"

Avery's voice pierces through the pause between songs like a sword. It suddenly feels like every Darla's eyes are glued to the two of us. Fighting with my daughter in front of one version of my mother is painful enough. Doing it in front of fifty-plus Darlas is hell.

Her eyes swell with the threat of tears, and her painted lips pull into a tight frown. All the joy and excitement that was bubbling out of her just moments ago is gone. "There's no point in talking." She wipes her eyes with the backs of her hands. "I'm stuck with you for two more years, but after those years are done, I'm gone. I'm leaving you behind just like you left Grandma and everyone else behind."

My body stills like a deer in headlights, waiting for impact and knowing that bracing for it won't change the final impact. I've had this fight before. Well, not this fight exactly, but pretty damn close. I've been on Avery's side of the argument. I've been the young girl who made big, loud threats and kept them like oaths. That's the thing about Day women. We rarely go back on the promises we make.

Chauncey's voice booms over the sound system, announcing a toast in ten minutes. I can vaguely hear Miles calling me. I think I see Kat walking toward me in her canary-yellow dress, but it's hard to tell through the tears. The only thing I see with absolute clarity is Avery's back as she walks away.

"Liza, I didn't mean to overstep—"

"Picture time!" Chauncey's voice rings in my ear like a fire alarm. "Let's get a picture of Ryomi and . . . oh, where did Baby Ryomi go? No bother. We'll do the whole family next."

Chauncey instructs someone to fluff my dress and somebody else to make sure we're in frame with the elephant in the background. We back up closer to the pool, which then throws off the lighting. Chauncey is uncompromising when it comes to making sure the pictures he takes of his event are perfect. I'm too emotionally raw to argue any of this, so I play along. I've already made one scene. No need to add a second to my résumé.

Scotty on the other hand feels different. "I've got to go get my kid," he says.

"Of course." Chauncey nods his head, but it's clear he's not listening. "Let me just get a few of Ryomi, and you can be on your way."

"You're not hearing me." Scotty tries to maneuver around Chauncey, but Chauncey holds his ground firm. "Buddy, if you don't let me go to my kid, we're going to have an issue."

"Please, it will just take one—"

I'm not sure what happens first exactly, but I'm sure somebody somewhere records it with their phone. One minute, Chauncey is trying to adjust Scotty's tie, and the next, both of them are in the deep end of the pool, which is awful enough in its own right. But to make matters worse, it's only when the two of them are in the pool that we suddenly realize Chauncey doesn't know how to swim.

Chapter 25

The crowd of guests breaks out in applause. Somehow, somebody gets the idea that the whole thing is a stunt. A little nod back to Scotty's *Sunset Breeze* days as a lifeguard. Chauncey rolls with it so seamlessly that for a moment, I question if it *is* all a stunt. George takes both men back to the Big House to dry off, leaving me alone with Miles and Kat, which is honestly the best place possible for me to be right now.

"So, how's your night?" Miles hands me a glass of champagne. "Judging by what just happened, I'm guessing it could be better."

"Yup." I down half the glass in one gulp. "Next subject. I don't want to talk about me. *Me* is a heavy, heavy subject right now. Tell me anything else."

"There's Rooster." Kat nudges me and nods toward a man with salt-and-pepper hair in a pale-gray suit. "He's here, and he hasn't run away yet. I'm going to call that a win."

"Did he see Scotty and Chauncey fall into the pool?" I ask. Kat nods. "And the fight with Avery?" She nods again. "He might be a keeper."

"Why is he called Rooster?" Miles asks.

"If I told you, I'd have to kill you." Kat wraps an arm around my shoulders. "Tell us what you need. Do you want me to go hunt down Avery so you can patch things up? Miles could help Scotty out in the wardrobe department, and we could try to salvage this night. What do you say? Sound like a plan?"

I want to say yes because I always want Kat's help for everything in life, but I tell her no instead. This is the first time Kat's ever brought a boy home . . . Granted this boy looks like he might qualify for AARP, but still. It's a big deal, and I want her to have her night with him.

"Have fun with Rooster," I tell her.

"You sure?" she asks.

"Go." I give her a little shove. "Or I'll push you in the pool next."

"Well, you've still got me." Miles leans back on his heels. "I don't have a date, and so far, I haven't seen anyone I might want to take back to the Casita with me for a cry about my failed marriage."

"Explain to me Chauncey's appeal." I finish the rest of my champagne and place the empty glass on a tray. "What attracted you to him?"

"He was the exact opposite of James." Miles sighs. "I thought somebody who didn't remind me of the man I love in the slightest might be what I needed to get over him. Also, I legitimately don't think the man remembers me, and I can't tell if that makes me feel better or worse."

"Well, my kid thinks she's the reason my life sucks." I grab another glass of champagne from a waiter passing by. "And I'm pretty sure she hates my guts."

"She doesn't hate your guts," Miles says. "She wants to be you, Liza."

"What?"

"When we were watching a movie together the other day with Kat, all Avery wanted to do was ask us questions about you. She wanted to know what you did when you were her age. She wanted to know how Mom got you started in acting and how the two of you ended up shooting *Sunset Breeze*." Miles looks down at the ground for a moment. "I was kind of surprised at how little she actually knows about the old you. Maybe open up to her a little more. Sometimes, feeling included goes a long way."

The mic taps over the sound system, signaling it's time for the toast. A slightly damp Chauncey makes his way to the stage with a thousand-watt smile. You'd never know the guy just nearly drowned at somebody's funeral. He lifts his glass in the air, and the crowd follows suit. Kat and Rooster join Miles and me just as Chauncey starts to give a speech thanking everyone.

"I'm going to look for Avery and Scotty," I whisper. "I'll be right back."

"No, wait." Kat grabs my shoulder. "Look."

Mom walks onstage in a classic black velvet gown that I vaguely remember Grandma Viv wearing to one of Mom's premieres. George is next to her, his arm gently guiding her across the stage. He's dressed up in a nice navy suit with a red tie. It's the most dressed up I've ever seen him. They meet Chauncey in the middle of the stage to a raucous round of applause.

Mom's glowing. She's waving to everyone, standing taller and prouder than I've seen in forever. Chauncey hands the mic to George and tries to exit the stage, but Mom grasps Chauncey's hand, insisting he take a bow.

When he finally leaves, a woman I don't recognize takes the stage. She's older—not as old as Mom, but easily in her sixties. She's dressed in costume, but you can tell she's a sharp dresser in everyday life. Her gray bob is precision-cut, and her glasses are a bold tortoiseshell frame. She raises her champagne glass and says, "My name is Debbie Houston. Darla and I did a few movies a million years ago, and recently we reconnected. When she asked me to say a few words about her tonight, I was honored to do so." She turns to Mom and holds her gaze. "Now if you'll indulge me, I wrote you a little poem. 'To some, you will always be Daisy. To others, you are forever Billie. You've been America's darling and, at times, a tabloid sensation. To your parents, you were Darla, and to your children, Mom and then Grandma. To me, however, you will always be the woman who saved me when I needed to be rescued the most. To me, you are a hero.'"

Debbie raises her glass, which looks decidedly like water, to toast Mom's glass of sparkling cider. A symphony of glass clinking fills the night air. I hold my glass toward Miles and Kat and then Rooster. All of us, minus Rooster, have the same befuddled look on our faces.

"How did Mom rescue her?" Miles asks. "I didn't even know the woman existed. I mean, I had a vague idea of who she was, but not a clue that she and Mom were close."

"Debbie Houston used to have trouble with drinking," Rooster says, out of nowhere. "She and her husband, Mack, are members of the same golf club upstate as me."

"You're besties with my mom's bestie?" Kat asks.

"Not exactly." Rooster chuckles. "I'm not that old. Anyway, she relapsed not long after her husband came down with some health issues. Maybe your mom was the one who helped her clean up her act."

Mom and Debbie step to the side of the stage, and the jazz band begins to play, as a grainy black-and-white video of a young man and woman dancing flickers across the screen. It takes me a moment to pull the scene into focus. A tall, good-looking man with jet-black hair and a slight, serious look on his face. The woman slightly shorter with pale hair and lithe features. He twirls her, and she dips. That's when I recognize the fireplace from the Big House. It's my grandpa and grandma, dancing in the living room. It's empty. They must've just moved in. Mom wouldn't even be born yet.

Grandma Vivian walks to the camera, putting her face up close to it and waving. She motions for Grandpa to do the same, and he does, but you can tell it's just to humor her. Grandma Viv looks giddy. She reminds me of Olivia Newton-John in *Grease*.

The video fades and leads into a new one. This one is in color. Grandpa is walking through the pecan orchard, dressed like he's an old cowboy. Mom said he was from Brooklyn, but you'd never know it. He had no accent to speak of. The camera pans away from Grandpa and toward the lake. Lake Vivian. Grandma is walking toward the camera, her hand holding the underside of her belly. Mom.

Kat reaches for my hand and squeezes it. She's not crying, but I get the sense she's making a mental note to put it on her calendar. Miles is halfway to a full-out ugly cry. I set my champagne flute down and take his hand.

The three of us stand linked together on the pool deck, just like we used to when we were kids. George would be in the pool, egging us on to jump. Kat was timid around water, and Miles was timid around everything. I'd take each of their hands and count to three. I'd close my eyes when I went to jump, because I was always a little afraid that one of them would back out and leave me hanging. I wasn't any braver than the two of them—water made me nervous too—but it was because of them that I could be brave. Never once did they not jump.

Clip after clip of Mom and Grandma and Grandpa on the ranch scrolls across the screen. So much life happened here before I even existed. The memories and secrets contained within the walls of the Big House, the groves, and the land, too numerous to count.

A wave of emotion hits me out of nowhere when I realize I don't have videos like this for Avery. Not that I think she'll ever throw her own funeral, but one day, when Avery wants to look back on her family, she won't have videos like this here at the ranch. She'll have videos that Scotty took and videos that I took, but nothing linking her to here. I hate that. This place is magical. It's been magical to my family for generations, and that shouldn't stop with me and Kat and Miles.

The show draws to an end, and the lights turn back on. Mom and Debbie return to the stage to thunderous applause. Chauncey hands Mom the mic, which only heightens the fervor of the applause.

"Does she look OK to you?" Kat whispers.

"Who?" I ask.

"Mom." Kat nods toward the stage. "She looks like she's lost."

The applause slowly dissipates. The mic shakes in her hand—not a lot, but enough to be noticeable. Debbie whispers something to her, possibly prompting her to say whatever she's prepared, but Mom doesn't look like she's listening. Mom looks like she's somewhere else entirely.

"I want to thank the Academy," she says, slowly. "It's an honor just to be nominated, but winning is always preferable."

The crowd chuckles. They don't realize this isn't a gag. To them, it's just a well-timed joke. I squeeze Miles's and Kat's hands tight.

"Anyway, I'd like to thank my agent, and of course my family." Mom squints, looking into the crowd. Kat holds up a hand and waves. "Ah, there they are. My children: Katherine, Liza, and Miles. They're the best production I've ever been a part of. I made a lot of mistakes with them." She pauses, scanning the crowd again. "Has anyone seen Eddie tonight?"

The pool deck falls silent. The veil has lifted. My heart sinks.

"We need to get her," Miles says.

Debbie pats Mom on the back and gently takes the mic from her. "It's been a long day," she says. "Who wouldn't be tired at their own funeral?"

A few people laugh, but it's not the upbeat laughter of just a few moments ago. Even if it were possible to ignore Mom's comments about Dad, it's hard not to notice the look of confusion on Mom's face. The sound of uncertainty in her voice. The timidness in her posture.

"Ladies and gentlemen, on behalf of our guest of honor, please dance, drink, and be merry. This is not only a celebration of Darla, but it's also a celebration of the Day family and this beautiful ranch they've called home for over seventy years."

Mom tries to grab the mic, but Debbie stops her. Chauncey takes the stage again and tries to reiterate that this is a party. He cues the band to play, and the slideshow of Mom from yesterday starts up.

The three of us make a beeline to go get Mom.

Chapter 26

I see Debbie lead Mom through the kitchen door into the Big House. The three of us follow them, fighting against a current of people trying to refresh their cocktails. Miles and Kat push ahead, as a woman I vaguely recognize as one of the production interns on *Sunset Breeze* corners me. I want to tell her to leave me the hell alone. Did she not see what just happened?

"Liza. Remember me?" The woman places her hand on her chest. "Dani Cooper."

"Hi," I say, stiffly. "Yes, I think so."

"I was hoping to run into you and some of the other cast from *Sunset Breeze*. It's been ages, hasn't it?"

"A long time." I make no attempt to hide my impatience. "I'm sorry, but I have something I need to take care of."

"Of course, of course." Dani smiles at me. Her understanding seems genuine, which kind of makes me feel like a jerk for being so short with her. "I'm sure you've got so many people demanding your time."

"Something like that." I take a few steps toward the kitchen door. "I'll catch up with you later."

"Well, if I don't see you again, I just wanted to tell you how happy I am that you and Scotty ended up finding your way back to one another."

This gives me pause. "What do you mean?"

"You and Scotty," she says. "I was always rooting for the two of you, and I'm so glad you guys got back together."

Maybe she saw Scotty and me talking earlier by the photograph display. Maybe she misconstrued our interaction as something more, though I find that hard to believe.

"Don't judge me"—Dani lowers her voice and rummages in her purse for her phone—"but I have a Google Alert set up for every show I've worked on." She taps on her phone screen, pulling up god knows what, and hands it to me. "I didn't even realize Scotty was here."

The headline on *Page Six* reads *Ryomi Forever*. Underneath, a series of photos of Scotty and me from tonight fill the screen. Photos of me twirling in my dress for Scotty, smiling like a teenager in love. Me pressing my hand to Scotty's cheek and biting my lip. And finally, the two of us from behind, staring at the photo of Avery and me. It looks like Scotty's hand is pressed against my back, but I know it wasn't. It had to be hovering. I would remember him touching my lower back, and he wouldn't do it without asking. Of course, had he asked, I don't think I would've told him no.

I don't read the article, not that there's much in the way of text anyway. I don't care what the article says, just like I know nobody else will. The photos are all that matter. That's how it's always been. A picture isn't worth a thousand words. A picture is worth everything.

"I've got to go check on my mom," I say.

I push past Dani and make my way through the rest of the partygoers and into the kitchen. With each step, the gravity of what's happened begins to sink in more and more. Somebody who was supposed to be here to celebrate Mom not only had the balls to take pictures of Scotty and me but also had the audacity to send them to a gossip blog. Who would do that?

I make my way through the kitchen and into the hall toward Mom's room, but George stops me.

"Where's Mom?" I ask.

"She's in her room with Kat and Miles," George says, calmly.

"OK. I need to see her." I try to move past George, but he stands in my way.

"Honey, Avery has been in her room in a state of distress for the past half hour. Scotty's been talking to her, but I think she needs her mom." He rests his hand on my shoulder.

She needs her mom. God, I wish that were true.

"Let Kat and Miles look after Darla while you check in with Avery."

"I think I'm the last person my daughter wants to see right now."

"No," he says, softly. "Just go to her. Please."

"I think I really messed things up, George," I breathe, shakily. "I think I tried so hard to protect my kid from everything I was afraid would hurt her the way it did me, and in the process, I think I ended up keeping a big part of me a secret from her."

He hands me his handkerchief. "Well, the beauty about messes is that they're temporary. Entire cities have been destroyed by war and natural disaster, but they always manage to get put back together. Do you know why?"

"No."

"Because somebody cares enough to clean up the mess and start again. The size of the mess we make doesn't matter so long as the size of the heart of the person cleaning it is bigger." He pulls me in for a hug. "Your heart is big enough to put back together any mess you might make."

"Thanks, George." I hold on to him a little longer than normal. He doesn't let go until I do. He never does. There's something special about people who hug you as long as you need it.

Armed with his handkerchief, I head down the hallway away from Mom's room and toward Avery's. The door is closed. I knock, and Scotty answers.

"Hey," he says, stepping out of the room and closing the door behind him. "She's having a rough time."

"George told me," I say. "Let me talk to her."

He looks uneasy. "I just got her to calm down, Liza."

I can tell by the pained expression on his face that he's uncomfortable. It's hard seeing your kid hurt, and this is the first time Scotty's seen Avery like this. He usually gets the highlight reel of her life.

"I don't want the two of you to fight," he says.

"We won't," I assure him.

"She wants to go with me, Liza."

"I know. George told me. It's fine if she wants to stay tonight with you at the motor lodge—that's what I'm here to tell her. She can come back in the morning, and we'll start fresh and—"

"That's not what I mean. She wants to stay with me permanently."

Every nerve ending feels like it's just been dipped in acid. I can feel every shred of control and calmness I managed to muster slowly disintegrate into nothingness. "What did you tell her?" I manage to ask.

"I told her that we don't make big decisions when we're feeling emotional," he says. "As a compromise, I told her she could stay with me at the motor lodge tonight if she wanted, and tomorrow, we'd sit down and have a talk."

"I just want to tell her good night and that I love her." My voice is barely a whisper.

Scotty moves aside from the door, and I slowly push it open. Avery sits on the window bench. She's out of her Daisy costume and is back in her own clothes. She looks so much younger. She also looks so much like me. I've sat in that same spot she's in. It's the spot where I used to practice my lines. It's also the spot where I cried my eyes out when Mom told us we were leaving Day Ranch for good.

"Hey," I say, softly.

She doesn't say anything back, which is somehow more painful than if she had yelled at me.

"Dad says you two are going to stay the night at the motor lodge. I think it's a good idea. You probably won't get much sleep here tonight anyway."

"That's not why I want to stay there," she says, with no emotion at all.

"I know."

I start to talk but stop. Something I remember Mom telling me before an audition crosses my mind out of nowhere. She told me to leave room in the scene for people to feel what you're saying. *People are so quick to fill silence with noise,* she said. *If you give people enough time to feel between heavy lines, the dialogue makes a bigger impact.* I decide to do just that. I let the room fill with silence, even though it hurts. Even though I just want to fix things. Even though all I want to do is tell Avery that I love her more than I've ever loved anyone. I stay quiet, and wait to follow her lead.

"You treat me like you don't trust me," she says, quietly.

"That's not what I want to do, Ave."

"But you do." She looks up at me with glassy eyes. "You know that day you caught me in your car with Matt?"

"I'm pretty sure that day will be forever emblazoned in my memory."

"That really was the first time I ever did anything like that. To be honest, it kind of freaked me out."

"Then why did you do it?"

"Because I was mad at you," she says. "In one car ride, you managed to control me being able to talk to Dad, and then when I asked you about the invitation, you just brushed me off like it was nothing. You talk about us being close, Mom, but the truth is I was always the one opening up to you. You kept so much of you away from me."

"I didn't mean to, Ave," I say, my voice breaking. "I didn't realize it."

"I've been wanting to make you mad just to get some real emotion out of you. You always say you're fine. You always say everything is OK, but I don't think you really believe that."

I don't. I probably haven't for a long time, if ever. I just didn't realize that the one person I was trying to put on a performance for was the one person who could see right through the act.

Chapter 27

Kat finds me first. It's always Kat.

I'm sitting on Avery's bed, holding her pillow against my chest, trying to breathe in every last bit of her. Scotty took her to the motor lodge shortly after we talked, and I've just been sitting here ever since, trying to figure out how to fix everything that's broken.

"How's Mom?" I ask.

"Sleeping," she says.

"I'm sorry I wasn't there to help you."

"Ditto."

"And Rooster?" I ask.

"He's staying at the motor lodge," she says.

"What happened to the mom-cake?" I ask. "Did they cut it after we French-exited Mom's funeral?"

"I got rid of it." Miles waggles his eyebrows and leans into the doorframe, cradling a loaf of George's sourdough like it's a baby. He looks absolutely exhausted. "If you head out to Lake Vivian, you'll find twelve ice chests filled with mom-cake."

"You took it all apart?" Kat asks.

"That thing never made it to the party," Miles says. "I may or may not have told the baker that the driver never showed up yesterday. I also may or may not owe that driver a new job."

"Genius," I say.

"Also, I've made a decision. From now on, I only attend funerals of people who are actually dead." He throws himself onto the bed, in between Kat and me. "Also, when I die, I've decided I do want my body to be donated to science. I don't care that they mail back the parts they don't use. I think it'll be a fun little subscription service for the two of you. Each time you go to the mailbox, you'll never know if I'll be there."

"Another reason to cancel my mail service." I yawn.

"I did a little research on different death options too." Kat falls back on the bed. "I'm going to have an open-air cremation."

"What the hell is that?" Miles asks.

Kat starts to explain the process in far too graphic detail, which results in the three of us laughing hysterically together. Most people would probably find us morbid or, at the very least, tacky. What could still be funny in a world where things like dementia and death and shitty childhoods and even shittier parents exist? Who can find humor after a night like this?

Survivors do. That's what the three of us are. Above all else, we know how to survive.

"What about you, Liza?" Miles elbows me. "What are we doing for you?"

"I'm old-fashioned," I reply. "Just put me in the dirt."

My answer surprises me a little. I've never given thought to what I want to happen when I die. Even through all the craziness of this weekend, I never once stopped to consider it. But something about being in one place in the ground where the roots can grow around me sounds like the only right answer.

We fall asleep, the three of us and a half-eaten loaf of sourdough, on Avery's bed. George wakes us, and at first, I assume it's to get us to go to our rooms, but the moment my eyes adjust to the light and I see his face, I know something is wrong.

"I can't find Darla," he says, his breath haggard. "I checked on her just after midnight when the party ended and I was on my way to bed. She was in her bed, asleep, but she's gone now."

"What time is it?" I ask.

"Nearly five a.m.," George replies.

We hurry out of bed, our bodies collectively screaming at us for falling asleep on a too-small bed in formal wear. I throw on a pair of slippers and hurry out the door behind Miles and Kat.

There's a thick layer of fog and dew on the grass. Fall has finally arrived. The chill in the air draws a veil of goose bumps across my exposed shoulders and back. The thought of Mom being out here for any amount of time makes my stomach churn.

"Where have you looked, George?" Kat asks.

"The usual places: the rabbit hutch and the barn. I even checked the Casita. That's when I realized the two of you were gone." He points to Miles and me. "Benny's gone too."

"Just Benny?" Miles asks. "Or are some of the other rabbits missing too?"

"Why does that matter?" I snip. "Who cares how many rabbits are missing? Our mom is missing!"

"Don't yell at me," Miles says, defensively. "I'm a publicist, not a detective."

"George, have you checked the groves? What about the lake?" Kat asks.

He shakes his head.

"Alright, why don't you and Miles check the groves? I'll take the lake. Liza, you go back and check everywhere that George has already looked in case she's on the move. Keep your phones on."

"Shouldn't we call the police?" I ask.

"I don't think we need to do that just yet," Kat says. "If we don't find her in the next half hour, then we call."

And with that, we take our marching orders and canvass the ranch.

I take a lap around the porch and decide to double-check all the rooms in the Big House before heading back out. It's a strategy from my days of playing hide-and-seek with Avery when she was a preschooler. She was an excellent hider, and on more than one occasion, I panicked, completely convinced that she had somehow snuck out of our condo.

Thankfully, she never did, but that's when I learned to totally clear one area before moving to another. It's also possible that I learned this technique from watching too much true crime.

Once I've cleared the Big House, I start to slowly increase the perimeter of my search. I cover the pool and the Casita. I check in Grandpa's barn. I even turn on the flashlight on my phone to search for footprints, but it doesn't help.

A million worst-case scenarios begin to form in my mind. George last saw her at midnight, after the party ended. Who's to say she didn't get out of bed right after? How long has she been outside in the cold? I checked the temperature on the old thermometer hanging on the outside of the barn. It's in the midforties now, but who knows how cold it actually got last night. I push an image of Mom huddled under a pecan tree, blue and shivering, out of my head.

My new phone pings with a text.

Miles: Anything?

Kat: No.

Liza: Nothing.

Kat: I'm going to check the road.

Miles: We'll meet you there.

Liza: I think we should call the police.

Kat: Not just yet. We've still got 5 minutes until our 30 is up.

I close out of my texts, frustrated. It's just five more minutes, I rationalize. How much can change in five minutes? Technically, I suppose a lot can change in five minutes. A baby can be conceived. You don't even need the full five for that. I'm pretty sure you can drown in that time. Oh god. What if she drowned in the lake?

My phone pings with another text, but this time, it isn't the sibling group text.

Scotty: Are you awake? I haven't been able to sleep a wink.

I call him immediately.

"I guess you couldn't sleep either," he says.

"My mom's missing." I can barely choke the words out. "I don't know how long she's been gone, but it's cold out here, and I'm freaking out."

"I'm on my way," Scotty says. "I'll leave Avery here, and I'll get there as fast as I can."

"No. Don't do that. I don't want Avery to wake up and you not to be there."

"Then I'll wake her up."

"No. She'll be panicked that her grandmother is missing, and she won't understand why, because I haven't told her what's wrong with Mom and—"

"Just take a breath," Scotty says. "Tell me what you need."

"I need to find my mom." My voice trembles. "She could've drowned or fallen in a ditch. It was cold last night; she might've frozen to death. The ranch is so big. I need a drone or something."

"Liza, that's it. Can you tell if any of the paparazzi are still out by the main road?"

I glance toward the hedges, which are now shaped like tropical birds. I can see a few cars out there. Probably people who were too tired to drive home last night.

"Yes," I tell him. "I can see a few."

"I'm on my way, but in the meantime, go see if any of them have a drone."

"Are you sure?" I ask. "I don't really want footage of my family in evening wear searching for my mom at five a.m. What if she's dead, Scotty? I can't—"

"If there's a pap who has a drone, you tell him that I will pay him double what he would get for selling whatever footage he shoots. OK? Go, Liza. This is the one time when these assholes might actually be useful."

"OK," I breathe. "I'll do it."

"You're going to find her, Liza. It's going to be OK."

"How do you know?"

"Because your mom is tough, Liza. Just like you are. Just like Avery. Day women are built different. They're strong." And in that moment, I believe him. "Call me when you can."

I hang up and run. I run to the edge of the road that I've avoided since being here. I run to the people that I've hated because of what their photos and words did to me and my family. I run as hard and as fast as I can, and after pounding on three different car doors, I find someone with a drone and a heart, and ten minutes later, I know where to find Mom. It's the place I probably should've thought of from the very beginning. She's in Dad's old truck. It's Benny's hiding place, and apparently it's hers too.

I stop about fifteen yards away from Dad's truck, and to my relief, I can see the top of Mom's head just over the steering wheel. On the dash, a white ball of fluff the size of a breadbasket is sprawled in front of her.

"I found her," I say into my phone. Kat and Miles and George are on their way, but it's just me here right now.

"Can you tell if she's awake?" Kat asks.

"No." I shake my head. "Stay on the phone while I check, please?"

"Of course," Kat says. "We're almost there. You can wait if you want."

"No," I say. "I can do this one on my own."

My legs feel like cement, but I force them to carry me to the driver's side of Dad's truck. The windows are foggy, which I think is a good sign. Fog means heat. I learned that one from watching the car scene in *Titanic*.

I tap on the window softly, trying not to startle her. She stirs, and I let out a cry of relief. "She's alive," I stammer.

I wait for Mom to open the door, but she doesn't. She just looks at me like I'm a ghost or something.

"What do I do if she doesn't recognize me?" I whisper.

"She doesn't need to recognize you to know that you're someone safe. Go around to the other side of the truck and sit with her."

"OK. I'm going to hang up now."

"We'll be there soon."

I end the call and walk to the other side of Dad's truck, steeling my nerves with every step I take. *I can do this. I'll know what to say.* I squeeze the rusted metal handle and close my eyes. *I've got this.* I'm not a scared girl. I'm a slightly terrified woman in a ball gown, but I'm also a mom, and that makes me strong as hell.

I open the door. "Hi, Mom. It's me, Liza. I'm your daughter."

"I know who you are, Liza." She says it like it's the most obvious thing in the world. "Are you OK?"

Am *I* OK? This woman is sitting in an old truck before sunrise with a rabbit the size of a damn terrier, and she's questioning my mental state.

"I'm fine, Mom," I say.

"Oh, I don't think so, honey." She takes my hand. Her fingers feel like ice. "I recognize that look. You give me a minute to grab my purse, and I'll get you in touch with my sponsor."

My alcoholic mom thinks I'm drunk. Well, this is going great.

She reaches across me and pulls down the sun visor. She motions for me to look in the mirror. I wipe the dust off it with George's handkerchief, which somehow made it into my bra last night. Sure enough, I look like I've spent the night at Studio 54. My mascara is smudged, my eyes are red and swollen, and my hair looks like I've been playing with metal spoons in electrical sockets.

I decide to change the subject. "Mom, what are you doing in Dad's truck? It's freezing, and you're still in your pajamas."

"I hardly think you're in a position to criticize my wardrobe." She points at my wrinkled dress. "I'm waiting for your dad."

My stomach flip-flops.

"I can't believe he didn't show up last night," she says. "But I guess I shouldn't be surprised. The man always knows how to let me down."

"Then why did you want him to be at the funeral—er, party last night?"

She looks out the window, resting her hands on the steering wheel. She looks so small, so helpless. Part of me wants to wrap my arms around her and cradle her, but part of me doesn't think I can. Mom's never been a hugger. I suppose that's why I'm not either, but god, do I want to be right now. Why aren't we a family of huggers? Why aren't we mushy and sentimental?

"I wanted him to see that he didn't break me," Mom says. "I had a good life, even without him. He's the one who missed out, not me. Not us."

"Mom—"

"I know what's happening to me, Liza." She crosses her arms over her chest. "I know that I'm slipping away in my mind. That's why I had the funeral. I know you probably think it's silly, but it was important to me."

I scoot to the center of the cab and rest my head on her shoulder. It's not a hug, but it's something. "You wanted to make one last memory for yourself. There's nothing silly about that."

"I wasn't trying to make a memory for me, love. It was for you." She kisses the top of my head. "I was trying to give you and your brother and sister one last good memory of us."

Tears slip down my nose, leaving marks on my blue silk dress, and before I realize it, I'm sobbing in my mother's arms. I can hardly hear her through my cries. Occasionally I catch a *there, there* and an *I'm with you*, but mostly I just focus on the sound of my mom's heart. Its soft beat reminding me that I'm not alone. I never have been. We've always had each other. Maybe not always at the same time, but never were any one of us completely alone.

That's a gift Mom gave us. She made us learn how to lean on one another. The three of us siblings and Mom, we took turns leading our family. We took turns caring for one another, cleaning up messes, and rebuilding the parts of us that broke. We never abandoned each other.

We were probably a little too dysfunctional to be pigeons, but we were certainly better than rabbits.

"You know what we are, Mom?" I reach across the dash and give Benny a pet. "We're like wolves. We stick together in a pack."

She smiles and chuckles a little to herself. "I never considered getting wolves."

"That's probably a good thing."

I pull myself together and realize I need to get Mom back to the Big House. She needs to eat and get warm. She probably needs a nap too. Honestly, everyone probably does at this point.

I try to get her to leave the truck, but she doesn't want to leave. Not without seeing Dad.

"You go ahead, honey. Get yourself a shower. I'll be up as soon as I get a chance to talk to your dad."

That's when I know what I've got to do.

"Mom," I say, softly. "Dad isn't going to show up today, or any day for that matter. Dad died a long time ago."

I watch her face carefully, trying to figure out what's going on inside her head. Her eyes look clear, no sign of confusion like there was last night and no welling up with tears. Her bottom lip doesn't tremble, and she doesn't show any sign of sadness. But then again, Mom is one hell of an actress.

"Are you OK?" I cup her shoulder with my hand.

"Yeah," she says. "He didn't break me or us?"

"No." I shake my head. "Not even close."

"I won, then," she whispers. "We won."

We did.

Chapter 28

It wouldn't be a family crisis if there wasn't a pot of hot tea and George's sourdough rolls waiting for us in the kitchen. The four of us—me and my siblings still in our formal wear from the night before and Mom gently stroking Benny on her lap—look like something out of a Wes Anderson film. I take my seat across from Kat and hold my cup of oolong close to my chest for warmth.

"That was some funeral last night," Miles says.

George suggested that we, for the most part, don't make a huge deal out of Mom's wandering right away. We don't want to make her feel ashamed or guilty for something that's out of her control. He suggested we focus on something neutral that wouldn't be upsetting. Neutral isn't anybody's strong suit at this table, but I have hope.

"Best funeral I've ever been to," Kat adds.

"Your sourdough is fantastic, George," I say. "I never thought to put cinnamon on it. It tastes amazing." I notice Mom's barely touched her plate. "What's the matter, Mom? Aren't you hungry?"

"Yes," she replies. "But I don't think this is what I want. No offense, George. The food is lovely, like always. I just have a bit of a craving for something different."

"Anything you want, I'll make it," George says. "An omelet. A soufflé. You name it."

A wry smile tugs at the corners of her lips, and there's a twinkle in her eye that I hope never goes away.

"Popcorn," she says. "The real kind, not from the microwave. The kind you pop on the stove that tastes just like it came from the movie theater. Can you do that, George?"

Asking George if he can make fresh popcorn is like asking da Vinci to do a paint-by-number portrait. He nods, enthusiastically. "Fresh popcorn coming up."

"Wait a minute," Miles says. "We can't eat popcorn without watching a movie."

"Ooh, I like that even better." Mom claps her hands together. "What will we watch?"

A debate breaks out around the table, while George starts heating the oil for the popcorn. Miles and Kat are adamant we should watch one of Mom's movies, while Mom insists that she'd rather watch C-SPAN than watch herself act.

"It's not enjoyable," she says. "I just watch myself and think about all the mistakes I made or the cues that I missed." Her gaze lifts away from the table and out toward the window overlooking the remnants of yesterday's festivities, some of which are now floating in the pool. "Sometimes, I'm glad there's never been a documentary about me or our family. I don't think I could relive all the mistakes I made in my life. All the ways I've let the three of you down."

"Mom," Kat starts.

"Don't," she says. "I don't want either of you to feel like you need to say something that isn't true to make me feel better." She inhales deeply, closing her eyes, as if this confession has taken all the strength she has left in her. "I just want you three to know—before it's too late for me to remember to say it—that being your mother is the most meaningful role of my whole life. If I had a second shot, there's a million things I'd do differently, but that's not how life works. Life is the ultimate casting director, if you think about it." She smiles faintly, her voice shaking ever so slightly. "It doesn't even let you audition."

"Even if it did, Mom," I say, in a voice just above a whisper, "we'd still pick you."

I reach for Mom's hand on the table and cover it with mine. Miles and Kat follow suit until all four of our hands are stacked on one another like we're about to do a cheer in some cheesy, half-hour family sitcom. But this moment doesn't feel cheesy, not one little bit. *This* moment feels like healing.

We let George pick the movie, because, in the end, we know he'll pick something that we'll all like. He delivers. The five of us spend the morning cuddled up in the living room watching *The Wizard of Oz*, a story about a girl who gets swept up in a big storm and just wants to go back home. Mom asks me if I want to have Scotty and Avery over, but I tell her that this movie is just for our family. The OG Days. The next family movie will be for all of us, and there *will* be a next time.

Not long after the movie wraps, there's a knock at the front door. I volunteer to answer it, while George is in the kitchen. I swing open the door and find Debbie and a man I don't recognize.

"Liza." Debbie smiles warmly. "Boy, I've thought so many times about what I would say to you if we ever got the chance to meet. I'm Debbie, by the way. I was your mom's—"

"Friend," I interject. "Best friend, maybe. The speech and poem were really beautiful last night."

"Thank you. I'm glad you enjoyed it. It was my honor." She turns toward the elderly man, dressed exceptionally dapper in a tweed sports coat and crisp slacks. "Liza, this is my husband, Mack."

"Oh," I gasp, connecting the dots. "Mack, it's so nice to meet you."

I hold out my hand, but he doesn't reach for it. His arm is firmly locked in the crook of Debbie's. He's smiling, but not necessarily at me. I notice the way he rocks on his heels, his body shaking ever so slightly.

"Mack has pretty advanced aphasia," she says, gently stroking the side of his face with her hand. "It's a form of dementia. I don't know how much your mother has shared with you about her . . . um . . . diagnosis."

"Just a little," I say. "There's still a lot I think we're all trying to learn and figure out."

"That's normal," she says. "It's overwhelming, especially when you're dealing with a big personality like Darla. Anyway, I know I wasn't around when you and your siblings were growing up. Your mother and I had some rough years—rough decades, really—between us, but she was there when I needed help getting sober. She was there when I needed someone the most, and I'd like to be more present in her life and her children's lives now. If, that is, you feel like you need a little help."

"I think we could all use a little help," I say. "Would you like to come in and have something to eat or drink? We have popcorn. It's fresh."

Mack's eyes light up, and he nods ever so slightly toward the inside of the Big House.

"That sounds great," Debbie says.

Debbie and Mack spend the next two hours with us. George keeps the popcorn coming, while Mom and Debbie tell stories that make us all laugh and even shed a tear or two. These women weren't just friends. They were like sisters. Debbie feels like a living, breathing journal filled with facts and details about Mom that would take me two lifetimes to learn all on my own. Before she leaves, we exchange numbers and emails. She also connects all of us with a support group for people dealing with loved ones with memory issues.

Mom and I walk the two of them to the door to say goodbye. We wave until Debbie's car isn't anything more than two taillights on the dirt road.

"Can I ask you something, Mom?"

"Go on," she says.

"Why didn't you marry Mack?" I ask.

"Because he wasn't my soulmate," she says.

"I didn't know you believed in soulmates."

"Of course I do. I knew Mack wasn't mine. He was Debbie's. She loved him a million ways better than I ever could, and I'm sure he loved her more than he ever could've imagined loving me."

"Does that mean you think Dad was your soulmate?" I can't help but make a face.

"Goodness, no." She yawns. "Not every soulmate is a romantic partner. Mine isn't."

"Who's yours?"

"George. It took me a long time to figure that out."

"At least you figured it out," I say.

"You have one too, you know." She loops her arm around my waist. "He's staying at the motor lodge."

"You once told me not to get involved with an actor. You said Scotty would leave me."

"You shouldn't take dating advice from a twice-divorced alcoholic." Mom shrugs. "But advice from a sober old woman with dementia? Now that's the kind of advice you should listen to."

~

I borrow George's car to go to the motor lodge. He offers to drive me—so do Kat and Miles—but this feels like the sort of thing I need to do on my own.

I crank up the radio and roll down the window. The morning fog and chill have burned off, and the sun is back out. There's something about the California sun that does a soul good. The cool air whips through my hair, while Stevie's *Edge of Seventeen* blasts through the speakers.

I pull into the half-full parking lot of the motor lodge next to Scotty's motorcycle. The motor lodge rooms face the parking lot, and I try to remember which room belongs to Scotty and Avery. I'm about to send Scotty a text, when one of the doors opens, and Avery's on the other side. For a moment, we just stare at one another, neither of us sure of how to break the glacier that's drifted between us.

I open the car door and get out. She leaves her post and takes a few steps toward me. By the time the door slams behind me, we're both on the sidewalk, with just a foot or two between us.

"Ave—"

"Mom," she interjects. "I'm sorry."

"That's what I was going to say."

"I shouldn't have made a scene like that." She tugs at the sleeves of her flannel. "It was Grandma's big night, and I was selfish to make it about me. I'm going to apologize to her."

"I think it's great you want to do that, but I don't think it's necessary. She didn't see it, honey. There was a lot going on."

I give Avery a brief rundown on the events from last night and this morning. She listens intently, asking questions about Mom's diagnosis, and I do my best to answer. It's the last question she asks, the one specifically for me, that catches me off guard.

"How do you feel about all this, Mom?" she asks.

"Oh, I'm fine," I say, automatically. Her face falls slightly, and I realize that I've slipped my mask—the one that insists everything is always OK—back on. "Actually, that's not really true. To be honest, I'm sad. I'm sad and I'm scared, and I don't know what's going to happen next."

She reaches for my hand, just like I reach for my mom's hand when she needs consoling. "That makes sense," she says. "Thanks for telling me. I know that probably wasn't easy for you to do."

People talk about how quickly babies grow. One night, you put them to bed, and they can barely hold up their heads, and then seemingly overnight, they're climbing out of their crib. It happens so fast. It happens *in the blink of an eye*, is what they say. Well, if babies grow while you're blinking, then teenagers become adults when your eyes are wide open.

"Thanks," I tell her. "I should probably try to do that more."

"I would like that." She squeezes my hand.

I pull her into my arms and hug her until my arms ache. "I love you, kid."

"I love you too, Mom."

Avery heads back into the room to start packing her things. She tells me Scotty is working on something in the lobby, the only place with reliable Wi-Fi in a five-mile radius, and I ask if she can pack slowly so that he and I can have some time to talk.

"Why don't I take George's car back to the ranch?" she asks, her eyes big and hopeful.

"Uh." My body tenses as a dozen possible scenarios, all of which ultimately end in a catastrophic accident, race through my head. "Well—"

"Before you say no, just remember I've had my license for months now, and I've never gotten into an accident. Also, none of my friends' parents still insist on driving everywhere with them. Not to mention, it's literally a straight shot from here to Grandma's."

"I don't know, honey. It's not my car."

"What if I call Papa George and ask?" she pleads. "Then?"

My gut reaction to say no starts to subside. Not because I'm suddenly not terrified of something bad happening to Avery, but because I think I've learned that never letting her experience anything isn't a recipe to keep her safe.

"OK." I toss the keys, and she catches them. "Call Papa George first."

"I will," she squeals. "And I know the rules. No music. No cell phone."

"Good," I say. She gives me another hug. "Actually, not good."

"What do you mean?" A concerned look casts across her face. "Did I forget a rule?"

"Stevie Nicks," I say. "If she's on the radio, you should listen to her."

"I will."

A bell chimes overhead as I enter the lobby. It's small and smells like it hasn't had a proper deep cleaning since the seventies. There's a kid behind the counter who can't be much older than Avery. He's got earbuds in, his attention focused on his cell phone. He doesn't acknowledge or greet me, which doesn't surprise me. The Heavenly Motor Lodge isn't the sort of establishment that looks like it prides itself on customer service.

I start toward him but stop short. There's a little meeting room off to the side of the main lobby. I catch a glimpse of Scotty sitting at an old laminate-wood table with a cup of coffee. I guess I won't have to bother the kid behind the counter after all. I make my way into the room when someone else catches my eye: Chauncey Hill.

Scotty is having coffee with Chauncey Hill. Why? What on earth could he possibly have to discuss with him?

Suddenly, I remember snippets of my brief interaction with the production assistant from last night. The familiar ick of realizing that a private moment had been made public without my consent. I can't remember the woman's name now, but I remember the *Page Six* photos she showed me on her phone—the photos of Scotty and me at the funeral looking like a couple moments before the fight with Avery broke out. Then he was there, demanding a happy family picture of the three of us. He probably saw the whole thing unfold. He had to be the one to take the photos. Has Scotty seen them?

I push the door open. "You!"

"Liza." Scotty stands abruptly, nearly knocking over a pile of bound papers on the table. "Is everything OK?"

I glare at Chauncey, ignoring Scotty altogether. "Why are you here?"

"I was staying here," Chauncey says, calmly. The usual bravado in his demeanor virtually nonexistent. "And the two of us happened to run into each other in the lobby. Apparently, we both like a crappy cup of coffee around lunchtime."

"Sure," I scoff.

"Am I missing something? Did I do something to offend you?"

"You took those pictures of us," I say. "You and all your Ryomi bullshit, acting like you were some superfan or something; meanwhile, all you really wanted to do was make a buck off of us. As if all the money

I'm sure my mom paid you wasn't enough for you and your bullshit experience-curator life. Why was there a pink elephant at my mom's funeral? Explain that to me." I'm rambling, which is common when my blood has reached a boiling point. "And the cake. Who in their right mind wants to eat a cake that looks like someone?"

"That part was actually your mother's idea," Chauncey says. "And not to be rude, but *Page Six* doesn't pay their sources. Even if they did, I wouldn't sell pictures of you two, or anyone, for that matter. I don't need to."

"Well," I say, the wind knocked solidly out of my sails. The heat from my boiling blood has now migrated to my cheeks. "Then I don't know what to say to you."

"If it makes you feel any better, I got them pulled for you," Chauncey says. "One of the perks of my bullshit experience-curating life is that every once in a while, I can ask for a favor. Oh, and the elephant was also a bar, and there's this whole connection between people getting drunk and seeing pink elephants that dates back to the early 1900s. I thought it would be a fun reference."

It's like someone's spray painted the word *ASS* on my forehead. It's awful when the person you want to vehemently hate actually ends up being a decent person. Well, mostly decent. The jury's still out on what happened between him and Miles.

"Oh. That's actually kind of cool. I guess." I take a step back toward the door, trying not to trip over my fallen ego. "I'll leave you two to finish your coffee, then."

"Actually, I think you might want to join us." Scotty pulls out a chair. "It turns out there's a lot more to Chauncey than meets the eye." He nudges the stack of papers on the table. I take a closer look at them and realize it's a script. THE LOVELY DAYS is written in bold letters across the front. "He's also a writer."

"It's a love letter to old Hollywood told through your family's life and legacy," Chauncey says. "Your mom gave me a bunch of her old journals and home movies. I've actually spent the weeks leading up to the funeral at the ranch with her. She's an incredible woman."

"So, then you know about her diagnosis," I say.

"I do." He nods. "The first time I called her was the same day she got it. I had no idea, of course. The universe's timing is funny like that. We've actually forged a little bit of a friendship."

"It's a good script." Scotty taps the stack of papers with his index finger. "I haven't read all of it, but what I have read is pretty fantastic."

"It's a script, not a book?"

"That's right." He nods.

"I'm confused," I say. "I thought you were the party guru. Now you want to write movies?"

"Look, it's hard to get noticed the old-fashioned way," he says. "There are a million people who think they can at least write a screenplay, and a million more who think their screenplay is the next *Good Will Hunting*. So I decided to find a way to stand out. I built a brand and a kooky little persona. I learned how to throw killer parties and how to photograph them to make people wish they were invited. My real name isn't even Chauncey."

"What is it?" I ask.

"Josh," he deadpans. "Josh Smith. You know what name doesn't stand out on a script or a résumé? Josh Smith."

"So this is all an act?" I try to reconcile the information he's given me with the Mad Hatter of a man I've spent the last two days watching and avoiding. "Did you even watch *Sunset Breeze*?"

"For Darla," he says. "She was the best part of the show." Scotty and I exchange a look. "Look, you two weren't bad. I watched the show with my grandmother. She was obsessed with Darla and all the Days, to be honest. So to answer your question, no. This isn't all an act. I wrote a movie about your mother and your family because the Days brought my grandmother and me joy before she passed."

I think back to earlier this morning. Miles, Kat, Mom, George, and me gathered around the TV, listening to Judy Garland singing. There was magic in that room. That's the beauty of movies and television. They create magic in a place where it's needed the most.

"Thanks for sharing that, Chauncey," I say. "Or should I call you Josh?"

"Under no condition ever call me Josh." He lifts his brow.

"Fair enough," I reply. "How can I help you, then?"

"Be in it." He nods toward the script. "And let Avery be in it too."

"The story follows your grandmother and Darla, both young and older," Scotty says. "He wants the three of you to be in it."

"But I don't act," I say. "Not anymore. Plus, Avery has school, and I don't even know if Mom's capable of doing this. I don't even know if she would like the idea. You know, she basically turned down Diane Sawyer's offer to do a story on her and our family. I don't think that—"

Scotty rests his hand on my arm. "One step at a time. Read the script first. Then, we can figure out the rest. You don't have to solve every problem at the same time, and you don't have to figure out anything alone. Unless you want to."

"Right," I say. "One step at a time."

I agree to take the script and look it over. I clutch the manuscript to my chest, and despite my best efforts to be practical, something inside me is giddy. It's as if just holding these pages with my family's name on them has somehow awoken a piece of me that's been asleep for way too long.

"Can I ask you something?" I ask Chauncey, as I walk with him to his car. "Do you remember going on a date with my brother, Miles?"

Chauncey's eyes grow to the size of saucers. "Thought I was going to get away without having to address that pink elephant."

"Is pretending not to know a guy that you went on a bad date with part of your brand?"

"No," he says. "But saying the exact wrong thing in an intimate moment is one hundred percent on brand for me."

"Can I tell him that?" I ask. "Unless you do actually think he's old and out of shape."

"I don't think that at all. Please tell him that."

"I will."

"And can you tell him something else for me?" he asks. I nod. "Can you tell him that if he ever wants to maybe go out again, I'd really like the chance."

"I can do that," I say.

Chapter 29

When I get back to Scotty's room, he's in the process of packing. Seeing his suitcase on one of the full-size beds creates a familiar knot in my stomach. It takes me back to the first time I watched him carefully extract himself and his belongings from the life we were trying to make as a family.

I didn't cry that day. Maybe I was too sleep-deprived. Avery was so tiny. Maybe I was just too numb. Or maybe that's when I first told myself the lie that if I kept saying everything would be *fine*, eventually, it would be true.

Now, looking back, I'm not sure it ever was. That's not to say that Avery and I haven't had a great life, or that us staying with Scotty while his career took off would've guaranteed us a life as a happy family. I just think that for far too long, I've fought to make myself believe that every decision I made was the right one.

"Where are you going?" I ask. "I mean, obviously home, but after that. What are your plans?"

"I don't have any." He smirks. "That's the beauty of being unemployed."

"I guess we have that in common."

"Yes, but you have a job offer." Scotty nods at my purse with the script. "Look at you, getting work before me. Finally, the rest of the world is catching on to what I already knew."

"And what's that?"

"You're the one with the talent."

We both chuckle a little, but eventually the room falls silent. There's so much that needs to be figured out, and not with Avery. After this weekend, it's painfully obvious that something has to change in Mom's life. Miles and Kat and I can't rely on George to take care of her like he has in the past. It's not fair to him, and it's dangerous for Mom. But the thought of Mom being in a nursing home or an assisted-living facility doesn't feel right either. At least not yet.

Kat and Miles live too far from the ranch to commute back and forth, and I don't think Mom moving in with either of them full-time would work either. Our family has too many big personalities to live in tight quarters together, and that's without Benny and his harem.

"I want to apologize," Scotty says, softly.

"For what?"

"When Avery didn't come out this past summer, I think I indulged her frustration with you a little too much. I may have vented my own frustrations too." His gentle, brown eyes meet mine; an apologetic smile turns up the corners of his lips. "I talked to her last night. I made it clear that while you and I have a difference of opinion when it comes to her pursuing a future in acting, we're on the same page when it comes to her needing to still be a kid. You and I grew up fast—even faster after she was born. I don't want her to do the same. She's got her whole life to rush through things. There's no need to start now."

He's saying everything I thought I wanted to hear from him, but listening to him now, I'm not so sure he's right.

"You don't owe me an apology," I say. "I should've listened to you. We should've come to a compromise together."

"Moving forward, let's do that," he says. "We make decisions about our daughter together."

There he goes with the *our daughter* again. A thousand butterflies take flight in my stomach, and I fight back the urge to tackle him.

"OK." I nod. "Then, if that's the case, I think we need to be open to Avery acting a little. If this script is any good, maybe we consider it.

Or maybe we look at her going to a theater school. I'm not sure what the answer is exactly, but I think we need to compromise with her a little too."

"I like the acting-school idea."

"Me too."

He furrows his brow. "And where would this hypothetical school be?"

"Here." I take a seat on the bed across from him. "I mean not *here* here, but California. Colorado wouldn't make any sense."

"So, you'd both move in with . . . me?"

"Avery, yes, but I don't think living in Malibu is in the cards for me right now. I think I need to move to the ranch for a little while to get things settled with Mom. Honestly, I probably need to get things settled with me too."

"And what about when those things are settled?" He moves from his bed to mine, our knees touching as we face one another. "Will Malibu be in the cards then?"

Every piece of my soul wants to scream *yes*, but I know better. I'm not the only one in the picture. I haven't been for over sixteen years.

"Scotty." I heave a heavy sigh. "If it were up to me, then it would be easy to say yes. The other night was great, but we've got a teenager we're trying to raise. Moving her to another city, a new school, basically changing her entire life, that's a lot for a kid to process. You can't add her parents dating each other to that mix. It doesn't seem fair."

"Why?"

At first, I think he's joking, but the look on his face is so earnest and sincere. The thought of so much change all at once is enough to make me break into a sweat and possibly hives, but Scotty seems totally calm.

"Scotty, my mom has dementia and lives with a small army of rabbits." I stand and start to pace between the beds. "My sister is ready to have a man named Rooster's baby or possibly just shop for sperm, and I know what it's like to shop for shoes with that woman. Finding the right sperm will be a marathon event if Rooster's not up for parenthood."

"I have so many questions about Rooster," Scotty says.

"And don't even get me started on what she'll be like during pregnancy. She'll probably schedule a C-section before she's even knocked up. Then there's Miles. He and James just split because Miles is terrified of having kids, but I think he and James might actually be able to work things out. Either that, or he and Chauncey might end up becoming a power couple. It's hard to say. It's an entire ordeal, and I'll need to be there to support him and Kat and my mom and—"

He takes my hands, lacing his fingers through mine, and pulls me in between his legs. "What are you trying to say, Liza?"

"What am I trying to say? Scotty, we just went to my mother's funeral. My living mother's funeral, where we all dressed up like her. My life literally just turned into a soap opera, and I'm not saying it's a bad thing; it's just a lot."

"Well, if that's the case"—he wraps his arms around my waist and stands, holding me firmly against him—"I would like to audition for a role."

"What role is that?" I huff. "You want to be a ghost? A guy in a coma?"

"I want to be the love interest. Your love interest," he whispers in my ear. "It can be a small role at first. Maybe just a few episodes each week. We'll see how the audience reacts to me." He kisses the spot just below my ear, his lips leaving a trail across my chin. "If it looks like the viewers respond well, then maybe we give me a character arc."

"And what if that goes well?" My breath hitches in my chest, as his lips hover just above me. "What then?"

"Maybe I become a series regular. Either way, there's no pressure. We're not planning a wedding. We're just seeing where things go." His lips graze mine. "You jump, I jump. You just say the word."

The thing about soap operas is they never end with a simple happy ending. Their storylines rarely ever end at all. Unlike sitcoms, which wrap each episode with a conclusion—minus the occasional *to be continued* cliffhanger—or movies, which leave audiences with one final scene, soaps just keep going. They keep evolving, and so do their characters. Sometimes for the better, and sometimes for the worse. And in that way, I think that's what makes soap operas relatable.

For years, I've tried to turn my life into something familiar and formulaic, because that seemed safer for me and for Avery. I tried to make our life a sitcom. But if this weekend has taught me anything, it's that predictability doesn't always equal happiness. Life was never meant to be a sitcom. It's too big and far too bold for that.

I won't pretend to know the secret to life, but I'm starting to think that maybe life, when it's at its fullest, is meant to be a soap opera. Maybe it's our jobs as humans to simply show up, follow the script, and be open to the possible plot twists.

I kiss Scotty and whisper in his ear. "Jump."

Epilogue

One year later

"Babe, we're going to be late," I shout from the bottom of the staircase of the newly renovated Casita. After Avery and I moved back permanently, Scotty got to work on modifying the first home we ever lived in as a family to something that could potentially be forever. "Avery, are you ready?"

She steps out onto the top of the stairs, dressed in one of Mom's vintage dresses. Her hair and makeup are the perfect combination of modern meets old-Hollywood glamour.

"You look good, kid," I say.

"I'll be down in a sec," Scotty calls.

I check my reflection in the mirror at the base of the stairs, adjusting my pink bow tie. "You know, I really hated this idea when Miles pitched it, but there's something kind of fabulous about going to a premiere and not having to wear a corset."

Miles asked an up-and-coming designer to re-create my little pink tuxedo that I wore with Mom during our variety act. The designer also designed Mom's matching tuxedo look, complete with a bedazzled top hat and cane.

"It's really cool, Mom," Avery says, applying a little lip gloss in the mirror.

"How do I look?" Scotty asks, as he glides down the stairs.

He stops behind Avery and me. The three of us stand together in front of the mirror like a living family portrait, and my heart swells so big it aches.

"We look good together," Avery says.

We do. It took over seventeen years to get here, but damn, was it worth it.

The number of offers Chauncey's screenplay received was historic. Most wanted to adapt it into a feature film, and some wanted to do a series based on it, but Chauncey stuck to his vision. He wanted the silver screen, and he wanted the Day women to play the leads.

Avery played young Darla so effortlessly, you would've thought she'd been preparing her whole life to do it. I got to tackle the role of mature Mom, which didn't come quite as naturally to me as I'd hoped. Looking back, that was actually kind of a blessing. Mom and I spent hours reviewing her old movies—a task she was willing to do only because she refused for me to portray her inaccurately—and in the process of all that, we became friends for the first time in our adult lives. Chauncey even made sure that the real Darla had a small part playing Grandma Viv. Mom nailed it, which was a surprise to absolutely no one at all.

The doorbell rings, snapping me back into the present moment. Our limo is here to take us to the premiere. I give my bow tie one more tug and start to head out the door when Scotty grabs my hand.

"You forgot something," he says.

"What?" I ask, genuinely unsure of what I might've missed. "I don't need tickets or something, do I?"

"No, silly. You forgot this." He pulls me in close and presses his lips to mine.

"Remind me one more time."

We kiss until the driver honks, and Miles rolls down the window to yell at us.

Inside the limo, there's champagne and sparkling cider and so much excitement it makes it almost hard to breathe. I'm squeezed in between

Avery and Mom, both of whom take turns holding my hand. I'm not sure if they're doing it because they're worried that I'm nervous or if they're doing it to quell their own anxieties. Either way, I take comfort in it.

We arrive at the downtown theater, where a crowd is waiting with microphones in hand and cameras flashing. Scotty seems relatively unaffected by the whole thing. He's much more accustomed to the attention. He files out of the car first, followed by Miles and Chauncey, who are soon to be officially family. He proposed to Miles three weeks ago, and they're already planning the wedding of the century. George comes out next, and then a very pregnant Kat and Rooster. I hold on to Mom's and Avery's hands, keeping us back in the limo for just a beat more.

"Mom, how are you feeling?" I ask. She's been on a new memory medication for a few weeks. It's hard to tell whether or not it's helping, but she seems to have more good days than bad. "Are you sure you're up for this?"

"Liza." Mom pats my hand. "We were made for this, darling."

With that, Avery leads the charge out the limo. Camera flashes greet her, and she smiles and waves like an absolute pro. She links her arm with Scotty's, and he leads her over to a reporter he's familiar with. I help Mom out of the limo. Miles takes her arm from me. We agreed that she would spend minimal time on the red carpet to keep her from becoming overwhelmed.

I stand alone on the carpet for a moment, watching as the two women who bookend me begin their waving and have their pictures taken. Miles purposely selected one of the oldest theaters in Hollywood. The entire place feels like something out of a different time.

"Mom." Avery takes my hand. "Look up at the marquee. Grandma, look up. That's us. We did it."

NOW SHOWING:
THE LOVELY DAYS

STARRING
AVERY DAY SAMSON
LIZA DAY
DARLA DAY

Yes, we did.
We absolutely did it.

ACKNOWLEDGMENTS

Dear reader, when I tell you that this book nearly broke me, I am not using hyperbole. Writers employ many different strategies when it comes to crafting a novel. My go-to technique seems to be this: write the book wrong four times, and then, when virtually no time is left, write the book correctly while forgoing sleep for weeks and subsisting on copious amounts of caffeine. I'm sure there are better strategies out there. I just also think my brain works best when it launches into survival mode. Thankfully, I have an amazing group of people who give me the time to write, the gift cards to stay caffeinated, and the shoulders to cry on when I hit a wall.

To my agent, Joanna MacKenzie, I am forever thankful that you are my publishing partner.

To my editors at Amazon, Selena James and Kristi Yanta, thank you so much for trusting me and my process, especially with this book. It wouldn't exist as it does now without your support.

To my critique partner, Falon Ballard, there's never a day that I write that I don't consider how lucky I am to have you in my corner.

When people ask me how I manage to write a book while also working two other jobs, I always give them the same answer: I have an incredibly supportive partner in my husband. Matt, I wouldn't be able to do this without you. Whatever books I'm lucky enough to publish exist because of you.

To Lucas, Brock, and Hattie, thank you for giving me time to write. Also, thank you for telling me that you're proud of me. I am in constant awe of each of you, and to know that I do something that impresses you is my favorite compliment in the world.

To Chelsey, I wasn't sure how I felt about having a sibling when I was ten. Now, at thirty-eight, I can't imagine how I would survive life without a sibling. You *get* me, and for that, I am eternally thankful.

To my mom, thanks for watching classic TV with me. Some of my best memories are of watching you laugh at Lucy and Ricky. I laughed too, but watching the joy they brought you is what I remember the most.

And finally, it's impossible for me to write a story about three generations of women without acknowledging my grandmothers. How lucky am I to have had you in my life for so many years? The stories you've told me about your lives are some of my most valuable treasures.

ABOUT THE AUTHOR

Photo © 2022 Alexandra Yarborough

Brooke Abrams lives in the Sonoran Desert with her husband, three children, three dogs, and cat. She's quite literally never alone. Not even now. You can find Brooke's socials and writing-related news on her website at www.akabrooke.com.